Rock Baby

'Even be[illegible] *Frog* ... a delightful am[illegible]ment and fast-moving

Books and Bookmen

[illegible] thriller of its season [illegible] comparison is unavoid-[illegible]odhouse has a pleasing vein of [illegible]bsurdity which Balchin never sought [illegible]endidly enjoyable book.'

The Times Literary Supplement

'Nice touches of wry villainy in both goodies and baddies.'

The Yorkshire Post

'A gripping, funny, convincing story ... Dr Yeoman is the most sympathetic hero for years, as readers of *Tree Frog* may remember, and his scientific approach strikes exactly the right note of blundering expertise. A fine shooting finish rounds off an extremely lively book.'

The Glasgow Herald

'A first-class piece of story-telling.'

Manchester Evening News

'You can't stop reading.'

The Observer

By the same author in Pan Books

TREE FROG

Martin Woodhouse

Rock Baby

UNABRIDGED

PAN BOOKS LTD · LONDON

First published 1968 by William Heinemann Ltd.
This edition published 1970 by Pan Books Ltd,
33 Tothill Street, London, S.W.1.

330 02441 8

To
M.R.C. A.P.U.,
who taught me many
of the facts of life

Printed in Great Britain by
Cox & Wyman Ltd., London, Reading and Fakenham

ROCK BABY

One

England, Germany, Austria

Prologue

THE LAST of the spring snow still lay in luminous patches here and there, in the lee of rocks. There was no wind. The plane which dropped Rock Baby flew high, pencilling ice crystals across the bitter night sky. The faint sound of its engines alerted the wild cat, and she laid her ears flat and screamed defiance at the thing that was drifting down into her territory. She had two kittens that year, hidden in a cave.

Rock Baby landed heavily, humming quietly and monotonously. The parachute and draglines were stowed. Rock Baby slowly stood upright, adjusting to the firmness of the ground; determined that all was well, and sent down a small drill-headed probe into the stony, thin soil.

The wild cat heard the humming and the sound of the little drill, but after an hour or so she stopped her low, wavering scream and set her ears upright again. Twice during the week that followed she circled Rock Baby cautiously, and finally gave up, finding no threat to her kittens.

All that dry summer it was quiet. Rock Baby collected data, recorded, analysed, and transmitted. All this was long before I ran across Rock Baby, but that's the way I always imagine it, with Rock Baby barrelling down out of the cold night sky and the cat screaming softly like a damned soul. By the time I actually clumped on to the scene, in studded boots and humping seventy pounds of electronic gear and survival kit, not to mention a couple of thousand pounds' worth of chocolate bar I'd stolen from Yancy Brightwell, the whole affair had become ten times more complicated and a hundred times more dangerous. Like an iceberg, most of it was under the surface, way under. They say that what you don't know can't hurt you. That's what they say, but they can't have been in this trade. In this trade, what you don't know can not only hurt like hell but very likely kill you stone dead.

ONE

IT WAS getting on for midnight.

'The trouble with scientists,' said Andy, 'is that they think they've got some private, personal hot line to truth.'

'I don't think it's exclusive to scientists,' I told him. He looked as though he might be going to pursue the matter, but he caught Driver's eye and subsided into his chair. Driver, it was quite clear, regarded him with the lack of enthusiasm of a CO surveying a junior officer drunk on Mess Night. Also, since Driver and McKellar were trying hard to sell me something, he didn't want Andy Dylan raising prickles on my back. As a matter of fact I could take a good deal more of Andy drunk than Driver sober, but I didn't say so since this was a Guest dinner and they were paying for it. I leaned back and stared upwards, waiting for somebody to make another pitch.

Guest dinners at the Hall of the Worshipful Company of Master Gunners are endurance tests backed by seven centuries of tradition. Tails are worn, of course, and probably the only hired ones in sight were mine. People are occasionally and discreetly sick in quiet corners, but nobody ever raises his voice.

Around me the walls of the Massingham Library in Gunners Hall – dedicated, the Warden will tell you, to the memory of Sir Josiah Massingham, the inventor of the earliest siege gun traversing mechanism – rose thirty feet and more and were lost in darkness overhead. From them great men, and the wives and the whores of great men, gazed down upon us in varnished disapproval. Stewards came and went. Driver was precise, military and persuasive and McKellar swivelled his head to and fro above his antique wing collar like a vulture.

I'd spent the evening saying no. I'd said it about as often as a virgin at a Hunt ball and it was getting to be a reflex. Driver thought I was being unreasonable, and McKellar thought I was wilfully avoiding my patriotic duty, but I didn't see it that way. The facts were simple; they wanted me to get them out of a technical jam. They'd used the word 'technical' about every other minute, but they wouldn't explain what, exactly, the jam consisted of. I didn't want to know, so this suited me fine, but they still went right on trying.

'You do understand, Dr Yeoman,' said McKellar, 'that it's purely scientific help we want?'

He craned his neck in my direction. He was a cadaverous Scot and I wouldn't have cared to guess at his age. He suffered from a delusion common among a certain type of Scot. The delusion is that since everyone expects them to be blunt and dour to the point of rudeness and loves them for it, they may as well string along with the Sassenachs and live up to the idea. I'd only met McKellar four hours ago and already I disliked him more than Driver.

'I know,' I said. 'So you've been telling me all evening.'

He worked out exactly how to put the next bit.

'What I meant,' he said finally, 'was that there will be no . . . difficulty involved.'

'By "no difficulty" I take it you mean "no risk",' I said. 'Nobody's likely to lose any blood. Is that what you mean?'

He coughed politely.

'I don't think you've done your homework,' I told him. 'You can't have conferred extensively with Major Driver before approaching me.'

'I'm afraid I don't quite follow you,' said McKellar.

'Because if you had, you'd undoubtedly know that the last time I was asked for help on a purely scientific matter – by Major Driver himself, as it happens – I wound up flying three-quarters of a ton of unairworthy plane around the African desert until somebody blew it up. This makes scientific operations very difficult to sell over my doorstep.'

Driver was glaring at me as though he were about to beat me over the head with the Official Secrets Act. I didn't mind. I might have been a bit unfair to him, but I wanted to make sure McKellar got the point.

'I don't like technical jobs unless somebody says clearly, and preferably in writing, exactly what they're about, where they take place and who I've got to work with. None of which you've told me yet,' I said. 'Thank you, but no.'

Driver leaned forward.

'I did warn you,' he said to McKellar.

'You did indeed,' said McKellar. 'But I had hoped, just the same.' He looked over in my direction.

'You're treading me into the ground,' I said. 'I can hardly believe you're serious about any of this. First, the only time I've had any dealings with Seeker Section, Driver here played yo-yo with me from beginning to end. I got mixed up with Security once before that and all it got me was dysentery. I'm fairly slow but I'm not daft as a brush.'

'This isn't a Seeker matter,' said Driver stiffly.

Seeker Section is Driver's stamping ground, and stamping is the word all right. Way back in the mists of time Seeker started out as a bunch of filing clerks who sorted out technical information, mostly on who was ahead of who in the post-war atom bomb stakes. Driver came out of the Marines, grabbed hold of Seeker with both hands and drove it to where it is now, with its own headquarters in a crumbling Bayswater terrace and an appropriation from the Civil List which nobody knows the size of except Driver – and maybe the Prime Minister, if he's really on the ball.

Driver was tough. Driver got things done and counted heads afterwards if there were any heads left to count. It was best to approach Seeker, assuming for the sake of argument that you had to, in a defensive frame of mind and with one hand held firmly over the crotch. I'd found out about Driver the hard way, and I wasn't going to find out any more if I could help it.

'This time he doesn't even want me to work for Seeker,' I said. 'But he's tried to sell you the idea that I'm just the man to unravel some complicated snarl the Department of Scientific Security's got itself into. A technical snarl, of course.'

'I didn't use the word "snarl",' said McKellar.

'I'm getting quick at reading between the lines,' I told him. 'Being around Seeker taught me that.'

I knew very little about the Department of Scientific

Security. Occasionally they sent round little bulletins to the Institute, where I worked. As far as I knew, their job was chiefly to stop scientists going on permanent holidays in Russia, China or Egypt, but apparently they did other things, too.

McKellar protruded his head still farther in my direction.

'And what have you read between the lines tonight?' he asked.

'All right, I'll tell you. D S S is in trouble. They're in trouble because Stimminson defected from Porton last year, and Bernado disappeared a few months ago and nobody seems to know quite what's happened to him. Stimminson was a top-weight and Bernado is important enough in particle physics for the Press boys to start writing those little articles.'

McKellar sucked his head back into the protective circle of his collar. He said nothing.

'Even leaving the Press out of it,' I went on, 'other people have started to wonder out loud whether D S S isn't falling down on the job a little. Two scientists inside a year is a bit over the ration of permissible errors. They want somebody's head on a pole, only it isn't going to be yours.'

'I'm glad to hear it,' said McKellar.

'It isn't going to be yours because you've been laying off your bets. You've been quietly setting up a little technical operation of your own, a showpiece, to set off against any boring little mistakes like losing a few physicists here and there. Never mind whether it's D S S's job to set up technical operations—'

'It's within our terms of reference,' said McKellar.

'Great,' I said. 'In that case, fanfare of trumpets, roll of drums, wave the wand and lift the cloth and what have we? Suddenly it turns out that D S S is a swinging outfit all the time and never mind a few missing persons.' Nobody said anything, so I went on. 'Of course, you aren't going to tell me exactly what this little operation is unless I sign on the dotted line. If I do that, I shall hear much more about it than I really want to know, because now it's going wrong too. Hence my use of the word snarl, which I will amend to read "slight political difficulty" if you like it any better. All right?'

I knew I was three-quarters right and probably right all the way. Dinner at Gunners Hall. Oak beams from before the Fire and before the Plague. Rule Britannia. Soften up the clod scientist and the clod scientist will haul you out of the soup.

'The only snag is that I'm not going to play,' I said.

'Why not?' said McKellar.

I nodded at Driver and Andy Dylan. Andy seemed to be asleep, but you could never tell.

'Because they're here,' I told him. 'If Seeker is within a ten-mile radius of this, then it stinks. That's why.'

Driver tapped the rim of his glass against the side of his jaw. Suddenly, for the first time that evening, McKellar raised a smile. It nearly cracked his skull in half, but at least it was there.

'Perhaps we've been guilty of a tactical error,' he said. I turned to Driver.

'What made you think I'd be interested in Scientific Security troubles?' I asked him.

He rolled the belly of the glass to and fro against his cheek thoughtfully, watching me.

'We wondered if you were finding your work at the Institute tedious,' he said. 'Valuable though it is, of course.'

'No. I don't find it tedious. The Institute suits me down to the ground. Nobody worries me and I get three square meals a day. It's March now and in June I have to produce the final draft of my tiny but valuable contribution to the High Altitude Symposium, and after that I'm going on leave.' He went on rolling the glass against the side of his face. In the end he said, 'Well, I said I'd do my best for you, McKellar.' I was beginning to get annoyed, which was stupid of me.

'What you need is a nice young Ph D all bright-eyed and bursting with enthusiasm to join your interdepartmental goodwill crusade,' I said. 'Not me. I'm part-worn and peaceful-minded, and I don't like the rules you play by, even when I can see what the rules are supposed to be. Which isn't often.'

Driver didn't say anything. He smiled slightly, an old smile and full of malice, but that was all.

'You don't like the rules,' said Andy Dylan from behind me. I'd almost forgotten he was there. He still had his eyes closed and sounded as though he were reciting something. 'You don't like the rules. Well, well, Giles. Do you know, sometimes you science boys turn me up.'

'You mean on account of our hot line to truth?'

'Yeah, that,' said Andy. 'And because you don't like the rules. Science is clean and pure and bright, and when you've got hold of the truth it stays the truth, doesn't it? Far different from us mucky political types. With us the truth varies from day to day, and sometimes we have to make do with the slice of truth we've got today because tomorrow it may be a different slice. Is that it?'

'Something like that,' I said, I still couldn't tell how drunk he was.

'Ah,' he said. 'Well, I tell you what, Giles. Let's just suppose, for the sake of argument, that you walk out of here tonight and you just happen to fall under a bus. Let's suppose they cart you off, bells clanging, and do something drastic, like, say, taking your leg off at the hip. You'd have to start playing by a different set of rules then, wouldn't you?'

'Are we still arguing about slices of truth, or have we moved on?' I asked him.

'About rules, mate. About choosing rules or having them chosen for you, that's what we're arguing about,' he said. 'You know what I think? I think you're a sort of philosophical Conchie, Giles. That about covers it.' His eyes were still shut. I could see that he'd got to the stage where the truth of the human condition was within his grasp. I wasn't going to have a debate with anybody who had the truth of the human condition within his grasp, drunk or sober; there's no percentage in it, as those Zen students were always finding out in between bashes round the head with willow cudgels.

'Have it your way,' I said. 'Right now I still have a choice.' I turned back to Driver and McKellar. 'No hard feelings,' I said. 'Just forget the whole thing.'

And that should have been that, only of course it wasn't. Something like the far-off tinkling of distant camel bells told me I was going to wind up sunk to the ears in McKellar's technical operation.

Half an hour later we were walking down Gunnershall Lane towards Fleet Street and a taxi. I felt McKellar's detaining hand on my elbow. Under the raw lamps his face was impassive, withdrawn, skeletal.

'We really do need your help, Dr Yeoman,' he said.

'Perhaps you do,' I said, 'I'm flattered. And I'm sorry, but the answer is still no.'

We stopped for a moment. Andy and Driver were twenty yards ahead, Driver marching stiffly and with precision, Andy skipping from side to side of the pavement in an attempt at a late-night soft-shoe routine. A gust of wind spattered raindrops across McKellar's starched, pearl-studded shirt front, spotting it with small, dim smudges.

'I think you misunderstand me,' he said. 'I was not repeating a plea. I was stating a fact. I think you should bear that in mind, Dr Yeoman.'

TWO

THAT WAS on Monday. Eleven the next morning found me in my room at the Institute with a small-to-medium hangover and a short temper, trying to teach a nice-looking girl the elements of electronics. I'd have taken out the temper on her except that she'd noticed the hangover as soon as she arrived and had spent the first ten minutes of the study period being sympathetic and amused.

Her name according to her supervision card was Amanda Grayle (Miss), and although I'd been doing my best for the last six weeks I didn't think she was suited to electronics. We were on inter-electrode capacitance this morning, a subject which failed to arouse any great enthusiasm in either of us, but I went on doing my best.

'The effect of connecting a capacitance externally between the grid and anode of a triode valve,' I said, 'is to add a small but proportional extra grid-cathode capacitance, to the extent of one plus M multiplied by C.'

Stirring stuff, blood-warming stuff. Miss Grayle evidently thought so too. She was looking out of the window at the

Institute tom-cat, who sat on a fir-branch looking back and lashing his tail. Him and me. I'd read somewhere that skirts were short this year, but the amount of Miss Grayle's legs on display was more than enough even so.

'Miss Grayle,' I said.

She turned back into the room. Her legs weren't by any means the only striking feature about her. She was studying social psychology, which is what girls study these days instead of deportment, and it had been decreed that all psychologists of whatever kind should be given a grounding in electronic technique as applied to laboratory work. An excellent theory, though it wasn't working out. Not that I minded doing my bit to prove the point.

She was the sort of girl you knew at once spent her summers skin-diving and her winters on the ski slopes. She had a cedarwood tan which looked as though it had cost about five hundred pounds of somebody else's money and high, almost Mexican, cheekbones. She was about five-seven at a guess and from here most of it seemed to be leg. I didn't think she was going to turn out to be much of an electronics engineer even by crystal-set standards, but who cared?

'I'm sorry, Dr Yeoman,' she said. 'I really am. What did you say?'

'Nothing of importance,' I told her. 'Nothing poetic, for instance. It's a losing battle. The University sees fit to pay me the laughable sum of seven guineas for twelve hours of trying to beat some basic electronics into your beautiful head and they're wasting their money. I'd say they were wasting my time too except that it's a pleasant way to waste it on Tuesday mornings. I don't think you're ever going to understand what goes on inside all that delicate and complicated equipment you're supposed to be learning how to use, assemble, and repair.'

'I think you're right,' she said calmly. 'But on the other hand, why should I learn anything about it?'

'In case any or all of it breaks down. Which happens on average about once every two days, I've found.'

'Well, I tell you what, Dr Yeoman,' she said. 'If and when it does, I'll shout for help. If I shout loud enough, perhaps it won't matter that I'm just a poor, weak, impractical woman. How does that strike you?'

I could see what she meant. I was more certain than ever that the University were wasting their money. Any time she opened her door even a few inches, she'd probably find a queue of eager beavers with soldering irons stretching from here to London. Among them would be me, most likely. I didn't get a chance to say any of this because the hour was up and Miss Grayle was folding pages of unreadable notes into her brief-case with an air of finality and triumph. She smiled sweetly as I held the door open for her. I watched her walking down the corridor until Binnie Abrams tapped me on the shoulder

'All right, Giles,' she said. 'You can slip your eyeballs back into place now.'

She grinned at me. She was carrying what looked like the rough draft of my High Altitude Research Group paper.

'What, me?' I said. She leaned against the door and swung it all the way open. I followed her back into my room and watched while she dumped paper all over my desk.

'You,' she said. 'And you look terrible this morning. Poor Giles. Rough evening yesterday?'

'Don't you start as well.'

'Why? Has Miss Whatsit been cooling your fevered brow too?'

'That and other things,' I told her.

'Lucky you. You make friends easily. The only thing is you can get fired that way, can't you? Or am I being old-fashioned?'

'I expect you're right.'

'Well, then.'

I wasn't sure what this was supposed to mean, except that I'd learned to recognize the tone of voice she used to clinch an argument.

'Why don't you get that bloody great Swedish ape to make an honest woman of you, Binnie?' I said. 'Then you could stop worrying about my brow and worry about his instead.' Time was when I could always get a rise out of her by teasing her about Rasmussen, but she'd stopped getting annoyed now and

I knew I'd been gently but firmly edged out into the cold. Oddly enough, I minded less than I thought I would.

'He's Danish, not Swedish,' she said.

'Same thing.'

'You tell him that,' she said. 'I'll get you an aspirin.'

'I've had an aspirin.'

'Another couple won't do you any harm.'

'Sometimes I begin to wonder why I bothered to waste all those years studying,' I said, 'when all it gets me is to be told by damned great red-headed—'

'Girls.'

'Girls, that what I need is an aspirin.'

'Poor Giles,' she said again. 'You really did have a rough evening, didn't you?'

'Yes. All right, I did,' I said.

'Was it Driver?'

'Driver, and Dylan, and a pre-Jacobite Scot from some Government Department or other called McKellar.'

I really wanted to talk to Binnie about it. At least she knew Driver almost as well as I did, having been at the rough end of one of his bright ideas herself. She had a three-inch scar across her temple to prove it.

She'd been sleeping with Christian Rasmussen for six months now and I knew that they were most probably going to get married, though I could never get her to come right out and say so. I still seemed to be caught in what I'd describe as maternal backwash, not that I minded. I thought, not for the first time, that Rasmussen was a lucky guy and that if I'd had any sense I'd have thought of it first.

'They've got a nerve,' said Binnie. 'They really have. What did they want?'

'They still have a retainer contract with us for technical advice.'

'Advice, yes. What else did they want?'

'About the same as they wanted last time,' I said. 'I'm only guessing, of course. They wouldn't tell me exactly what.'

'Of course they wouldn't. I hope you told them to stick it up—'

'Don't worry. I did.'

'Good. I wish we'd never had anything to do with them. They're absolute bastards.'

'I'll pass it on to them.'

'You do that. I might even do it myself. Now look, Giles, these experiments. Are you paying attention?'

She started to deal the High Altitude papers into three piles. There were times when I knew she could have organized anybody from the United Nations down. I wondered how much organizing Christian Rasmussen needed; I'd only met him a couple of times, and liked him on sight. He was a metallurgist, his hair was the same shade of red as Binnie's and he was about seven feet tall and six feet across the shoulders. His healthy Scandinavian laugh tended to rattle the pictures on the walls when he found life funny, which seemed to be most of the time. Binnie seemed very happy with the whole arrangement, and it looked to me as though she'd put on about eight pounds all in the right places. She was a big girl to start with.

'These are fine,' she said, tapping one of the piles of paper. 'These are lists of references, the ones I've been able to find in the library. These are the ones I haven't checked yet. Have you got that?'

'Yes,' I said.

'All right then. Tell me if there's anything else. And keep your mind off your girl students and on your work.'

'Yes, Miss Abrams.'

'Oh, and there's a telegram for you down in the office. I'd have brought it up with me but my hands were full.'

Telegrams make me nervous. I know all about those people who are always tearing them open with shaking fingers and I'm right behind them. About one telegram in a million tells you you've won the pools. The rest tell you about battle, tempest, sudden death and brief-cases you left in the Gare du Nord. This one told me that Captain Yancy Brightwell was in the Lady Adderly Memorial Nursing Home near Colchester after a serious accident and had asked to see me.

I had an appointment with the Director of Research immediately after lunch, but I phoned through to his secretary and cancelled it. I locked my room, went down and grabbed three cheese buns from Fred's coffee swindle trolley, left ninepence in the tin mug on the lower shelf, and headed the car eastwards in the uncertain spring sunshine.

THREE

HAIL DRUMMED on the hood of the car as I drove through Colchester and out towards the coast. Then the sun came out, the road narrowed and ran between hedges, and I overshot the narrow entrance with the black-lettered sign which was all that showed where the Lady Adderly Memorial Nursing Home came into tentative contact with the great wide world outside. I backed and turned on to rutted gravel. A hundred yards from the entrance the drive had turned twice around islands of rhododendron bushes and the gate was lost from sight. I drove on gently for another half-mile. Melting hail-stones lay in small drifts against the grass verge, and a little old man looked up as I passed him and then went back to studying the broken stems of the early tulips.

The front of the Lady Adderly was battered Regency, except for an afterthought wing added with a piece of somebody's will. The afterthought included pine-plank facia work and picture windows and looked terrible.

Inside it was sterile and efficient with obligatory flower vases. A porter led me past small Gothic-lettered fingers pointing the way to *Operating Theatre, Consultant Physician,* and then stopped under one marked *Matron's Office*. He knocked and showed me in, and Matron asked who I was and then gave me a cup of tea.

'Mr Wylie is with Captain Brightwell at the moment,' she said. 'Perhaps you wouldn't mind waiting.'

'How is he?' I asked her. She smiled briefly before telling me that Captain Brightwell was doing quite well, meaning that he was anywhere between being dead and ready to go home tomorrow morning. Matron looked over forty and under seventy, as close as I could get it. She also looked as though she'd been running the Lady Adderly Memorial Nursing Home, the way she wanted it run, for longer than I'd been around on this earth, but then I have never come across a Matron who looked any different.

'What sort of an accident was it?' I asked.

'I'm afraid I don't know the exact details. He was in some sort of explosion on board a boat at sea, so I gather. This was four days ago. Captain Brightwell was transferred here as a private patient, under Mr Wylie, our consultant surgeon. His condition was quite serious when he arrived.'

'I see,' I said. 'Thank you, Matron.'

'Not at all. Mr Wylie will be able to tell you a great deal more, I expect.'

Mr Wylie was a large and languid man who walked with a slight stoop. He wore the regulation suit which seemed to have been run up out of somebody's old billiard cloth dyed battleship grey. He picked things up and waved them about in the air vaguely when he talked. It was hard sledding, but after a while I got him to say something definite.

'Well.' He pinched the bridge of his nose hard and shut his eyes. 'Admitted four days ago,' he said. 'That was down in the town, at the General, you know. My registrar did most of the donkey work, thank God. Four in the morning. He's American, not my registrar, of course, I mean Mr Brightwell, Captain Brightwell.'

He opened his eyes and looked at the ceiling.

'That's right,' I said.

'Yes. Had concussion,' said Wylie. 'Also half-drowned; they pulled him out of the sea. Local man pulled him out, chap called Telford, plays golf. Yes. Well. Several burns, nothing serious. Apparently the fuel tanks on his boat blew up, he was fishing or something.'

'At four in the morning,' I said.

'Mm. Anyway, metal splinters in right thigh and buttock, we took them out in theatre here yesterday, though we might have waited a bit longer, I suppose. Three fractured ribs, pneumothorax on the right, aspiration pneumonia on the left, inhaled water, you know. Thought we might have to do a thoracotomy for a bit, but we stuck sundry needles into him, you know, sucked out his chest on the right and it turned out to be mostly sea-water, so we gave that a miss. Drain and water-seal, antibiotics, all the rest of the circus and he's doing all right now, considering. He seems to be a fit man to start with, which helps, of course.'

'But he is going to be all right?'

'Oh good heavens, yes,' said Wylie. 'Why on earth not?'

'Thank you,' I said. 'Will it be all right if I talk to him?'

'Yes of course. Don't have him doing full knee bends and reciting Shakespeare, his lungs won't really like it yet. Reminds me, I must get in the physios chop-chop. What branch are you in, Dr Yeoman?'

'Research,' I told him.

'Research? Really? How interesting.' It was clear he didn't think so. Clinicians traditionally regard research people as slightly soft in the head, and maybe they're right, at that. 'What sort of research?' he asked.

'Physiology, psychology, engineering.'

'Really. Really. Well.'

'There's one thing I'd like you to tell me if you could,' I said. 'Has there been any sort of investigation yet?'

'Investigation?'

'Well,' I said. 'There was an accident at sea. What about insurance? Or the police? I don't know exactly what the form would be about reporting fire on board ship, but I wondered if there were any sort of clear account of what happened.'

'Now let me see,' said Wylie. 'Let me see.'

He went over to an antique wooden filing cabinet with moulded brass handles; his office, now I came to look at it, was like a film set for an early H. G. Wells, but it obviously went with his personality. Papers were cascading to the floor in droves. Wylie stood in abstract thought saying 'No, no, no,' to himself while I scrabbled around his feet trying to collect them together again. Perhaps he had a secretary in the morning, or perhaps he did it all by guess and by God. Finally he dumped Yancy's case-notes on top of the cabinet with an air of triumph, took the bits of this and that I'd collected, and stuffed them all back into the second drawer down. He banged the drawer shut with triangular paper ears sticking out from it on all sides, selected a couple of quarto sheets from the folder and gave them to me.

'There we are,' he said. 'It's all there. Why do you want to know, Dr Yeoman?' A thought seemed to strike him. 'Not your boat, was it?' he asked.

'No,' I said. 'I'm just curious, that's all.'

'Fine. Fine. In that case I'll leave you to it, if you don't mind. That all right?'

He headed for the door, nodding like a rear-window car mascot and looking everywhere except where he was going. He turned in the doorway and stabbed a finger in my direction.

'Mr Brightwell, *Captain* Brightwell,' he said. 'Five doors along there, on the right.' He swivelled his finger. 'Nice chap, don't tire him out, there's a good fellow.'

He gave me a final nod of benediction and strode off down the corridor before I could thank him. I went back to the flimsy typewritten sheets he'd given me. About the fifth carbon, at a guess. They represented Telford's account of the incidents of four nights ago. The man who'd fished Yancy out and who played golf. Commander Henry Telford, no less, now that I came to look at the top sheet of his report.

Commander Telford to: Coast Guard, was the heading. The language was an odd mixture of semi-officialese and conversational reporting, with Commander Telford's personality showing through in ragged patches. I skimmed through it once and then again, looking for something that might tell me what sort of fishing Yancy had been doing.

Commander Henry Telford, of *Wind's Eye*, had seen and heard an explosion about a quarter of a mile offshore at three-thirty AM on, etcetera. He had dressed immediately and taken out his own cabin cruiser. Conditions, cold, Light Air B'ft One. NW, no sea running, some high cloud, some surface fog, heavy in patches, etcetera. Had spotted floating wreckage almost immediately, had come across survivor clinging to buoyancy bag some minutes later, in rather poor condition and semi-conscious. Survivor was Captain Brightwell. Captain Brightwell said there was no other occupant of what he described as a fishing boat, but which Commander Telford identified, provisionally, and from such pieces of the wreckage as were still afloat, as a Fairey Huntsman offshore cruiser. (*Commander* Telford? Did this mean he really knew what he was talking about, or just that he wanted everyone to know what an expert he was?) His report then described what was left of the boat, that the engines appeared to have sunk, and so on. Telford had taken Captain Brightwell back to *Wind's Eye* and from there had driven him at once to the General Hospital. Had discouraged Captain Brightwell from talking more than necessary, but Captain Brightwell had told him that he had been fishing and that the fuel tanks of the boat had exploded following a fire in the galley compartment. Commander Telford had no opinion to offer on this explanation of the accident beyond the fact that it agreed with what he had observed from shore.

All in all it was a reasonable account. I wasn't clear why Commander Telford had been scanning the horizon for possible incidents at sea at three-thirty in the morning, but perhaps he was a man of lightning reflexes and had been woken by the bang. I left the report on top of the desk and went along the cool, wax-scented corridor to Yancy Brightwell's room.

'Where are the grapes?' asked Yancy. 'I always thought grapes were traditional over here?'

'No grapes,' I said. 'Sorry.'

The room was pale blue and totally dust-free, with fourteen-foot high walls and arched windows looking out over a lawn the size of Wales. They vacuum-cleaned the air three times a day and you could have shaved in the shine on the parquet.

Yancy Brightwell leaned back against stacked pillows and panted like a dog on a hot afternoon. He didn't look too bad, and he had the tail-end of a grin on his face, but just the same he'd been closer to the edge than I'd care to go and it showed on him.

'What does the boss say?' he asked. 'Nobody ever tells you anything in this god-damn country.'

'Don't worry,' I said. 'It's tradition. Like grapes.'

'Okay. You tell me, Giles.'

He talked about the way you'd expect a man to talk on a

lung and a quarter. The right side of his face and hair was scorched and he was still wearing a surgical gown, so I guessed they were still dressing body burns here and there.

I'd known Yancy a long time, ever since we met at an Aircraft Instrumentation Conference at Malmo just after I qualified. We could count on bumping into each other about twice a year on average, because once you're on the technical conference circuit you're there more or less for life, though as it happened the last time I'd seen him was in the back of a refrigerated truck in the Sahara. We didn't send each other postcards and we didn't need to. I thought he was a fake scientist and he thought I was an ivory-tower don, so we got on fine. At times we even kidded ourselves that we talked the same language, though it's always a dangerous assumption between Americans and Englishmen; the words are the same or most of them, but there's a difference between a collection of words and a language and sometimes you realize it.

Yancy had found himself in U S A F Intelligence via a comic-opera PhD and a three-year stint on helicopters. He had a wife and three children somewhere in the middle of the North American continent, but I'd never met them. Right now I was pleased to see him, though I didn't know what he wanted.

'I'll put it in layman's terms, shall I?' I said. 'Wylie thinks you ought to be dead. He thinks that if you were just an ordinary lad like us you would be, only since you're a home-grown, vitaminized, tall-walking, all-American boy you're going to live to spread the word about socialized medicine. Now what did you get me all the way over here for?'

'I wanted you to put something in the mail for me.'

'There are a couple of dozen able-bodied nurses here who'd do that for you,' I said. 'Why me?'

'Because I don't want you to mail it right now but in a couple of weeks. I'd like you to keep it till then. And because you're stupid enough to do it without asking questions.'

'Oh, fine,' I said. 'What is it you want me to post?'

'Jewellery.'

'What sort of jewellery? Stolen? Smuggled?'

'That makes four questions already,' Yancy said. 'Maybe you're not as stupid as I figured.'

'All right,' I said. 'I'll post it. Now let's change the subject and try something else. How was the fishing?'

'Didn't catch a thing. Look, it's over there in the locker. One of the girls here wrapped it up for me, but I'd rather you addressed it.'

I thought it over. I'd known for some time, since he'd saved my life in fact, that Yancy was more involved in Intelligence work than just debriefing Starfighter pilots. He knew that I knew, and he knew my general feelings on the subject of intelligence. But he was a sick man, and likely to stay a sick man for several weeks to come yet. All he wanted me to do was post something for him and, by implication, to keep its destination to myself. It was fair enough, in a way. I should have left it at that, but of course I didn't.

'That's all there is to it?' I asked him.

'That's all. You know me, Giles. I'm just a simple Wyoming farm boy. You mail it the end of next week because the guy I'm sending it to won't be there until then, and I'll buy you a beer when they let me out of here. Right?'

'Okay, farm boy,' I said. 'There's one thing about Wyoming, though. I've never been there, but they tell me it's not great territory for sea-fishing. Too far from the sea, or have I got my geography all wrong?'

'So.'

'Look, Yancy,' I said. 'I've heard three times so far that you were out fishing at four in the morning and your fuel tanks exploded. That may be fine for Wylie and Commander Telford—'

'Who's he?'

'The man who pulled you out of the North Sea a while ago,' I said, 'and I'm not even sure it was a good enough story for him. It certainly isn't for me.'

He shifted slightly against the pile of pillows and said nothing. I shouldn't have been arguing with him, but I wanted to know what it was all about before Matron came in and shooed me out like a chicken.

'Commander Telford says that the boat you were out in was a Huntsman. Not that there was much of it left, he says, but that's what it started out as.'

'Okay, Giles. It was just a boat.'

'Right. Now just let me take you through the next bit nice and slowly, Yancy. The standard engines for the Fairey Huntsman are turbocharged Perkins diesels. Diesels run on diesel fuel. Diesel fuel does not explode, not even if you light a bonfire under the tank and shove your distress flares in for good measure.'

'So how come we exploded?'

'How the hell should I know?' I said. 'Maybe you were torpedoed by an Excise launch, armed to the teeth and looking for jewel thieves. Or maybe you can dream up a better story.'

Commander Telford could have been wrong, of course. It needn't have been a Huntsman, and even if he was right it could have been fitted with petrol engines. But I didn't think so. Yancy lay there and shut his eyes, and his fingers moved to and fro on the bed cover. The breath hissed gently in and out of his damaged lungs, and I waited for him to make his mind up.

'You ever hear of a man called Jissock?' he asked finally. 'He was with me. I ferried him across from France, from the Pas-de-Calais. How does that sound?'

'It's a good opening line,' I said.

He opened his eyes again. He looked angry, but not as angry as he was tired. He turned his hand over on the bed, palm up, and the movement made him wince.

'Okay, Giles,' he said. 'You want to know all about it, I'll tell you. Only get it through your skull first time around, because I'm sure as hell not going to say any of it twice over. You don't remember Jissock? He was a geologist. And a nut case, at least according to your boys. It's down in writing.'

'Wait a minute,' I said. 'Jissock. Wasn't he in the papers a couple of years ago? Shouting the odds because nobody would give him a grant to develop something he'd invented, or have I got him mixed up with somebody else?'

'That's him.'

'Believed in the migration of souls. Is that him too?'

'That was him. *Was*. He's dead and I was lucky. Funny thing was, he kept saying they were out to kill him but I never really believed him.'

'Because he was a nut?'

'I guess so. Maybe he wasn't a nut but he acted the part as though he wrote it himself. You want me to tell you or don't you?'

'Tell me.'

'Right. Two years ago Jissock was an obscure geologist with emotional problems and halitosis. Also he didn't want to be a geologist any more but a physicist. Also he'd invented something, something of extreme military importance, so he said. You can see how popular he'd have been. Your boys, by which I mean British scientific top brass, talked to him and then gave him the thumbs-down. From what I hear they were pretty thorough. Then Jissock wrote to all the papers. It was flying-saucer season and one or two of them wrote him up and weren't very serious about it. He got mad, went on holiday in Milan. After that, nothing, except that on his way to Milan he talked to us in Paris.'

'What sort of us?'

'Me, as it happens,' said Yancy. 'I was in Fontainebleau at the time and they hauled me over to do an evaluation.'

'And you said he was a nut too.'

'That's right. Even if he hadn't been a nut we couldn't have done anything without irritating you British. Jissock screamed, said the USA was stupider than Britain and the whole world was conspiring against him. Went on to Milan and then *pow*. Vanished. Nobody knew where to, nobody knew what for.'

'He was gone for eighteen months? Up to last week or thereabouts?' I asked.

'Right. Up to last week. Then he rolls up in Paris again squealing that he wants to go home. So I took him home, or started to.'

'You mean just like that, you started to take him home?'

'Well.' Yancy closed his eyes again. He looked as though he was about ready to start talking again, only just then the door opened and a tiny indomitable nurse came in. She pushed pillows briskly, took Yancy's pulse, frowned at me and told me I was to be sure not to let him talk. I nodded and waited until she'd gone, and Yancy opened one eye and grinned.

'What happened was Jissock phoned the American Embassy,' he said. 'You can guess how glad they were to hear from him, after they'd shuffled through a few files. After a bit they got hold of me and I contacted him in a café. He was as nervous as hell, had two people with him, a girl and a smooth upper-crust guy, one of you lot, know what I mean? Talked as though he'd got a ping-pong ball in his mouth. He pretended not to know me, Jissock, this is. After a few minutes he went to the can and I joined him. He said he wanted to get back to England and would I help him? This guy was scared witless. No passport, he said the girl had it. Lots of money, he practically threw wads of the stuff at me. He said the girl and the guy he was with were all set to kill him but he knew where he could get a boat and would I take him back across the Channel? I said nuts.' Yancy paused. After a few seconds he muttered, 'It was a foul-up. God, what a foul-up. Next time I swear I'll go by the book.'

I waited again. He'd run out of breath and was fighting to get it back. I went over to the locker by the window and pulled the door open. On the top shelf was a smallish parcel wrapped in plain brown paper; it could have held, say, a tube of toothpaste.

'Is this it?' I asked.

He nodded. I turned it over once or twice, weighing it in my hand, and Yancy suddenly said, 'He paid his fare.'

'This?'

'Yeah, that.'

'And you ferried him across in a Fairey Huntsman?'

'How do I know?' he said irritably. 'You're the great maritime nation. Me, I don't know from Chris Craft. It belonged to some friends of his, he said, called Marris and Braun. Maybe they were his friends. Maybe. I fixed to see him again that evening. I didn't want any part of it but I had to stay in the game. He came that evening all right, with his terribly ever so British playmate after him and we had a fight. This smooth British playmate had a gun. When the argument was over Jissock gave me that little item you're holding there and I said okay, I'd ferry him across the damn Channel if that's what he wanted. I'd already called some friends of mine in the UK. I thought I'd have a nice long chat with him on the trip over and then give him to British Intelligence in case they wanted him. I thought maybe they'd give me a medal or a knighthood or something.'

'You don't have the right accent,' I said.

'Anyway we picked up this cruiser from his two friends Marris and Braun at Le Touquet, and I hauled him across in it. Only they must have followed us over. Most likely they'd put a marker on board.' He waited for me to ask what a marker was. 'DF beacon,' he said.

'Who must have?'

'The girl. Or the public school playmate. Or Braun and Marris. Or all of them.'

'And they crept up on you and blew you to bits with a large naval gun they had around?'

'It was foggy, dark as Satan's ass, Giles. We didn't have very accurate navigation either. Consol, and how would you expect a farm boy to handle that? I was waiting for daybreak so I could take her into the Blackwater estuary. I was having a rest in the forecabin and they lobbed two grenades into the cockpit. One phosphorus, one fragmentation. Must have blown Jissock into little tiny pieces.'

I looked out of the window. Alternate bands of sun and shadow drifted across the impeccable satin lawns and the *petit-point* flowerbeds. Somewhere about half a mile away I could hear the persistent chug of an idling tractor, occasionally screwing itself up to a two-thousand-revolution clatter and then falling away again. Behind me Yancy went on with his small account of piracy and murder in territorial waters, and if he hadn't been lying in bed six feet from me with two damaged lungs and various burns and scars to prove it I wouldn't have believed him. One phosphorus, one fragmentation. There spoke the true and trained Intelligence Officer. Where possible, be precise.

'I can't recall much after that,' said Yancy. 'This guy who pulled me out, Commander Whatsit.'

'Telford,' I said. 'Commander Henry Telford.'

'Him. Did he put in some sort of report?'

'Yes,' I said. 'Two pages, closely typed, for the Coast

Guard. Don't worry, you said all the right things and none of the wrong ones. It must be a great thing to have a trained subconscious. His report wouldn't perhaps be quite good enough for a Lloyd's investigation, but it doesn't sound to me as though there's likely to be one.' The sun went in, the invisible tractor coughed into final rattle and died away to silence. I came away from the window, balancing the package in my hand. 'They're going to bust you back to pfc or whatever it is, aren't they?' I said. 'Ceremonially. In front of the massed ranks of U S A F Intelligence.'

'It could be,' said Yancy. 'It was a foul-up all right.'

I tapped the package with a finger-nail.

'Oh well. We all make mistakes,' I said.

'I'll give you the address for that. Ten days, right?' said Yancy.

'Fine. Ten days.'

'And try not to lose it on the way to the mailbox. I've been to a lot of trouble to get it here, one way and another.'

'Not as much trouble as Jissock, though,' I said. He started to cough, in small, painful explosions of sound.

'No,' he said. 'There's that, of course.'

I drove away from the nursing home. On my way back I dropped into the casualty department at the General, where they'd done the emergency work on Yancy after Telford brought him in. Yes, they said, now that I mentioned it, Captain Brightwell had arrived with something strapped to his thigh with plaster. They brought out a check list of its effects. One watch, some small currency (French, German, Swiss). Fifty dollars American in metal clip. One lump query sailmakers' wax secured to outer aspect R. thigh.

I know about a thousand other places where they'd have taken a closer look to see what it was Captain Brightwell had taped to his thigh, but not here, of course. Sister Casualty would never have thought of it, or allowed anybody else to think of it either.

I considered dropping in on Commander Telford at *Wind's Eye,* but in the end I decided against it. The rain had set in for the rest of the evening and night, and I drove home slowly and steadily because of the leak under the scuttle which would gradually fill my left shoe if I didn't.

FOUR

LONG AFTER dark I threaded my way down Stiles Lane and into the stables, switched off and climbed out into the tangle of rope, firewood, skis and empty oil cans I keep meaning to clear up tomorrow, or some time anyway.

Stiles Lodge was old and decaying and I lived in the attic. The rest of the house was empty, and had been for years. The floors sloped, the walls only stayed upright because they built things better in those days, and the stone boundary wall which ran along one side of the lane carried a message in white-wash: CLLR WARBURTON IS A COMMUNIST. This piece of rural politics was what had attracted me in the first place. The negligible rent was what kept me there, though the fuel bills were ridiculous. The Lodge was a half-hour drive from the Institute and there was nobody around to talk to, which suited me fine. I was most likely classified locally with Councillor Warburton as an eccentric. I was building a seven-inch reflecting telescope in the summer-house, and Binnie had painted all the interior walls of the attic in pale orange, just to show she was still fond of me in spite of having shacked up with Christian Rasmussen.

I climbed all four flights of stairs with the milk, the morning and evening papers and a dozen eggs all from the tin trunk in the hall which was my delivery box. I had a bath, ate my way through three-quarters of a pound of steak and watched four eminent men on television discussing an issue of world-shaking importance until disbelief and inertia set in. Then I went to the desk and wrote the address he'd given me on the outside of Yancy's parcel: *to await collection, C. V. Melrose, 96 Lancelot Crescent, London W8.*

I went slowly downstairs and out into the garden. The rain had stopped but the trees still dripped and pattered. I collected three gear wheels from the equatorial mounting of the telescope and brought them back into the house. Several of the teeth were sticking slightly and I worked on them until a little after midnight, wondering how long it would be before I could afford a new screw-cutting lathe. Then I picked up Yancy's package again and started, slowly and carefully, to open it.

I remember all this quite clearly and I also remember feeling no sense of guilt whatever about it. It would be neat and moral to claim that if I hadn't done it, none of what followed in the next weeks would have happened and that the whole thing was therefore my own fault, but it wouldn't be true. It's a moot point whether I'd have been better off or worse and the fact that Yancy undoubtedly meant me to open it is neither here nor there.

If I'd been more scrupulous I'd have left it where it was for ten days and then posted it. If I'd been more competent I'd have gone to 96 Lancelot Crescent, waited for C. V. Melrose to show up and then asked him politely what the hell went on.

All this is speculation. What I did was to lever the brown sealing tape away from the end of the parcel with a scalpel, and I was just sliding the cardboard box inside on to the desk top when the phone rang.

It was Andy Dylan, Driver's understudy at Seeker Section. He had reason to believe, he said, that I'd visited Captain Brightwell in hospital. Was this so?

'Yes,' I said.

'I think you ought to come up and talk to us,' said Andy.

'Why should I do that?' I asked him.

'Just a little advice, offered in the friendliest possible spirit.'

'Or else what?'

'No listen, Giles,' he said. 'I know how things stand. Just come and talk to us. What does it cost to talk?'

'I don't know,' I said. 'What did it cost last time?'

'Okay, last time. This is this time.'

'No thanks.'

'I would if I were you. I'm only trying to save time, trouble and energy all round. There's a certain amount of reckless opportunism about and some of it I don't agree with. If you change your mind, call me, will you, Giles? I'll give you a number.'

He gave me a number, and rang off. I wasn't sure I liked the bit about reckless opportunism, but I was still nowhere near wanting to talk to Seeker.

I slid Yancy's parcel all the way out of its wrapping. Whatever it was, he'd put it inside a shaving-soap carton. I flipped the end open and shook out a chocolate-coloured bar loosely packed in tissue paper.

It was about an inch across and five inches long, a rough cylinder which rolled to and fro slightly before rocking to a halt. I scraped at it experimentally with a finger-nail. The surface, at least, was wax of some sort all right, just like the Casualty report had said. Cobblers', sailmakers' wax, maybe.

I balanced the little cylinder in the palm of my hand, trying to guess what might be inside the wax. Diamonds? Suppose Yancy had been telling the truth?

I picked up the scalpel again and picked at one end of the cylinder. When the tip of the blade grated against something hard I stopped. I switched on the desk lamp and held the bar under it, trying to see what I'd struck.

Then I carefully stripped about half an inch of the cylinder free from wax and looked at it some more.

It took me a couple of minutes to work it out, but what Jissock had handed over as his boat fare was a laser rod.

It had a central half-inch core of ruby, with an eighth of an inch of sapphire fused on to it like a jacket. The end I'd cleaned was ground flat as a mirror and I knew the other end would be just the same. The whole thing was about three-quarters of an inch in diameter under the wax top-coat.

I was doing a bit of mental arithmetic trying to figure out its probable cost – apart from one man's life, that is – when the phone rang again and I nearly dropped it on the floor. It wasn't my night for opening other people's parcels.

This time it took me a second or so to identify the voice at the other end of the line. Then the thin Scottish accent popped a switch in my brain and I could almost see McKellar, batwing collar and all, hunched over the receiver.

'Dr Yeoman?'

'Speaking,' I said.

'This is McKellar here, Dr Yeoman. You'll remember me, I expect. I'd like you to call at my office, if you could find it convenient. I would suggest about half past ten tomorrow morning. Would you do that, Dr Yeoman?'

I seemed to be very popular all of a sudden.

'Where is your office?' I asked.

'Whitehall Chambers. Department of Scientific Security, as I'm sure you'll recall from our meeting at dinner.'

'Will Major Driver be there, by any chance?'

'Of course not.'

'All right,' I told him. 'I'll be there.'

'Thank you.'

I put down the phone and went back to the desk, wondering why I found McKellar more persuasive than Andy Dylan. I collected together the wax I'd scraped off the laser crystal, swept it on to a sheet of paper and put the whole lot in the desk drawer; wrapping paper, carton, and the expensive piece of ruby and sapphire which had once been Jissock's and was now either Yancy's or C. V. Melrose's (whoever he might be) or, just conceivably, nobody's at all.

Then I went to bed. I slept so late that I only just made it to D S S on time, the next morning.

The offices of the Department of Scientific Security are near enough to the seat of government to be guarded, along with twenty or so similar departments, by a commissionaire and no less than three glass-fronted porters' lodges.

The difference, therefore, between the Department of Scientific Security and Seeker is that D S S officially acknowledges its own existence, whereas Seeker Section does not, a point which I brooded over in the lift.

McKellar sat behind an Inventory A desk and in front of a window looking out over a whole lot of roofs. Inventory A pigeons dipped about in the morning sun on a lead-flashed gable outside. McKellar stood up as I was shown in.

'Sit down,' he said. 'I want to talk to you on a serious subject.'

I sat down.

'Yesterday afternoon,' he said, 'you visited Captain Yancy Brightwell in a nursing home in East Anglia. Is that correct?'

'Quite correct,' I said.

I found this omniscient opening move irritating, particularly since this was the second time I'd had it tried on me. Pawn to king four, Yeoman, we know what you've been up to and don't bother to conceal anything from us, even the size of your socks. Just sign this and we needn't bother you any more. Give your watch to the officer on your way to the cell and try not to rattle the bars.

'Thank you,' said McKellar. 'How did you know he was there, Dr Yeoman?'

'He sent me a note.'

'At the Institute?'

'Yes.'

'Thank you. Might I ask what you talked about?'

'This and that. He wasn't in very good shape,' I said.

'I'm sorry to hear that. Could I put it another way? What was Captain Brightwell's reason for asking to see you?'

'He's an old friend.'

'I see. How long have you known him?'

'Ten years or so,' I said.

'Thank you. You do know that Captain Brightwell is an accredited officer of U S Air Force Intelligence, don't you?'

'Yes, I do.'

'How long have you known that, Dr Yeoman?'

'Since last year. We ran into each other on a project which you already know all about, I believe.'

'That would have been Project Tree Frog?'

'Yes,' I said. McKellar looked as though he were ticking off a set of invisible points inside his head, or perhaps he was trying to unsettle me. Or both.

'But before last year,' he said, 'you didn't know?'

'No, I didn't. Why?'

'You've discussed various topics, scientific topics, perhaps, with him? Over the course of the years? That would be fair, would it?'

'Very fair,' I said, 'considering we've been sitting on the same committees.'

'Yes of course,' said McKellar. 'Have you ever discussed military projects with him, before Tree Frog?'

'I don't know what you'd classify as military,' I said. 'We've been discussing altimeters, for instance, for about five years now. Altimeters are used in military aircraft. Yes, I suppose you could say I've discussed military projects with him.'

'Under authorization, of course.'

'Of course.'

'Three years ago, Dr Yeoman,' said McKellar, 'you were working on a certain project in conjunction with various bodies, the Royal Aircraft Establishment and so on. This was a fast, low-level strike aircraft project.'

'Aren't we going to use its proper name?' I asked. 'Or would that be a serious breach of something or other?'

'Please try to restrain your sense of humour. Did you ever mention this project in conversation with Captain Brightwell?'

'Yes,' I said.

'Was that wise?'

'Wasn't it wise?' I asked. 'As I recall it, we weren't at war with the Americans. Look, McKellar, suppose you tell me what's on your mind, otherwise we could be here for hours.'

McKellar drummed his fingers on the desk and looked out of the window.

'Security can present difficult problems,' he said finally. 'If it were always a case of people passing on photographs or plans to known enemy agents, life would be much simpler, don't you agree, Dr Yeoman? But that seldom is the case. Usually it's a question of people talking to each other, and of our having to decide whether they were supposed to or not. It's difficult sometimes. What sort of things might you have said to Captain Brightwell about . . . this low-level strike project, for instance?'

'I said it wouldn't work,' I told him.

'Did you, now?'

'Yes. I also said it to a whole lot of other people.'

'Yes, so I believe. And I expect Captain Brightwell discussed American projects with you, sometimes?'

'And with the French, and the Germans, and the Swedes and the Australians. Yes. That's the way we stupid naïve scientists work. We talk to each other, about planes and goldfish and pictures and Unidentified Flying Objects, McKellar. Didn't you know? I realize that Scientific Security would like us to communicate with each other solely by means of written notes, preferably all relayed through this office and suitably stamped, but that isn't how life works. It's very tough for you, I can see that. Now do you arraign me for treason or what?'

'What sort of American projects would Captain Brightwell have discussed with you?'

It was impossible to put him off. I could see how he'd climbed to the upper branches of his own little tree, and how difficult he'd be to dislodge now that somebody was shaking the trunk.

'Well,' I said. 'He talked about vertical take-off aircraft once or twice.'

'Oh? What did he say about them?'

'He said they wouldn't work,' I leaned forward. 'He said that if Providence had meant us to take off vertically, we'd have been given propellers on top of our heads,' I told him.

McKellar drummed his fingers some more. 'I see,' he said. 'I see. I think perhaps now, Dr Yeoman, you had better tell me exactly what it was you discussed with Captain Brightwell yesterday afternoon.'

'No,' I said.

'I must warn you very seriously. Your association with Captain Brightwell could have grave consequences. Things can be made very difficult for you. Very difficult indeed.'

'No they can't,' I said.

I was quite wrong, of course. You can make things difficult for a man without having him arraigned for treason; all you have to do is talk to one or two people, here and there. I walked down to the Embankment and wondered how long it would be before an extra high tide with the wind behind it came flooding over the new river wall opposite Millbank. Or through it. I expect McKellar was already talking to one or two people, here and there, because a week later I was out of a job.

FIVE

MICHAELSON WAS as nice about it as he could be, of course. I sat in his office and watched him shuttle to and fro across the room, raise and lower the venetian blinds, shift books around on the desk and blow dust from where they'd been lying and in general go through the necessary act of a Director who has to offload one of his staff and is embarrassed about the whole thing.

I didn't help him out, though I liked him and I knew all about the position he was in. He was a politician all right, but he hadn't reached the stage of complete surrender to expediency and I didn't think he ever would.

He talked about the historical background of my post at the Institute, or at least that was the way he put it. His heart wasn't really in it.

'Originally, you'll remember, your work was directly financed by the RAF,' he said.

'That was seven years ago,' I pointed out.

'I know. I know. But that's where the money originated. We get our research grants from all over the place, Giles, and it just happens to be your bit of the money that we've lost this year. I suggested that the Ministry of Aviation might take over the commitment, but they wouldn't. I'm sorry, but there it is.'

He stopped weaving about and sank into his chair.

'But surely,' I said, 'we aren't divided up job by job and grant by grant, are we? I can see that somebody's cut the total by about three thousand pounds or so, but I'd have thought that just meant three thousand less for the Institute as a whole.'

'I know,' said Michaelson. 'That's what I would have thought myself, but apparently not. You're not established, remember, Giles.'

I wasn't, though I didn't really see what difference it made. About half of us were, the others either hadn't got around to it yet or, like myself, didn't want to be established. If you're established, of course, you can only lose your job if you go berserk and shoot someone, or that's the theory, but even if you're not, you're supposed to have security of employment, otherwise everybody would be running off and getting another thousand a year for the same work somewhere else.

'I need hardly add that it's nothing to do with your work,' he said. 'You know that.'

'I should damn well think not.'

'Quite. Quite. As a matter of fact I think you're being badly treated and I've said so. Apart from anything else the notice is discourteously short. Your contract was due for renewal next month.'

He fished around inside his coat and brought out his pen. He started to twist the cap round and round irritably.

'The only bright spot I can see is that you'll easily get another post, Giles. University or industry. You'll get the best possible recommendation from us, of course. Least we can do.'

'I don't want another post,' I said. 'Oddly enough, I rather like it here.'

The pen came to pieces in his hands rather suddenly, and he bent down behind the desk to look for some part of it or other which had sprung out and fallen to the floor. While he was out of sight I said, 'What it comes down to is that someone up top has put the boot in. That's right, isn't it?' and he straightened up.

'I wouldn't allow anybody to dictate to me,' he said.

'I know,' I told him. He wouldn't, either, but doing battle with the sort of people who'd have put the boot in would be like trying to punch holes in fog.

I could easily get another post all right, and I knew just where. All I had to do was lift the phone and call the number Andy Dylan had given me. I began to have the sensation of running down an alley between high walls. I couldn't see where I was running to but Andy and Driver and McKellar could, I was quite sure. Michaelson wouldn't allow himself to be dictated to, but he ran a research establishment, research establishments need money, and he could easily wind up selling flags from a tray to get it without having been dictated to one little bit. So he spent another twenty minutes being sorry and I listened, and we shook hands and that was that. I expect everybody spent twenty minutes apologizing to Jonah, too, before the big fish got him.

I turned over my current series of experiments to McTeague, who works in the same field as me or near enough. He said he was sorry to hear I was leaving. So did everyone else, from Dinsdale in Radar to Fred in the tea-room. So did Miss Amanda Grayle when I told her she'd have to learn the rest of her elementary applied electronics from somebody else. I was pretty sorry about that myself. I suggested that McTeague might take her on, after which McTeague came and apologized for ever having doubted my generosity of nature. I got a half-pint pewter beer-mug as a leaving present and a formal letter of thanks from an office in the high hundreds at the Ministry of Defence.

I took the car one afternoon and drove to the Lady Adderly Memorial Nursing Home again. It was the day I was due to post Yancey's parcel. Yancey wasn't there. Matron said that he'd been transferred to a private hospital in London two days earlier, and handed me a foolscap envelope which she said Captain Brightwell had left for me.

'He didn't say where I could contact him?' I asked.

'I'm afraid he didn't, Dr Yeoman,' she said. 'I gather he was being flown back to America almost immediately and didn't know where he might end up. He said you would understand.'

Back in the car I shook out the contents of the envelope on the passenger seat. There was no letter. Just five photographs, four of them of men and the fifth of a good-looking blonde, around thirty, I'd say. She was wearing a dark-coloured cocktail dress. There was nothing to show when, where or how any of the photographs had been taken, who they were of or what they'd been taken with. None of them was a studio shot.

I drove home thoughtfully.

I was an unemployed scientist with a small overdraft, a smaller private income and prospects which you'd need a strong light and a magnifying glass to pick out. My qualifications weren't good enough to get me a reasonable academic job and my temperament would keep me out of industry. For the first time I realized accurately how well the Institute fitted me and how sorry I was to be out of it. I'd been running a bright, upstaging little war with Driver and McKellar and patting myself on the back every other minute thinking what a clever, independent-minded lad I was, but when it came to counting up the casualties the total seemed to be one. Me.

I put the car away in the stables and walked down to the village feeling sorry for myself. The Dog and Duck was full of visiting darts experts and their supporters from Barnwell. I stood at one end of the bar and drank Pernod until closing time, which is what I drink when I have no other aim but eventual coma. Nobody much looked in my direction except the landlord. He knew I'd lost my job, the way people in villages know everything.

I left upright but totally detached, and more than ever convinced that Pernod is the best, if one of the foulest-tasting, solutions to the troubles the world faces today. I marched back along Stiles Lane to the sound of internal and martial music, watching the moon wheel across the faces of the puddles, and plodded upstairs to my flat.

I pushed open the living-room door, and a fraction of my sodden brain alerted me to something I couldn't place and lacked the will to pay attention to anyway. I lit the gas fire and looked around the room. Then I took off my jacket and went through into the bedroom. I flicked the light switch but nothing happened; and as I stood in the doorway forcing myself to remember where the spare light bulbs were, I blinked myself into the realization that there was somebody in my bed, hunched under the covers.

My feet floated me across the room, almost without volition. I took hold of the top edge of the blanket and turned it down.

For a couple of years I looked at what I knew must be Jissock, at the waxwork face and the gaping, bloodless wounds like grinning mouths sliced by the fragmentation grenade which had killed him. Then I carefully turned the blanket up again and went back into the living-room to sit by the fire.

SIX

I COULDN'T sit there for long, I knew.

There was no reason why I should feel anything, particularly, about the cold thing in my bed next door. I have done the necessary number of post-mortems, dissected the necessary number of cadavers, I am familiar with the dead. There was no reason why the corpse of a man I'd never met should throw me off balance. And yet I sat and stretched my hands out towards the fire and felt the sweat grow on my forehead, and there was nothing I could do tonight but run, get out and away, as far away as I could.

In the morning it would be different. In the morning the sun would be shining and I would have a headache. In the morning the lark would be on the wing and the snail on the thorn, and the grey thing in the bedroom would be the remains of the machinery of Jissock and nothing more than that.

But that would be in the morning, and tonight was now. I stood up and turned the fire off and humped myself into my coat.

There was one thing I had to do before I got out. I pushed the bedroom door open, slowly, until my shadow in the rectangle of light spilled from behind me lay across the bed.

In my coat pocket were the five photographs Yancy had left me. I dragged them out and shuffled through them until I was sure that one of them was a picture of Jissock. I went over and pulled the blanket away again and looked until I was quite certain of it, and then I laid the back of my hand against the grey shoulder nearest me.

Jissock was cold. He'd been dead a fortnight, so why not? But he was, I thought, colder than death; cold as the morgue, cold as ice. With the tip of my index finger I pushed against the flesh and half an inch under I could feel the fat was frozen hard.

I went out of the bedroom and locked the door. I did the same with the living-room and the hall, went down the stairs and plodded out into the night. I walked for an hour or two while the alcohol drained away from my brain and left me with a raging dehydrated thirst.

In the morning he would, very slightly, be starting to smell.

I reached the outskirts of town and walked steadily on down the yellow suburban streets.

You have a corpse and you need to keep it. Fair enough. Pack it with ice, or put it in the cool chest in the mortuary. But there is something obscene about deep-freezing it, something which implies you want to keep it around for ever, or at least until it just happens to be convenient to thaw it out again in a fortnight or a couple of months or a year.

I was getting near the middle of town, passing the terraced fronts of tidy houses belonging to tidy people with tidy problems, not including defrosting corpses in the bedroom but probably just as unpleasant. I had a dead geologist, they had mortgages and patches of rust on the car and all of us were losing sleep.

I turned into a narrow mews and climbed some stairs and rang the doorbell of Binnie's flat.

After about three minutes a light came on in the hallway and the door opened. Christian Rasmussen, in vast striped pyjamas and a navy raincoat, examined me with suspicion.

'Can I come in?' I asked.

I must have looked more or less the way I felt. He stood aside.

'I think maybe yes, you'd better,' he said.

I stumbled in through the door. Binnie appeared from the bedroom, blinking sleepily, red hair swinging across her pleasant, ugly, competent face. She did a bit of silent telegraphy with Rasmussen while I leaned against the wall.

'Not so good,' I said. 'Not good at all.'

'All right, Giles,' said Binnie. 'It's all right now. Whatever it is.'

'Good,' I said, and started to slide. It was great, all of a sudden, not to have to bother any more.

'I think you been tying one on, hey?' said Rasmussen. He picked me up. I felt as stupid as hell about it, but there was nothing I felt like doing and it was easier than getting dragged. He probably carried Binnie about the place now and then when she felt kittenish, and I was no problem at all to him. He dumped me on the divan in the front room, Binnie came in behind him and dropped rugs all over me and I shut my eyes.

'Drunk like a pig,' said Rasmussen tolerantly.

'Giles is not drunk,' said Binnie.

'I'm drunk,' I told them as they went out and left me. 'Believe me, I'm drunk.'

I heard Rasmussen saying 'See, I told you,' as they shut the bedroom door. I started to count and got as far as eight.

Next morning nobody asked what the hell I thought I was doing barging in on an ex-mistress in the middle of the night. Binnie gave me coffee in a pint mug, and Rasmussen had to make do with four eggs and only half a dozen rounds of toast because I was there. He slapped me on the back and laughed, poured coffee on the tablecloth and laughed again when Binnie hacked him on the leg. Each time he laughed my skull bounced an inch or so in the air.

'You were drunk as a pig, buddy,' he said. He shook out the morning paper and told me there was an international athletics meeting at White City in the evening and that Denmark would undoubtedly thrash the pants off us.

'Do you want to tell us what's wrong?' Binnie asked me.

'I don't think so,' I said.

'It's not losing your job?'

'No,' I told her. 'Not that. And thanks.'

'You ought to get married, Giles,' she said.

'You think that might fix everything, do you?' I said, 'or did you have somebody in mind?'

'Don't answer back,' roared Rasmussen. 'I don't get to answer back, why should you? Sure, you get married, then you won't get drunk and ring doorbells at night, hey?' Binnie stood just behind his chair and they both grinned at me.

I collected my coat and said goodbye. Binnie kissed me on the cheek and Rasmussen shook hands and laughed some more. It was too early for anything to be funny, but I felt better. They were two of the nicest people I've ever met. I haven't seen either of them since, because a few weeks later they got married and Rasmussen dragged her off to Denmark, where they settled down to raise a brood of giant red-headed hammer-throwers and champion free-style swimmers.

I caught an early morning bus out into the country, which left me with a two-mile walk home.

All I had to do was to stop at the police station in the village and tell them everything. I'd have to answer a lot of awkward questions, but would they be more awkward for me than for Driver, or McKellar, or whoever had arranged for the frozen body of a former scientist, killed in an unsatisfactorily explained accident off the east coast, to be dumped in my bed?

I had no doubt at all that Seeker was responsible. With or without the cooperation of the Department of Scientific Security, and for all I knew the Special Branch and the Ministry of Agriculture and Fisheries. Reckless opportunism was how Andy Dylan had put it. He might also have called it cutting their losses.

Yancy had telephoned 'friends in the UK' before he'd set off across the Channel with Jissock. Who his friends were I didn't know, but Jissock was a scientist and the matter must have wound up in Seeker's lap. I could picture the disappointment all round when they steamed off to the coast and got nothing but a few bits of cruiser and a dead body, but evidently Driver was the sort of person who never threw anything away in case he should need it later, and that went for dead bodies too.

I still didn't have to buy it. Our policemen are wonderful, and Sergeant Gittings would listen sympathetically while I told him it was all a sort of Secret Service practical joke, really, and nothing to do with me even if the body did happen to be in my bed.

The snag was, of course, the fact that I was already connected with Jissock. You know nothing about the deceased, Dr Yeoman? Nothing at all. Oh, except that an American friend of mine who unfortunately can't be got hold of to give evidence told me all about him and I seem to have this package and these photographs. And what does the package contain, Dr Yeoman? Well, a laser rod. Why? I don't know. I see, Dr Yeoman. Now, one of these photographs seems to be of the deceased. Yes, I know. The post-mortem shows, Dr Yeoman that he met his death in some sort of explosion involving phosphorus burns and fragments of shrapnel. Can you give us any enlightenment about this? Well, you see.

What I had better do was to bury the package and burn the photographs. I was an innocent man trapped in the machinations of a bunch of devious psychopaths. I wanted nothing to do with them and I could say so. Everything would straighten itself out in the end. Nobody knew about the laser rod and the photographs except Yancy and myself.

Did they?

What I had better do was to phone Andy Dylan and tell him okay, I was tired, I couldn't keep up, I was a good boy now and would they please get this body out of my flat while we talked about what, exactly, they wanted me to do.

On my way upstairs I collected a PVC groundsheet from the stables. It was a sharp, sunny morning, and going into the flat was like unlocking a museum.

In the bedroom I took off all the clothes I was wearing except my shorts and rolled the top blanket all the way down. What was left of Jissock was dressed in a ripped shirt and bleached, bluish trousers. There was nothing much I needed to know about the body. I spread the groundsheet on the floor by the bed and eased the bedclothes, body and all, down on to it and rolled the lot up into an untidy bundle. Everything was damp because thawing was almost complete, but otherwise I didn't have too much difficulty.

I crossed the passage to the boxroom and dragged out the

wooden linen chest. I unpacked it and put the contents in the hall cupboard.

The chest was metal-bound and lead-lined and would, I thought, do the job perfectly. It was hard work getting the rolled PVC bundle into it, but not messy. When I'd finally managed it, the only sign left in the room was a damp patch on the mattress. I tried to recall what I knew of forensics and decided it didn't matter for the moment.

I went into the living-room and telephoned Arfon Jones at the local garage.

'Home Rule for Wales,' I said.

'And bloody early in the morning for it, too,' he said. 'What is it then?'

'Got a job for you and the van, I have,' I told him. He said he'd be round with the boy in about an hour if I didn't mind him finishing breakfast. I said that would be fine.

I dragged the linen chest out of the bedroom and into the hallway. I was still in my shorts, and as an afterthought I took them off, opened the lid again and stuffed them down beside Jissock's body.

I closed the lid and locked it, and then took a fifteen-minute shower, as hot as I could bear it.

Then I called the telephone number Andy had given me, and Driver himself answered.

'Hello, Dr Yeoman.'

'I'm in trouble,' I said. 'I'm coming up to see you.'

'Now?' he asked.

'I'll be there in about three hours.'

'I'm very glad indeed. You'll come to us in Bayswater?'

'No,' I said. 'Not at Seeker. I'd feel uncomfortable there. McKellar's office, twelve noon, was more what I had in mind.'

He thought that one over.

'I don't know if that would be quite as convenient,' he said. 'Prefer it here, much better.'

'I dare say. But I'd prefer McKellar's office,' I said, and rang off before he could argue some more. It wasn't much in the circumstances but it was a gesture.

What I needed badly was more coffee, but I didn't make

any. The whole flat seemed to stink of the charnel-house, though of course I was only imagining things.

After a while Arfon Jones came round with the boy who helped him with most of the mechanical butchery which passed for car repair work in the village, and I told them what I wanted done. They bumped the lead-lined chest on every single stair, going down. Halfway, Arfon said 'Extremely heavy, this is,' and I nodded and waited for him to ask what I'd got in it, a body? But he didn't, and they fought it out to the van and drove off.

I backed the car out of the stables and headed for London. I still had a headache, but I could feel it getting better every minute.

SEVEN

'WE WANT you to find one of these and dismantle it,' said Driver.

He handed me a sheet of drawing-paper. While I tried to decide which way up I ought to hold it everybody in the room sat back, in so far as they could on their slatted folding chairs, flipped open cigarette packets and bent their heads to other people's lighters. McKellar's office seemed a bit on the overcrowded side, though there were only five others in it apart from me. I flicked a corner of the drawing Driver had given me and looked across at the man from Telecommunications Research whose name I hadn't caught first time around. He was earnest and rotund and festooned with felt-tipped pens. I held the sheet of paper out towards him.

'What is it?' I asked.

In the corner nearest the door by the filing cabinets Andy Dylan was pouring out corrosive tea. Cups with brown detergent heads on them were being passed round. The man from Telecommunications reached out and tweaked the drawing from me.

'Rock Baby,' he said.

'And?'

'It's an automatic recording seismograph,' he said. Somebody put a hand on my elbow and I turned. It was Andy. 'Sugar?' he asked. I told him two and went back to the Telecommunications man, but he wasn't with me any more, he was getting his cup of tea from Conrad who was sitting next to him. Conrad was from Defence Intelligence Six; I'd run up against him before with painful consequences and the fact that he was here at all confirmed all my worst fears about the operation, as if they needed confirming. The man from Telecommunications Research had rolled up the drawing of Rock Baby and was tapping Conrad on the chest with it, emphasizing some point or other. I tried McKellar.

'What for?' I asked.

'I beg your pardon?' said McKellar.

'This, er, this seismograph,' I said. 'What exactly is it for?'

'Aye, well. It's for detecting underground nuclear explosions,' he said. 'Excuse me.' He tried to stand up behind his desk but found Driver's knees in the way. 'Maybe if I were to start a bit further back you'd understand more clearly,' he said.

'That sounds a good idea,' I told him.

All things considered, Driver had collected a lot of people together for this session; I hadn't given him much notice. The man from Telecommunications, whose name, I now recalled with an effort, was Higsbee, had taken longest to get here. While we waited for him to travel in from whatever godforsaken bunch of Nissen huts he worked in, Driver, McKellar, Conrad and myself had spent an hour reaching a rather tortuous and largely unspoken bargain whereby they would get me out of any little difficulty I might have found myself in and I would undertake a piece of so far unspecified work for DSS and Seeker combined, DI6 and Conrad intervening, as they say in the law reports. It was now well after lunchtime. The pigeons outside on the roof fluttered up on to the sill as McKellar fought his way genteelly around to the front of the desk. By the time he'd made it, two of them had got inside the room in a decorous, nodding hunt for biscuit crumbs. Driver flapped a hairy hand at them, teacups clicked and the small plastic fug-stirring fan on the desk corner whirred busily as though waiting for take-off instructions. It was all very reassuring, but none of it reassured me.

'Most of this goes back to 1958,' said McKellar when he'd levered himself into position. 'In 1958 there was a Geneva conference on methods of detecting underground nuclear explosions, in case there should be an agreement to stop tests altogether instead of merely the atmospheric ones. All that emerged from this conference was that nobody knew very much about detecting explosions underground – as opposed to earthquakes – and the major powers went away to study the matter.

'As a result, various seismographic stations were either built from scratch or expanded and adapted from existing stations, with the expressed intention of distinguishing explosions from earthquakes. These stations include, for instance, Eskdalemuir in Scotland, Yellowknife in Canada, and Pole Mountain, Wyoming, together with a new seismic array installed by the United States Atomic Energy Commission at Billings, Montana.

'All in all,' McKellar went on, 'detection of underground explosions by seismographic means has now reached a high degree of sophistication.' It was a terrific build-up. I began to wonder what had gone wrong, that would be the really interesting bit, but obviously I had quite a while to wait yet.

'It was felt that we could play a very full part in the project here in Britain,' said McKellar.

'After all we invented seismography,' said Higsbee from Telecommunications. 'As usual.'

'If you don't count the Chinese, yes,' I said. 'They were detecting earthquakes eighteen centuries ago.'

'It was felt,' said McKellar, 'that this was a project in which we could play a very full part.' He'd done his sentence construction better this time. 'We have a good deal of experience and some excellent sites for instruments.'

'Also it doesn't cost much,' I said. 'Not like sending things to the moon.'

'Relatively speaking, relatively speaking,' said Higsbee.

'However, during the last few years some difficulties started to arise, which Major Driver will explain to you,' finished

McKellar, giving way to the military with the air of an elderly schoolmaster who isn't getting the respect he's used to. I was beginning to take to Higsbee, felt pens and all. I held out my hand and he looked at it blankly for a second or two and then beamed at me brightly and passed over the rolled-up drawing of Rock Baby, about which doubtless I was going to be told something in the fullness of time. By now Driver was all set to go.

'Difficulties arose,' he said, 'when it became clear that research in nuclear explosives was concentrating on small weapons rather than big ones. Tactical rather than strategic, if I may put it that way. In fact it's very nearly true to say that these days there's hardly any need for testing megaton weapons. We know all about them already, you see.'

'But it still impresses people when you let one off,' I said.

'Yes, you mean the Chinese,' said Driver, 'inevitable, inevitable, yes.'

'The Chinese and the rest,' I said. 'What we need is a system where anybody who wants to join the nuclear club builds his bomb and then throws a party for everybody else to come and have a look at it. Then we all go into committee and decide whether it would go off *if* they pressed the button. If we all agree that it would we pass our cigars all round and give them a little membership card, nicely engraved and stamped, and invite them in without anybody having to make a bang at all.'

'If you wouldn't mind,' said Driver.

'No, that's interesting, though,' said Higsbee. 'Doubt if it would work.'

'Please,' said Driver. McKellar sat behind his desk and watched him with something like a satisfied look on his Tutenkhamen face. Higsbee nodded at Driver, who went on.

'There's nothing very difficult about telling an explosion from an earthquake,' he said. 'There are marginal cases, about six or eight a year, when we're not quite sure. What really started to bother us, and our friends across the water of course' (Driver hardly ever mentioned the Americans by name) 'was that nobody could pick up small explosions, say a kiloton or less, at all, not against the background of general seismic noise anyway.'

'You mean storms and landslides and people stamping around in their cellars?' I said.

'That sort of thing, yes. And anyway there are certain ways of damping down the shock waves from small underground explosions, such as setting them off inside caves or in alluvial rock rather than granite. Do you follow me?'

I did. I told him so.

'Right, well,' Driver went on, 'we found ourselves in the position where we could detect and identify nuclear explosions, big ones, which weren't of any particular interest because, ha, ha, they were usually reported in *Pravda* the next day anyway. But we couldn't do a damn bit of checking in the field which mattered most, the field of small nuclear devices such as might be used in mortar bombs or artillery shells.

'This was where we'd got to about two years ago. Then a man called Mikulicz got in touch with us with a proposed device he'd designed which seemed to be just the ticket. In essence,' said Driver, reaching across and tapping the rolled-up drawing I was still holding, 'that thing you're holding there.'

I unrolled the sheet of paper and studied it, feeling rather like a herald with a proclamation. It could have been almost anything. It showed a drawing of what amounted to a sphere standing on three cantilevered legs, from the underside of which a long rod or tube projected vertically downwards. There was no indication of what material the sphere was made of, nor of the scale of the drawing. A second diagram beside it showed a cutaway section of the sphere with a great deal of complex equipment inside it.

'You see the real point was that we needed seismographic stations nearer to the probable areas in which nuclear testing was being done,' said Driver. He slithered round behind McKellar and there was a sudden clatter as the blind fell across the window, darkening the room. Since I couldn't see the drawing of Rock Baby any more I swivelled round and looked at Higsbee instead. He was fiddling around with the slide magazine of a projector with the air of a man who is quite sure that the first slide is going to be upside down however hard he thinks about it. It wasn't, though. A map of Europe, Russia and the Far East sidled its way on to a square patch of light on McKellar's office wall, right side up and with the wording so you didn't need a mirror to read it. Higsbee coughed once or twice.

'The main testing sites in the USSR are at Novaya Zemlya up here, and at Semipalatinsk here,' he said. He had a faint Lancashire twang. 'What we need to do is to set up a chain of earth tremor detectors all round *here*.'

He struggled out from behind the projector and over to the map on the wall. He swept an arc with a stubby finger, starting in Scandinavia, curving downwards across the face of Europe, through Turkey and the Caucasus and onwards through northern Iran, Afghanistan, Kashmir, Tibet and into China. It looked a fairly tall order to me.

'Ideally of course we'd like to crowd in a little closer,' Higsbee went on, crowding a little closer with his cupped palm to the map as though it were as simple as that. 'We'd like to set up stations in Georgia, Turkmen, Uzbek, Kirghiz and the Sinkiang Autonomous Region. That would be marvellous.'

I watched his hand shaping around the bright patch on the wall. Almost for the first time I realized how much of the earth's surface is covered by Russia.

'You see?' said Higsbee. 'Let's suppose they set off a bomb here, at Semipalatinsk. Smack in the middle of the continent. Now what we want is a whole lot of coordinated detectors to pick up the explosion, all within, let's say, three or four thousand miles. Then we could correlate all the signals picked up by these detectors and pinpoint where the original explosion was and how big it was. But there's a snag.'

'They won't let you set up a chain of seismographs on their territory,' I said. 'Too bad.'

'And that's where Mikulicz came in,' said Higsbee. 'He designed a small, self-powered automatic seismograph which we have called Rock Baby. It didn't need anybody to operate it and we could drop it from an aircraft, or even a rocket if we felt like running to the expense. It carried its own parachute, stowed automatically and it was self-righting. We thought it would work and we went ahead.'

I turned the piece of paper I was holding around to catch

some of the light reflected from the wall, and tried to squint at it. But I needn't have bothered; Higsbee pressed the remote control on the projector and the map slid offstage and gave way to a photograph of Rock Baby. For the first time I could tell what size it was, because Higsbee was standing beside it in the photograph. It seemed to be about a foot or so across, and was standing on a metal table. Higsbee had his hand resting on it as though it were something he'd just shot.

'That's me with Rock Baby,' said Higsbee unnecessarily. 'Of course this chap Mikulicz, he's in France or somewhere. He only designed it and we had to iron out the snags and get it into production. But there it is.'

'Let me get this straight,' I said. 'That thing is a robot seismograph. How many of them have you made so far?'

'Thirty.'

'And you drop them all over the globe—'

'Well, not all over,' said Higsbee. 'Or not yet anyway, we've only had them operational best part of a year. We've concentrated on Europe so far, that is until we ran into a little spot of bother.'

'I don't want to hear about the little spot of bother yet,' I told him. 'These things do what? Record continuously until their power supply runs out?'

'That's it. Twenty-five months we reckon. As I said, they come down by parachute, you see, and set themselves upright on the ground. Not all of them make it, as you'll see in a minute, and it depends a bit on the ground texture. Then they send down this long probe here,' Higsbee pointed to the rod or tube underneath the sphere, 'and that contains the actual sensors which pick up any earth tremors. Makes a record inside here in the guts of the thing, and retransmits the record to us. Nice. We used a lot of techniques developed in satellite work, of course, the transmitters and recorders and that.'

'It can't transmit continuously, though, surely,' I objected. 'Otherwise they'd have the detector vans out in a flash and pick it up in no time. What does it do, transmit in squirts?'

'That's right. Stores up its recording for about a hundred hours or so and speeds it up. What we actually do is, we've got this Shackleton we've nobbled off Coastal Command. It goes up, does a bit of a tour round in range of all the seismographs in one particular area, that would be say five hundred miles radius. Sends out a triggering radio signal and they all send off their recordings for the last five days or so.'

'Taking how long?' I asked.

'About five minutes.'

That seemed reasonable. Five minutes would be far too short a time for anybody to spot a transmitted signal, let alone to track it down by DF.

'What happens if one of them lands on somebody's roof or in their cucumber frame?'

'Doesn't happen,' said Higsbee. 'We aren't ruddy lunatics, let alone the fact that we couldn't overfly any towns in the first place.'

'All right then, somebody's farmyard muck-heap,' I said. 'Or do you mean to tell me that you've dropped thirty of these things and nobody's found one yet?'

'We don't know. Can't distinguish tampering from failure to operate, the same thing happens, but it's most unlikely. Look,' said Higsbee, 'the damn thing's only a foot across and camouflaged. If I were to sprinkle them all over Yorkshire you'd never find one except by accident, and that sort of accident only happens once in a hundred years.'

'Fine,' I said. 'Forget about the hundred years. What happens if somebody finds one tomorrow?'

'This,' said Higsbee.

Another picture edged its way into the light. This time it was in colour and showed Higsbee again in grubby overalls and surrounded by what looked like a bit of the tank training ground on Salisbury plain. He was also wearing a bright red balaclava and gave the impression, all told, of being a refugee from Grimm's fairy tales. He was pointing at another of the spherical recorders, or maybe the same one, which was lying on its side in a patch of long grass.

There was a whirr and a click and the picture changed again. Higsbee was still pointing at the thing on the ground and grinning at the camera like an overfed demented gnome. A cloud of pinkish-maroon smoke was spurting from the thing's side. Maybe he'd put a spell on it.

The projector clicked again and Higsbee was frozen in the act of backing away from Rock Baby, which was still lying in the same position on the ground and was now burning with a searing, whitish glare. 'Thermite,' said Higsbee from behind the projector. In the next shot he'd gone off-set, the camera had moved in or changed to a long-focus lens and Rock Baby was reduced to a twisted mass of ash and molten metal, still glowing merrily, and the last shot of all made it quite clear that anybody who tampered with Rock Baby would get nothing for his trouble but a nasty surprise and a smallish pile of unidentifiable debris.

'Self-destructive,' said Andy from his corner of the room. 'Nobody gets hurt, but nobody gets to find out what the hell it was he tripped over either. Okay?'

'Looks fine,' I said. 'How many of them has that happened to?'

'Eleven so far,' said Higsbee. It surprised me a bit.

'Eleven out of thirty?'

'Ah well, we expected it you see. You've got to realize they activate the "destroy" circuit if they don't land on suitable terrain either, down a rabbit hole or something I mean. Either they're transmitting or they jack it in.'

'Bit like hara-kiri on a mechanical level,' said Andy.

'All right you've convinced me,' I said. 'You've got an operation going. Now what's the catch?'

Driver reached across and rolled the blind up again, washing the room through with sunlight.

'What about after lunch then?' said Higsbee.

'I have arranged for sandwiches to be sent up,' said McKellar frostily.

I was with Higsbee all the way in theory, but as it happened I was quite willing to settle for McKellar's sandwiches because I had a small but essential timetable to keep to. In any case, as with so many other things lately, I had no choice. The sandwiches came and were full of exciting substances, among them mashed pilchard and processed-cardboard ham, and there was a quarter of an hour's relative silence while we all chewed our way through them.

At ten past two we started all over again.

'Of course it works,' said Higsbee. 'Very well, considering.'

'You've got records from nineteen out of the original thirty of these things, then?' I asked.

'Yes. Well, more or less. Up to two months ago, and then one of them went dead. As a matter of fact it was one of the first ones we dropped and it had been transmitting for between eight and nine months by the time it stopped, so we thought fair enough,' said Higsbee. 'We more or less wrote it off as component failure, though our component reliability was very high indeed during trials. However.'

'Go on,' I said.

'Well,' said Higsbee. 'We knew we'd have to expect one or two failures. Or it could even have been somebody finding it and tampering with it, though as I said that isn't statistically likely. Any road, we crossed it off the list and forgot about it for about a fortnight. Then it came back on the air again.'

'Some sort of temporary fault,' I said.

'I suppose so.'

'What do you mean, you suppose so?'

'Well, temporary failure has happened several times with space satellites, so it was on the cards,' said Higsbee. 'Power supply failure, often, then a bit later it puts itself right and transmission starts up again. So of course the first thing we did was study the new lot of recordings it was sending back to us. Just to check that it was working properly, you know.'

'And was it?'

'No, it wasn't. Not only that, but the recordings led us to believe it had been messed about with. At least that's what I thought and I know more about the damn things than anybody else in this country.'

'But I thought,' I said, 'that if anybody tampered with a Rock Baby you got one of those firework displays you were showing me pictures of earlier? No, wait a minute.' It was beginning to sink in.

'That is not, I think, exactly what Mr Higsbee has in mind,' said McKellar.

'You think it was found by somebody who knew what they were doing? Somebody picked it very carefully to pieces, avoiding the self-destroy circuits, and then put it back together again a bit differently, all during the fortnight it was off the air,' I said.

'That's exactly it,' said Higsbee. 'And I must say I'd give a lot to meet the fellow that did it and shake him by the hand.'

'Don't say that sort of thing out loud here,' I told him. 'It goes down in the files.'

'Get away,' he said, grinning. 'I'm not a Communist.'

'I'm not a Communist either,' I said, 'but you'd be surprised how little good it's done me so far.'

He was the sort of technician you'd give your back teeth to get hold of, I could see, except that you never would because everyone else would have the same idea. He was about fifty and nothing would ever shake him because he'd always know that he was right. He would smoke a pipe and drink a pint and a half of beer some evenings in the week. He would have a plump, cheerful wife who used to teach in primary school; he would be worth three thousand pounds a year of anybody's money and he'd never get more than thirteen-fifty, and when he came up for retirement he'd dig his garden and believe me, the PhDs would miss him like hell.

'You're fairly sure about this?' I asked him.

'Bloody certain,' he said.

I turned to McKellar. He had edged his chair gradually closer to Conrad of DI6, and they now sat shoulder to shoulder, subtle, indestructible, academic.

'And this is the operation DSS put up the money for?' I asked him. He nodded. I remembered the persuasive dinner at Gunners' Hall, and McKellar's bleak warning to me in the rainy street afterwards.

'Well,' I said. 'Do you buy the idea of skilled electronic tampering with your little toy?'

'We are considering it as an hypothesis,' he said.

'And what do you want me to do?'

McKellar and Conrad turned their heads in unison to where Driver was sitting. He screwed the bowl of his pipe around on the stem several times and then suddenly jumped into gear.

'Tell us whether or not Mr Higsbee is right,' he said. 'Find the thing. Disassemble it yourself, carefully.'

'No pink smoke,' I said.

He squeaked his pipe around another couple of revolutions.

'It might not be pink smoke, of course,' he said. 'Not now.'

I could see what he meant. If somebody with a technical sense of humour had gone to all the trouble of dismantling Rock Baby and putting it together again, why bother to reset the destroy mechanism? There were other possibilities, too, of course, in the realm of what they might have done, but I didn't want to think about them now. A man could get discouraged that way.

'Right. I unpick it,' I said.

'That's all,' said Driver. 'Examine it, tell us whether or not it's been readjusted to send back a false signal pattern. If it has, then we shall have to do some serious rethinking about the whole operation. If it hasn't, we simply write it off as a malfunctioning unit and call it a day.'

'And the best of luck,' said Higsbee behind my back. I'd been paying attention to Driver and McKellar and I hadn't noticed he was all set to go. He was about the only man in the room who remotely resembled an ally and I didn't want to be left to the sharks. He packed away the last of his colour slides in a scarred and wrinkled briefcase and began to unhitch a sad fawn raincoat from the stand by the door.

'Wait a minute,' I said.

'Not me, lad. I'm off,' said Higsbee. He tugged the straps of the briefcase firmly through the buckles and made for the door.

'Thank you for all your help, Mr Higsbee,' said McKellar.

'Any time. Any time,' said Higsbee. In the doorway he turned. '*Nil carborundum,* eh, Dr Yeoman?' he said. 'Is that right? *Nil carborundum.*' His shoes squeaked off down the corridor. Andy reached a foot out and tipped the door shut again and everybody sat still and looked at me. *Nil carborundum* all right, I thought. Don't let the bastards grind you down, like it says in the books, but how was I to set about it?

'Where exactly is this malfunctioning recorder?' I asked.

'Yugoslavia,' said Driver.

'An operational procedure has been worked out for you to follow, Dr Yeoman,' said Conrad. He would be the man for working out procedure. 'The details I'll give to you later, if I may. The operation should take between six and ten days, depending on how long it takes you to locate the unit. Can you spare us that length of time?'

I told him, controlling myself carefully, that I thought I could.

'Good, good,' said Conrad. 'That's what we thought.'

There seemed to be no point whatever in pushing it any farther. Besides, something else had just struck me.

'Do you mean you don't even know where the damned thing is?' I asked him.

'Of course we do. Roughly speaking.'

'How roughly?'

He looked around as though he were trying to collect a fast vote on it before committing himself.

'Shall we say within a radius of five miles or so. It was dropped from a high altitude. Drift, you know.'

I sat back, thinking for a moment how reasonable it sounded. Then I did a brisk calculation in my head and stopped thinking it was reasonable. What he was talking about was something like a hundred square miles. I began to realize what Higsbee had meant when he said it was unlikely that anyone would trip over a Rock Baby by accident. Sixty thousand acres, was it, or a bit more? I tried to visualize what an acre looked like in my mind and then gave up.

'We shall issue you with a portable direction-finding set locked to the frequency of the Rock Baby unit in question,' said Driver. 'Our surveillance Shackleton will also arrange for the unit to transmit in five-minute bursts, as before, but at intervals of approximately twenty-four hours instead of its previous one-hundred-hour cycle. I say approximately because if it turns out that nobody has tampered with it after all, we don't want anybody except yourself to home on it.'

'Especially not while I'm there,' I said.

'We shall arrange a random schedule which only you will know,' Driver went on. 'I shouldn't think it will take you more than three or four DF bearings to find it. Is that clear?'

I caught a few more mental pictures. Yeoman with a little portable DF set, sitting in the middle of sixty thousand acres of moor, forest, bog, scree? Twiddling a little loop aerial round and round, looking for an overgrown golf ball?

'It still seems a lot of ground to cover,' I said.

'I'm sure you won't have much trouble,' said Driver. 'Depends on the nature of the terrain a bit, I know. It's mountainous, almost totally deserted so far as we know. Depend on your resources, what? You're a mountaineer, you can look after yourself, not many chaps can these days. But a piece of cake for you, with your background, which is why we asked you, of course.'

I got up and edged my way past McKellar and Conrad to the window. I opened it and looked out. Pigeons flapped into clattering take-off and whirled away into the sky. There was no view after all, just a long sloping pitch of roof with another window at the far end, behind which a man who looked like a faded picture of Lloyd George lowered a teacup from his lips and stared back at me in pursed disapproval.

I drew my head back into the room.

'It hardly seems worth the trouble of dumping a corpse in my bed,' I told them.

'We're doing you a favour,' said Andy.

'A favour? Such favours I can do without,' I said.

We were in the Rose of York tea-rooms, and Andy was playing at being young and earnest, just the way Driver had most probably told him. I knew better, but I needed a break from McKellar's office and at least we were a quarter of a mile away. I was having tea and muzak and he was having chocolate, poached egg on toast, egg-and-cress sandwiches, doughnuts and muzak. All around us men in daring dark grey four-button suits read the *Financial Times* and bit their way through Danish pastries. It was half past four and in Whitehall that is the beginning of the ebb-tide to Wokingham and Redhill and Brentwood, but we had a couple of hours ahead of us yet, I knew.

Andy stabbed his fork in my direction.

'Face facts, Giles. You didn't think you were going to spend the rest of your days at the Institute, did you?'

'That was the way I'd planned it,' I said. 'Why not?'

'Because you aren't made that way,' he said.

'Is that what it says in my file?'

'It's what I say. Why not stop kidding around? You're a competent scientist but not that good. You wouldn't even have got as far as Deputy Director.'

'Assuming for the moment I wanted to,' I said, 'why wouldn't I?'

'Because you're a bum,' said Andy. 'A knowledgeable bum, but a bum just the same. You don't hold your knife and fork right, and it still matters even these days; you've got no manners, you haven't got the faintest grasp of politics, you can't talk to anybody for more than five minutes without putting their backs up. None of which would matter if you were a genius, but you aren't. You're a solid, second-rate research scientist because you're too bloody idle to be anything else, and even at that you aren't satisfied with it because a millimetre under the skin what do we find?'

'A bum,' I said.

'A thirty-year-old juvenile delinquent,' said Andy pleasantly, 'and that means we love you like a brother.'

'I'm your kind of folks, is that it?' I said.

'That's it, cock.'

'It's not exactly the picture I have of myself. But thanks for the instant analysis.'

'You're welcome.' He looked at his watch. 'We ought to be getting back,' he said. 'I mean it, Giles. We're doing you a great favour.'

'Just like last time?' I said.

'Last time we conned you, all the way. I admit that. But you still did us proud. This time we need your full cooperation.'

'You're going a hell of way about getting it. This time you got me fired from my job and stuck a thawed-out corpse in my bed just for encouragement.'

'I don't know what you're talking about,' said Andy. 'What corpse is this?'

'Skip it.'

'You'd have died of boredom at the Institute.'

'But at a ripe old age.'

He drank the last of the chocolate. 'Those whom the gods love,' he said. 'You're on or you're not on, which?'

'Oh, I'm on,' I said. 'But just before you go back and collect the congratulations of all concerned at Seeker, I'll show you something. Watch.'

'Okay, Giles.'

I picked up the teapot and raised it slowly in front of me with my left hand. Andy surveyed me with indulgence but I didn't care, I had a point to make even though I knew it was a waste of time. When the teapot reached the level of my forehead the chewed-up bone splinter that hadn't quite healed yet in my shoulder caught me, just as I knew it would, and the spout of the teapot tilted towards him.

'Watch it,' he said. 'What's that supposed to prove?'

'Hallcraft tells me that in another six months or so I ought to be able to straighten my arm all the way above my head,' I said. 'That will bring it to just over a year since the last time I did something for you.'

'Okay, you're full of bullet holes,' said Andy. 'Other people have ulcers.'

'There's a difference,' I said. 'Only I'm not sure how I'd set about explaining it to you.'

He assembled a neat pile of coins on the table and stood up. 'Work on it,' he said. 'Some day I'll buy you a drink and you can try to get it across to me. How about that?'

We collected our coats.

'You go on ahead,' I said. 'I've got a phone call to make.'

He looked at me doubtfully. Maybe he thought I might still make a break for it and run screaming down the street, but after a moment he nodded and went away in the direction of Whitehall Chambers.

I rang the garage in Putney where I knew that Arfon Jones must have been waiting for the last hour or so. In the background I could hear what sounded like a power chisel pecking through a boiler and somebody whistling.

'Look, I can't hang about all bloody afternoon, man,' he said. 'What do you want me to do then?'

'It's all right, you'll get home for dinner,' I told him.

'There's handsome,' said Arfon. 'Right. Tell me all about it.'

I told him, and then went back to Whitehall Chambers against the growing stream of early commuters.

They'd decided to do the whole thing in relays from now onwards. We still used McKellar's office but now there was only Conrad facing me across the desk.

'We'll have to get you a passport,' he said.

'How about using mine?'

'We considered it.' He tapped a rhythm on the underside of the desk top with his fingers. 'It would be simpler of course, but I'm afraid we had better start thinking in terms of your being, shall I say, known in other quarters by now.'

He picked up a ballpoint and ran it down the side of a scribbled list on a desk jotter. 'Equipment,' he went on. 'Higsbee will deal with that side of things, but perhaps you'd tell us what instruments of your own you think you might require. Voltmeters and things.'

'I think I can battle on without a voltmeter,' I said.

'Whatever you say. Give me a list, will you, some time tomorrow? Right. Name. What name would you like your papers in? It's more satisfactory if the operative picks his own name, particularly, ha, don't misunderstand me, inexperienced operatives.' He looked at me without the trace of a smile. 'If you forget it we can say it was your fault.'

'Carstairs,' I said.

'Carstairs. First names, any preference?'

'Benjamin William.'

I watched him print 'B. W. Carstairs' in the margin of his jotter. He drew a precise oval around it. His lips moved slightly as though he were saying something to himself. 'Very well,' he said out loud. 'Now tomorrow morning we'll get you over to the Bayswater place' – he was referring, I supposed, to Seeker Section HQ – 'and I'll introduce you to your Number Two. Joint briefing on the admin. side before lunch, Higsbee's coming up to town again in the afternoon—'

'Just a minute,' I said. 'Number Two? You never mentioned any Number Two.'

He looked surprised.

'Of course,' he said blandly. 'You'll need some help on what I might venture to call the deception side of the mission. Posing as tourists and so on. It's purely for convenience.'

'Convenience nothing,' I told him. 'Nobody's coming with me. What the hell do you think I am? If I've got to spend most of my time climbing mountains I'm not going to make it more difficult by trailing some twit on the other end of a rope.'

'Please don't be difficult,' said Conrad.

'I'm not being difficult. I'm telling you the facts. If I'm doing this at all it'll be my way, and don't look as though the whole thing's a terrible surprise because you knew I'd object or you'd have told me earlier.'

'I assure you,' said Conrad. 'You'll admit you're not experienced in this sort of thing?'

'Never mind that. All I need is a phrase book with the Serbo-Croat for "I demand to see the British Representative, I have done nothing wrong" in it somewhere and I'll get by.'

He stood up and sidled around the desk like a crab, looking at me as though he might at any moment press the button and have me taken away.

'There's the question of possible defusing of the unit,' he said. 'I take it you're not a BD expert, Dr Yeoman?'

'You're not worried about whether I can handle a spot of bomb-disposal on the side,' I said. 'I take it this Number Two would be your boy, wouldn't he? I mean a genuine DI6 lad, sent along to wipe my nose if it runs and just in passing to see that I do the job right, meaning right according to DI6, in case I suddenly remember that you've got me into this operation with a crowbar? I might start to get ideas above my station, mightn't I? Your file will tell you how irresponsible and undisciplined I am.'

He thought it over.

'I see,' he said finally. 'I suppose we ought to concede your right to be suspicious of our motives.'

That was a charming way to put it, all right.

'Just so long as we know where we stand,' I said. He looked at me, sensing the beginnings of compromise in my voice. He was quite right; the ghost of an idea was forming at the back of my mind, or maybe it was just that I was starting to learn, slowly and painfully, when to stick my heels in and when to relax.

'Could we leave your final decision until after tomorrow, Dr Yeoman?' he said.

'All right.'

He took his checklist and folded it in two. 'I'll see you tomorrow,' he said, and went out.

Driver, of course, just went right on assuming that they'd got me in a big screw clamp and that if I raised my voice all they had to do was tighten it a few more turns. He strode up and down the office, eyes slitted against the limitless infinite, recalling the days when he said jump and everybody jumped.

'You'll fly to Zagreb in four days time,' he said. 'Then by internal transport to Ljubljana. Is that clear?'

'Yes.'

'We've arranged for you to stay with a man of ours who's a spelaeologist. He'll take you both to the caves at Postojna in order to give you some sort of circumstantial cover for your later excursions into the mountains. Look at the map, please.'

He spun round in front of the wall chart and pointed. There was an uneven circle marked on it, I saw, in the north-western bulge of Yugoslavia where it bordered on Italy and Carinthia. He unclipped the map from the wall and handed it to me. It was one of the Wanderkarten series by Freytag-Berndt of Vienna, scale one centimetre to the kilometre; as I'd expected, the area he'd blocked out was huge, but on the other hand, as he'd said, there was nothing there but mountains.

'Take it away with you. Study it,' said Driver. 'Leave the matter of approach route to you. Conrad's assigned you an assistant—'

'I haven't accepted an assistant,' I said. It was like talking to a brick wall.

'I expect he'll be capable of the simpler forms of mountaineering,' Driver went on. 'And of course you won't be doing anything too energetic because of the equipment you'll be carrying. Right?'

'It isn't, but we'll go into that later,' I said.

Driver tapped the map. 'Most probable areas have been marked in, here and here. That's according to the rather limited direction-finding our Shackleton people were able to do. They can't go winging about all over Yugoslav territory so I wouldn't bank too much on their readings, but an indication, eh, an indication?'

'Fine,' I said.

'Right then. Detailed briefing tomorrow, eleven hundred hours. Remember I want you in fast and out fast, Dr Yeoman. The quicker and less complicated it is the better we'll all be pleased and the sooner you can relax, is that clear?'

'Yes, sir,' I said. He looked at me suspiciously and pulled open the door. When he turned back to me his manner was suspiciously quiet.

'We wanted Jissock, you know,' he said.

I'd forgotten about Jissock. Alive, that is to say.

'Who's Jissock?' I asked. It seemed to be my turn.

'We wanted him badly,' Driver went on gently, 'and because of you and your friend Captain Brightwell of the US bloody Air Force we lost him. It was nothing to do with all this, of course, but I'd like you to remember that. You mucked us about, Dr Yeoman, with your bloody amateur schoolboy approach to our affairs. Which you affect to find so dirty. So next time you're feeling self-righteous and hardly done by, just chew it over.'

He went out. It was a good exit.

It sounded as though he knew about the laser crystal. It seemed possible, or at least it seemed possible that he knew there was a package strapped to Yancy's thigh when Telford pulled him out of the water, because the hospital casualty report said so. Though presumably nobody but Yancy knew he'd passed it on to me. That's what I hoped anyway.

The building was beginning to empty. The daytime people were being shelled out of it like peas, leaving the evening people behind; the quiet men and women with keys, for whom the office has become more homelike than the Kensington flat, and for whom the routine of work is now lover, friend, husband or wife, the people who drift and patter down the whispering corridors when the tide has receded. McKellar was one of the evening people. He was back in possession now, shrugging the room around him like an overcoat. He passed me a slip of paper.

'Here's the address,' he said. 'It's quite comfortable. I hope you'll excuse our taking the liberty of arranging somewhere for you to sleep in town, but we thought perhaps you wouldn't want to return home tonight. We'll clear things up, of course.' He laughed, or perhaps it was a sudden attack of asthma. 'It's been a long day, hasn't it? I think I ought to be getting along home myself.'

I stared at him in disbelief. I knew he didn't go home. I knew that after I'd left, someone would come and carefully lower a perspex dome over him, and that in the morning they'd lift it off again and dust him lightly before pressing the starting button.

I went out into the corridor. To left and right of me people strode briskly towards lifts and stairs. Opposite the door of McKellar's office there was a tall window, and I looked out and downwards. My watch said five-forty, and sure enough, seven floors below, I could see the rectangular blue roof of Arfon Jones's van pulling in to the kerb in front of the main doors. I rubbed my chin and went back into the office.

'Is anything the matter, Dr Yeoman?' said McKellar.

'Nothing. Nothing at all. I wonder if you'd like to step across here with me,' I said. He pushed himself upright and we went back to the corridor window again. I pointed.

'Down there,' I told him, 'is a man called Arfon Jones. A Welshman.' He nodded. 'He appears to be delivering something to this building. I don't know if you can see from this distance, but it looks to me like something the size of a trunk.'

'So I see,' said McKellar. He nodded again.

'If I were you, McKellar, I'd get down to the hall fairly smartly, before anybody starts wondering what they ought to be doing with it. It's got your name on, so I don't suppose the porter would go so far as to open it, but you can never be quite sure. Thank you for all your help. I'll see you tomorrow.'

I went off towards the lift. Nothing I'd said had altered the expression on his face by a millimetre. At the lift doors I glanced back along the corridor just in time to see him come away from the window and cross over to his office. It seemed to me there was a certain cheerful briskness in his walk, and he had his hands in his pockets. I couldn't see why, unless maybe any sort of action was a relief from the long and tedious day we'd all had. He didn't look in my direction.

The lift pinged softly and I let the doors gnash shut and swallow me down to the ground floor. There was a fair amount of activity in the entrance hall, what with one thing and another, but I couldn't stay to help. I beckoned to Arfon Jones and we left them all to it.

EIGHT

IT TOOK me until seven-thirty to get rid of Arfon Jones. It also cost me six pints of beer and the losing end of a discussion about the iniquity of the Birmingham Corporation Reservoir scheme and the likelihood of its turning central Wales into a desert. Arfon Jones argued about water tables with grim determination and I told him I didn't think it was possible to take more water out of Wales than fell into it during the course of an average summer, and when I left him he was opening the question all over again with three Australians in Earls Court.

The traffic had thinned and the roads were dry. I snaked the car out into the country and thought what a clever lad I was. The feeling didn't last long. I'd been a clever lad all right and I'd shown the professionals a thing or two. Sure. But where exactly had it got me? Like Gully Jimpson said about amateur art and farting Annie Laurie through a keyhole, it may have been clever but was it worth the trouble?

Well, perhaps it had bought me a little elbow room. Not much, but a little. And I was beginning to have ideas about how I was going to play the Rock Baby affair, as opposed to how Driver and Conrad thought I was going to, so I needed all the elbow room I could get.

Of course the whole scheme might be an enormous, highly

coloured, well-documented lie, or a means of getting Seeker Section a corner on the world supply of ball-bearings, for all I knew. There was always that possibility with Seeker around. The most I was prepared to admit so far was that the operation was feasible on a technical level, if you had a lot of money to throw around, and I was sure they had that.

Higsbee was the man to talk to.

There was something attractive, in an off-beat, screwy sort of way, about the idea of psycho-analysing a brain-washed robot, which was how it came out if you squinted at it from certain angles and with your eyes half closed. I must talk to Higsbee.

It came on to rain as I drove through the village and swung off the main road into Stiles Lane. I was a clever lad all right, but still when I saw the other car parked twenty yards beyond the run-in to the stables, my first thought was what a damned stupid place to leave it because it would make it impossible for me to back and turn out of the drive in the morning.

My mind is clearly ill-trained for the sort of job everybody seemed to think I should be doing, but after a while it sank in. I had a pair of 6×25 ex-Army spotter glasses in the glove compartment, and when it had finally penetrated my thick head that nobody in their senses would leave a brand-new BMW 2000 a quarter of a mile up a muddy lane on a wet night for fun, I got them out and scanned the front of the house until I saw a faint halo of light move behind one of the top-floor windows.

I am not by nature a violent man.

I lowered the glasses and thought a bit, while the rain dripped in a steady trickle down inside my collar.

It didn't seem likely that it was one of Driver's boys. Surely McKellar must have phoned him as soon as I'd left and told him nobody needed to clear up my flat because I'd done it myself?

It could of course still be one of Driver's boys looking for something else. It was probable they knew that Yancy had arrived in this country with something strapped to his leg and if so it was more than possible that they'd think I had it. They wouldn't find it. I'd stuck the laser rod into a flower bed on my way out that morning and I was going to have a little difficulty finding it again myself among the bindweed roots and old bricks.

I backed the car quietly down the lane and out into the main road. I switched off the engine and plodded back along Councillor Warburton's wall until I could clamber over it and into the orchard. The grass was knee-high and soaking wet.

I am not a violent man, except in so far as all men are violent by instinct. But one thing was clear; I couldn't be halfway violent. Either I could stay clear until they'd finished the job – whoever they were – or else I could go in without bothering to knock.

I worked my way around to the back of the house. My eyes were getting dark-adapted, and I stood in an angle of the outhouse wall and saw the faint flicker of a torch as somebody moved from the bedroom to the study, thirty feet above me.

I was wearing soft-soled driving shoes, which were just what I needed for climbing. I levered myself on to a rainwater barrel and from there on to the guttering of the outhouse roof. The tiles were slippery with damp and the scramble up the pitch of the roof to the ridge gave me a little trouble, but after that I could straddle my way along the ridge to the point where it joined the rear wall of the house itself. I stood upright, carefully.

Two lead overflow pipes and the bowl of a drain got me eight or ten feet higher up, and a shortish pitch of the sloping pipe that fed the bowl took me up and sideways for another five. Climbing the side of a house is both easier and more difficult than an equivalent rock ascent, though all the same techniques can be practised by the enthusiastic. A steady deluge of rainwater poured down into my face as I looked upward for the next move and I reminded myself to get the gutter mended.

I leaned sideways, both hands spread delicately against the rough brickwork, until I could stretch my fingertips and hook on to the lower sill of a second-floor window. There were deep cracks in the wall where it needed repointing, and twice I managed to get the thin end of half an inch of toe in between courses of bricks, but just the same the next ten feet or so sideways were a hand-traverse and left me hanging from the bathroom sill over a longish drop. When I'm feeling fit I can manage a straight-arm pull from my fingers, but I wasn't feeling fit tonight. I was very glad indeed to find the head of what felt like a coach-bolt with my left foot, and a couple of seconds later I was kneeling on the sill. I thought the window made a noise like a portcullis when I pushed it up, but nobody came and shoved me off the sill, so perhaps it only sounded that way to me.

I stood in the bathroom doing deep-breathing and trying to listen at the same time. There wasn't a sound, and nor was there any point in wasting time.

I edged out on to the landing. There was a faint rim of light under the study door which faded almost as soon as I noticed it. I took a last deep breath, walked along to the door and pushed it open. The torch would dazzle me anyway, so I snapped on the light and got into the room fast.

He was a slightly built, athletic-looking man. Traditionally dressed, which is to say black canvas shoes, dark blue jeans, a heavy black sweater and nylon stocking stretched over his head. I wondered why. He spun round to face me as I jumped towards him. I hit him, once, as hard as I could, just below the edge of the ribs.

He slipped and crashed back into a bookcase. Paperbacks showered around him. He was even fitter than he looked; I was hoping he'd collapse in an untidy winded heap, but he did nothing of the kind. He didn't even drop the heavy rubber-cased torch he was holding, and as I moved in again he swung it upwards at my groin. I dropped my left hand in reflex protection and the edge of the lens ripped an inch-long flap of skin off the back of my knuckles before it sank into my stomach. He looked a right idiot in that stocking mask, like something out of a Francis Bacon picture. I couldn't feel anything in my left hand and it refused to answer any messages my brain tried to send it.

He came away from the bookcase and tried to push past me to the door. He was smaller than I was. Not much smaller, but I'm no giant. I threw my right arm across his chest and twisted from the hips to get my right leg behind him in the movement Judoka call *osotogari* but I call a cross-buttock throw. On a mat or grass it's one thing. In a room full of furniture it's quite another, and the results depend on what your opponent hits on the way over and down. I hoped it might be the edge of the desk.

It wasn't, because the moment I'd got my arm across and gripped a handful of sweater it became clear that I wasn't fighting a smallish man but a quite ordinary sized woman, and it altered my outlook immediately and fatally. I know it shouldn't have made any difference, but I still give up my seat on crowded tube trains to women of all ages and I'd had very little practice in fighting with girls. I took my hand away from her left breast as though I'd been stung, and in the half second it took me to wonder what to do next she drove her elbow into my stomach at exactly the same spot she'd hit with the torch and I found I didn't have any decision to make. This time there was nothing I could do but double up and fight for air, and she had all the time she wanted to swing the torch over again on to the back of my head. No girl should be without an armoured-rubber torch. I didn't quite black out but after that a reasonably tough two-year-old would have been fighting way above my class. Anyway, what was the point? All men who fight with girls do nothing except try to grab hold of their wrists, looking pretty damn stupid, and with this girl you could get a nasty injury that way. It was almost a relief to find I couldn't have grabbed anything even if I'd tried. She trod on my left hand again on her way to the door, but I couldn't tell if it was malice or accident. I was almost straightened up again when she switched off the light; by the time I'd cursed my way past the coffee-table and the armchair to the switch all I could hear was the slam of the front door, two floors down.

I went into the bathroom and stuck the flap of skin back across my knuckles. It bled steadily and profusely. As I turned on the cold tap I heard the BMW start up and growl down the lane in low gear.

I thought of telephoning Driver and telling him that I'd just been beaten up by a girl a bit smaller than myself armed with a torch. Maybe he'd see the whole thing was doomed to failure and call it off.

She could have belonged to Seeker, of course, but I didn't think so. The BMW wasn't really a Seeker Section type of car and if Driver had wanted to search my flat he could have done it himself, or sent Andy Dylan. Neither of them would have bothered with a nylon stocking over his head.

NINE

IT WAS clear that I was in trouble. Two separate and distinct lots of trouble, though they seemed to have areas of contact, notably in the person of Jissock, deceased.

First there was Yancy Brightwell trouble. Unknown and recently designed form of laser crystal, at least four unknown and unfriendly people in Paris, and a bombed-out cruiser. Plus of course the aforementioned John Aloysius Jissock (according to the Register of Scientists), one-time disappearing geologist and well-known nut-case.

Second, Seeker trouble, hereinafter referred to as Operation Rock Bay. Department of Scientific Security, Conrad of Defence Intelligence Six intervening; malfunctioning recording seismograph in Yugoslavia. Plus, again, J. A. Jissock, or at least his dead and deep-frozen body.

Two sorts of trouble. My recent visitor belonged to one or other sort, but I wasn't clear which.

Question. Are these two sorts of trouble related on any level other than a common interest in Jissock by both Yancy and Driver? Good thinking, but unfortunately there is lack of evidence either way. Your Honour. One of the parties who could probably throw a good deal of light on the matter, Captain Yancy Brightwell, has, in legal parlance, pissed off to Yankee Land and cannot therefore be questioned as to any such connexion, which shows a good deal of forethought for a Wyoming farm boy. The ball is therefore in Yeoman's court. Also the laser crystal.

I got up, nursing my left hand, and went down to the garden. It took me half an hour of ill-temper to find the crystal again, and I brought it back upstairs and washed it under the kitchen tap.

There was no real reason to suppose that Driver's interest in Jissock had anything to do with his interest in Rock Baby. Seeker Section, formerly the Scientific Section of the Department of Special Intelligence, had been in existence for twenty years, and they must have opened a file on the original disappearance of Jissock, even if nobody wanted him at the time. It must follow that when he turned up again, Driver would have been the man interested in getting hold of him at the British end. If so, then we had certainly fouled him up. Irritated by this, he had used Jissock's corpse, acquired purely in the line of duty, to press-gang me into Operation Rock Baby. Andy Dylan had described this as opportunism, and on balance I thought that was just what it was.

On the other hand, they had gone to a lot of trouble just to make sure I toed the line, their line. A hell of a lot. Once they'd got as far as dumping the body on me there was nothing I could do to implicate them, but it still seemed a lot of bother. Not to mention the administrative chore of putting me among the unemployables.

It was late. My hand throbbed, my stomach muscles ached and I needed sleep. I needed it badly.

The man to see was Higsbee. I'd see him first thing in the morning.

I wasn't going to have any part of Conrad's 'colleague'. Not if he turned out to be the most competent active agent they'd got and could defuse bombs with his teeth. The whole operation was beginning to look far messier to me than everybody was trying to make out, and my instinct was to have nobody around to screw things up except me. No matter how you cut it up, I was going to be looking for an illegal piece of equipment on the soil of a country which, while not exactly unfriendly, still wasn't going to take kindly to pseudo-tourists with forged passports dismantling spy devices. I know the Secret Police in Yugoslavia is being cut by two-thirds to a mere seven thousand chaps and all that, but no thanks.

A man on his own can melt into the landscape. If he knows how, and I knew how. A man on his own, suitably equipped for mountain climbing (and I was suitably equipped) can cross frontiers without anybody being a penny the wiser, if he avoids the high huts. It's embarrassing if he later gets caught, but then if I got caught working with my little screwdriver on a secret atom-bomb detector it would be fairly embarrassing anyway, and illegal entry on top wouldn't make it much more so.

The decisions a man by himself takes are decisions for himself alone. They are based on what he alone knows of his own abilities and shortcomings.

I knew what my shortcomings were. As an agent I was out, I was nothing. I was the man who got laid out by any girl with a rubber torch. But I like the open country, and as a backwoodsman I might get by.

It was after midnight. I set the alarm for half past four, stripped, took a shower and went to bed on the divan. I was too tired to eat, though I knew I needed to. The sleep of a labouring man is sweet, whether he eat little or much, says Ecclesiastes, and I'd laboured enough in the last thirty-six hours to drop off on a bed of nails.

At half past five the next morning I was in the kitchen, heating coffee, frying things and melting a quarter-pound block of chocolate over the stove. The rain had stopped during the night and the sun was just beginnning to lift above the dawn cloud layer. Apart from minor damage here and there I felt great.

My frame rucksack was packed and ready. In half an hour I'd be out of the house and I wasn't coming back. I champed my way through bacon and eggs and hoped she hadn't had any bright ideas like letting down my tyres or removing the distributor cap.

I scraped nearly all the wax away from the laser rod. In the early sunlight it glowed alternately deep red, pink and mauve. A one-off job, that was certain. I wondered who had spent the days of trouble, the weeks of experiment that had gone into it. How had he achieved the bonding of the two layers of crystal, the ruby and the sapphire? There were all sorts of things it would be interesting to know, like what the hell it was for, but I had more pressing problems.

I dropped the rod into a jug of ice-cubes and let it cool for a minute. Then I took it out and dried it carefully. I stood it on end in a saucepan and poured melted chocolate over it. When it had set I picked it up carefully and dipped the uncoated end in what was left. I stood around while that set hard, too. It didn't look right, somehow, and I sprinkled Rice Krispies along it and dipped it again. That left me with a somewhat improbable candy bar worth a couple of thousand pounds. What I needed was some sort of wrapper for it, but for the moment I rolled it up carefully in waxed paper.

Everything would be fine so long as I didn't get absent-minded and take a bite out of it. You could break a couple of teeth that way.

The trouble was I hadn't spent an even halfway adequate amount of time getting ready for this trip. Or even on thinking out the implications, but if I spent much time doing that I'd see how hopelessly impractical the whole idea was and give up. I turned everything off at the main, locked a few of the more obvious doors, and humped the rucksack down the lane to the car.

The Telecommunications Research Unit at Abingdon turned out to be an outcrop of pink-washed concrete huts surrounded by geometrical lawns and disciplined privet hedges.

I got there about eight. They were changing shifts behind the tall wire gates, and a security guard came over and told me Higsbee lived down by the river. I drove off again.

When I finally found the place I did a certain amount of quick mental revision about Higsbee. I'd ended up in one of those curious floating caravanserais one finds every now and again on the Thames. I parked the car on a rubble patch, got out, and threaded my way downhill through budding thorn bushes to the edge of a wide riverside basin full of pondweed. Boats were drawn up against the rim of the basin; fibreglass cruisers, converted barges, square cedar-planked houseboats and faded Edwardian river steamers. Boats that would be gone tomorrow and boats that would never go anywhere again, tarred, varnished, flaking, rotting, trellised and fenced, gleaming with new paint, shabby with years of neglect.

Higsbee's floating home was called *Stumbo III*. It might have been a Dutch botter before he'd converted it. He'd done it well.

I edged warily along the gangplank and looked around the deck. There was a smell of frying bacon. A small girl appeared from nowhere and surveyed me in silence. She had that particular blonde beauty which no woman ever recaptures after the age of two and a half, though a lot of time and energy gets expended trying.

I gave her a brisk thumbs-up and she went on staring at me impassively. Higsbee clumped up the after companion ladder, or maybe the back stairs, in a brown suit and green and orange flowered tie.

'Morning,' he said.

'I'm sorry to disturb you,' I told him.

'Don't think twice, Doc. Come to give me a lift, have you? Very nice. I don't much like the train service to town. Go down to Mummy, Barbara.'

'I'm not going to town,' I said. 'At least, not all the way.'

'Is that so?' said Higsbee.

I said, 'If you'll give me a cup of coffee I'll tell you why not,' and we went below. The small blonde girl backed down the steps after us, using her hands and knees with unbreakable concentration.

'You're off on your jack then?' said Higsbee. 'Just like that?'

'That's the idea.'

'They aren't going to like it much.'

'Nor they are. But they are going to have to lump it,' I said.

We'd wound up in his study, workshop, ham radio station all rolled into one. It smelled partly of the ancient smell of a ship and partly of soldering fluid, swarf, oil, charred systoflex sleeving and other things that go to make up the indefinable smell of home-made electronic gear. Component charts, ABACs, frequency tables and curling graphs of this and that were stuck all over the walls with tacks and tape. The single hooded eye of an oscillograph peered from the shadows behind a watchmaker's lathe on the corner bench.

'I don't know,' said Higsbee. 'I don't know. You've put me in a bit of a spot, like, haven't you? I mean, where does my duty lie, eh?'

'I can tell you that in two seconds flat,' I said. 'You should be getting on the blower to Seeker for instructions.'

'What makes you so sure I won't?'

'I listened to you yesterday in McKellar's office,' I said. 'And watched you. You don't give a damn about the way Seeker runs things.'

He refilled the coffee cups. Out of sight the rest of the family were having an early morning conversation, or perhaps plotting a mutiny.

Higsbee searched around the corner bench and pulled a bottle of Ballantine's from behind the oscilloscope. 'Sun's over the yardarm,' he said.

'It's only half past eight in the morning.'

'That's right, lad. Sun's over the yardarm going up, not coming down. Do you want one or not? No. Well then.' It was beginning to look as though Higsbee was rather more complex than his Whitehall face showed.

'Look,' I said. 'I have to do this job, but I don't have to do it any way but my own.'

'Right, right,' said Higsbee.

'I know they've had years of practice at these things and they've got their own routine,' I went on, 'but I haven't. I don't see myself blue-assing all over Yugoslavia with a false passport, counting ten before I give my name to anybody in case I can't remember what it says under the photograph.'

'And pretending to be fascinated by caves,' said Higsbee. He sipped delicately at the whisky in his glass. His flowered tie looked as though it might throw out suckers any minute now. 'You're right, lad,' he went on, 'we see that lot on telly every night, don't we? If they want to play silly bleeders, let them. We're technicians. What do you want me to tell you, Doc?'

I breathed out, slowly. I hadn't been quite sure. Almost, but not quite.

'There was going to be a technical briefing later today,' I said. 'I want you to give me the same briefing, right here and now.'

He went over to the door. The small blonde girl put her head round it at about knee level and smiled at me. She was terrific. Higsbee spread his hand over the top of her forehead and pushed gently. 'Go to Mummy, Barbara,' he said, and closed the door firmly. He came back. 'Right then, Doc,' he said. 'Here it is then.'

It didn't take long. Good briefings never take long. He gave me a pencilled list of the times Rock Baby would be transmitting over the next three weeks, a set of three small Allen keys for the socket screws in the casing, and a read-out probe for the magnetic recording cylinder.

'No bother about transmission frequencies,' he said. 'The DF set is locked on to just the one. How do you reckon on getting hold of the set, by the way? Don't tell me if you'd rather I didn't know. I'm just asking out of interest.'

I suppose I'd been prepared for it, but it was still a bit of a facer. I'd been nearly certain Higsbee would have the radio himself, as tame technical wizard to Operation Rock Baby. I told him so.

'Not a hope,' he said.

I swore. He looked towards the door as though his daughter might hear.

'What did you think?' he said. 'There's only just the one set.'

'You built it. I thought you might have it here.'

'Up to yesterday you'd have been right,' he said. 'Matter of fact I was working on it. But I left it at that place in Bayswater before I came away.'

'Damn,' I said.

He sucked in his breath, through his teeth.

'Course,' he said. 'What you could do is still go to the briefing. Pick it up there and then scarper. I don't know why I should sit here giving you helpful suggestions, but that's what I'd do.'

'I can't afford to go anywhere near Seeker,' I told him. 'I

need a head start, and the last thing I want is to have to shake off Conrad's man first.'

Somewhere else on the boat the telephone started to ring. Higsbee went over to one of the wall charts. Its lower corners were starting to curl upwards where he hadn't stuck them down properly. He pushed things here and there on the bench and at last came up with a drawing-pin.

'Maybe it's a blessing in disguise,' he said.

'How?'

'Oh, not for you,' he said. 'For me. What I mean, they aren't exactly going to love me for telling you all this down here instead of waiting till we get to Seeker and it's all official like. But I can flannel my way round that all right.' He pushed the pin into the chart. 'But if I'd turned over the DF equipment to you, well that'd be something else again, wouldn't it? No authorization, no inventory, you see.' He came back to the table. 'Bit hot on authorization, are that lot,' he said.

'I can imagine.'

'Still, that's not helping you.'

'No.'

He flipped open the lid of the coffee percolator and let it fall again. There was a knock at the door and he went over and opened it; I heard a woman's voice and he turned back to me. 'Hang on,' he said. 'Phone.' He went out.

It was a pity about the DF set, because without it I would simply never find Rock Baby. I changed my mind and poured some of Higsbee's Scotch into a paper cup. A thin grey layer of dust floated to the surface. I'd have to go and argue with them; Higsbee was quite right. In the last resort I could refuse to have Conrad's bomb expert along with me, I supposed. I'd left the matter open. Conrad would then dream up some other way of keeping an eye on me, but I was fairly confident of being able to shake off anybody who tried to follow me.

The snag was that I didn't want to shake off everybody. I might have to talk to some of them.

If I added up the number of people who probably wanted to contact me, to keep an eye on me, or just simply to know where I was it would make quite an impressive total, which was the penalty for doing two things at once. What I needed was to identify the people who were all tangled up with Yancy Brightwell and his cross-Channel trip, and to get a long way away from anyone to do with Seeker, and once I was lumbered with Conrad's friendly DI6 man I didn't see how I could manage it.

I could forget about Yancy and the laser crystal, then I wouldn't be doing two things at once. Except that it didn't depend on me, as last night's episode underlined. Nothing depended on me, that was the trouble. In research laboratories, psychologists with time on their hands build mazes and run rats through them. It is virtually unknown for a rat to decide that today is not a maze-running day. There is no consultation.

Higsbee came back.

'My only soul, Doc,' he said. 'You don't care, do you?'

'What about this time?' I asked him.

'You never let on about any dead body, that's what it's about.' He pushed the door shut and leaned against it. I looked at him a bit more closely and I could see he was trying not to laugh.

'You horrible man, you've been messing them about, haven't you, Doc?' he said. He was shaking. His face didn't change but the buttons on the front of the brown suit gave him away. 'You horrible man,' he said again. 'You know what they did with it?'

'Put it back in the freezer,' I said.

'That's right,' he said. 'That's just exactly what they did. They wanted to know where you were. On the blower.'

'I expect you told them.'

'Don't be daft, Doc, of course I told them you were here. I had to. Otherwise how could you get to know about all the stuff in that briefing I just gave you? Of course I had to be a bit circumspect, like. They reckon you're halfway to being a dangerous lunatic.' He reached behind the table and picked up his briefcase. 'Come on,' he said.

'Where to?'

'Look, Doc,' he said. 'I told them you were giving me a lift up to town. I'm supposed to reckon you're a dangerous criminal myself but they've decided I can manage to get you as far as Bayswater. Mind you there's not much else they can do right now, is there?'

'So?'

'So if you want to hop on a plane, like, to Klagenfurt or wherever you've got in mind, I should get on with it smartish.'

'What about you?' I asked. I couldn't see why he was sticking out his neck for me and I wasn't going to ask. Seeker must think he was too valuable to axe. I wished they felt the same way about me.

'Drop me somewhere near a station,' said Higsbee. 'About three hundred yards, I'm fatter than I've a right to be and I don't much fancy walking.'

'What are you going to tell them?'

He dragged at his briefcase and started to bang his way irritably over to the door. 'What the hell do you think I'll tell them, Doc? If you're clever enough to drop their own body back in their laps then you're clever enough to con a simple man like me into getting out of the car to look at a tyre or something, aren't you?'

I couldn't think of much to say. He hauled open the door and squeezed out into the passage.

'Are you coming then, Doc?' he said.

'What about the DF set?' I asked. 'There's not much point my dashing off in all directions without it, is there?'

He led the way along the dark, narrow corridor which ran like a backbone the length of the ship, thumping his briefcase into doorknobs and kicking toys out of the way with his feet. Just before he started to climb into the damp riverside air, Higsbee looked over his shoulder at me.

'I thought of that,' he said.

We were somewhere in Hounslow.

'This'll do,' he said. I pulled over to the kerb, leaned across him, and pushed the nearside door open.

'See, I only developed the thing,' he said. 'The direction-finding stuff I mean. There's that mad old sod in Bavaria designed it in the first place. You remember.'

'Mikulicz?' I said.

He nodded. 'That's him. Mikulicz. He's barmy of course,

but he'll have a radio set, must do. Part of his test gear, do you see. He's the lad to get hold of.' He winked, screwing up the whole of one side of his face. 'Don't tell anybody I said so, will you, eh, Doc?' he said. He started to laugh again as he hauled himself out of the car.

'What happens if he's not all that barmy?' I said. 'Supposing he hits me over the head with a sock full of wet sand and calls Seeker to come and collect me?'

'He won't. He won't.' Higsbee slammed the door, rocking the car like a ship in a squall. He leaned on the sill, peering in at me with a Cheshire-cat grin.

'Where in Bavaria?' I asked him.

'Don't panic,' he said. He stood half-upright and undid the massive straps of his briefcase. 'That lake outside Munich, well, I say outside, bit of a distance really,' he said. 'Boats and swimming and that. Steinberg something.'

'The Starnbergersee,' I said.

'Aye, that's right. Well I've marked the map about where I think he lives, somewhere around there. Big old whatsname, country house, schloss, you know, Doc? Like a birthday cake.' He gestured, nearly dropping the case. 'With towers,' he said. He passed the map through the window to me. 'He's barmy, like I said, but clever, is Mikulicz. You ought to get on just fine with him.'

He shoved his head and shoulders in through the car window again leaning confidentially across the passenger seat. It was like sharing a small cage with a grizzly bear. 'Remember this is your ruddy idea, Doc,' he said. 'Not mine. What I mean, if Driver catches up with you, say nowt. Course he might start taking your finger-nails off, I wouldn't know, but if you drop me in it there'll be another body in your bed and this time it'll be yours. Give me a sixpence.'

'What for?'

He looked at me pityingly. 'I'll have to find a phone box and tell them what you did to me, won't I?' he said. 'Thanks, Doc. Keep your eye on the ball.'

I watched him shamble off into the ten o'clock shopping crowd. It was time I got to the airport, even though it looked as though I needn't book beyond Munich now. At least I knew which way to face for the moment, which was something.

TEN

I LEFT THE car in Feltham and took the bus from there. The sky was streaking over with low, trailing cloud and the tyres hissed on the wet tarmac as we drove through the slums at the back of London Airport where all the real work is done.

I didn't see the BMW. It needn't have been there, of course.

I collected my ticket and got myself processed through the machinery which sucks in people and spits out passengers. I thought for a while about having myself called over the Tannoy system, but I decided against it. They weren't incompetent. We all had a mutual interest in getting together and they'd followed Jissock and then Yancy and then they must have followed me. They'd tried to search my flat.

I couldn't believe they weren't still keeping track of me, BMW or no BMW, though of course they might all be cleaning their nails outside Seeker in Bayswater right now. But I thought not. All I wanted was to keep things simple, because that way I stood a faint chance of being able to follow the game myself.

I took part in the usual guessing game on the transfer coach and picked the right exit door for once. Somebody must be going to open proceedings and I hoped it would be soon. Left to myself, my own inclination would have been to sprint like a hare as soon as they opened the door at Munich and vanish into the countryside, only I couldn't do that without collecting the DF set first.

I wondered if Driver could possibly be organized enough to have me stopped at Munich airport, which would solve the problem in a way. Then I remembered he wouldn't know I was at Munich unless and until Higsbee got around to telling him. The tranquil girl at the top of the stairs welcomed me into the padded, gently humming interior of the plane and I looked around for a seat.

As it happened the whole thing was very easy. I usually sit on the crossed ends of my own seat belts and try to strap myself in with my neighbour's, so by the time I'd given the girl who sat next to me her bits of webbing back and apologized we were practically getting to be old friends. Her name was Mercedes, she'd been covering a conference on land drainage for a West German newspaper, and she was several shades less blonde than Yancy's picture of her showed. Land drainage seemed unlikely, but I reminded myself firmly that it was a bit more artistic than caving, which is what I'd have been doing if I'd listened to Driver and Conrad.

We fought our way upward through grey cloud and then white cloud and then into open sunshine above regular ploughed fields of vapour. The captain's voice told us where we were going, in case there was somebody who'd forgotten. After a while I got up and went back to the lavatory to check on Yancy's pictures, just to make sure. I considered, not for the first time, how well Yancy knew me, though I wished he'd gone the whole hog and written some names on the backs of the photographs. I'd trimmed off all except the heads, which at least made them easier to carry, but you have to be a policeman to recognize people from photographs of their faces, as is proved by wanted notices all over the country.

This time there was no doubt, though. I came back to my seat and Mercedes lent me her copy of *Stern*.

The aeroplane had turned the world into a chessboard. London is a square, Berlin another square, New York, Rangoon, Melbourne, Kingston; all are squares now, separated not by seas, forests, mountains and fields but by thin oblong books labelled BOAC, KLM, PAN-AM and filled with the carbon copies of symbols which describe our moves from square to square. I drank black coffee and wondered what the state of play would be when we touched down on a square labelled Munich, and from how many pieces I should find myself under attack. The stewardess announced our landing, Mercedes stopped writing shorthand on the back of *Water and Water Engineering*, and we slid down towards drifting plumes of smoke and municipal spider-webs of roads and railways a mile below us.

ELEVEN

MUNICH WAS damp and sunny and the pavements breathed soft streamers of steam into the drifting air. We looked at picture galleries until noon, and then Mercedes went off to meet somebody big in land drainage and I made one or two small arrangements, like hiring a Taunus and leaving it accessibly near the Hauptbahnhof. The sun shone, girls in flared trouser-bottoms and blowing curtains of hair carried make-up boxes up and down the Leopoldstrasse, and I ate spaghetti for lunch.

At ten-thirty I met Mercedes again in front of the Town Hall and we plunged into Bavarian night-life. She'd been to the hairdressers in the afternoon and was fractionally blonder than she'd been on the plane, but still not as blonde, even now, as her picture in my passport pocket.

Munich is an organized city. It is true that in the battle between organization and Bavarian cheerfulness organization often loses, but the effort is there. The traffic is controlled by computer and television monitor, which gives Munich the biggest and best computer-controlled traffic-jams in Europe. The beatniks go home to bed at midnight so as not to worry their parents. It was long past midnight when we wound up, drinking reasonable Scotch at reasonable prices, in a first-floor nightclub called Bei-Willi.

The room smelled faintly of dust. Regulation pink three-watt lamps struggled pathetically with the warm, blanketing darkness, and on stage a big healthy girl took off many of her clothes to the accompaniment of what sounded like one of the Brandenburgs. She looked happy and thoughtful, like somebody's sister doing it for a bet, and beyond her and out of the spotlight I could see the green corner of a ping-pong table. Bei-Willi you could build a healthy body by day and relax your mind by night.

I have little interest in nightclubs, though some in the people they contain. Mercedes sat opposite me, wearing a severe white blouse and a skirt which I remembered as being dark green when I'd seen it by daylight. She was discreetly scented, like good soap. She watched me without expression as I peered around, trying to adapt my eyes to the prevailing level of illumination. Three tables away a heavy man in a dark suit nodded without interest in our direction, as though I were somebody he thought he recognized but didn't want to talk to, and then swung his attention back to the stage.

'You are going to climb mountains,' said Mercedes.

'I beg your pardon?'

'Would you find me a match, please? I said, you have come to Europe to climb mountains, is that so?'

I nodded.

'Where?'

'Austria,' I told her.

'It is something I don't understand. To get to the top of a mountain, what for? For the view? There are cable-cars. I don't understand.'

'I don't understand it myself,' I said. 'But lots of us go right on doing it, just the same.'

'But why?'

'God knows. You take a lot of time, effort and trouble on the way, it's fine when you get there, you come all the way back and wonder why the hell you took all the bother but next time you start the whole thing over again. It's a lot like it is with girls, only you get colder doing it.'

The music stopped. Heads swivelled momentarily towards the stage, where the big girl stood abstractedly as though running through a mental shopping list. There was a patter of applause and she walked off.

'Is that all?' asked Mercedes.

'I don't know,' I said. 'Nobody knows about lemmings either.'

'Lemmings?'

'Small furry animals,' I said. 'They run into the sea.'

'Why should they do that?'

It began to look as though this could go on for ever. 'I just told you I don't know,' I said. 'Scientists all over are baffled. *Weltschmerz*, maybe.'

She reached across the table and took hold of my sleeve.

'Now you are laughing at me,' she said. 'Is that really all you have come to do? To climb mountains?'

'Yes,' I said.

She began to look annoyed, or at least I thought so. With the spotlight off it was darker than ever. 'Stupid,' she said, almost to herself. The heavy man in the dark suit was pushing his chair back, looking in our direction again. Mercedes said, 'You are not making things very easy for me,' but I wasn't really listening to her. There was something about the heavy man. He was still holding his napkin, and dabbed at his mouth with it. Mercedes tightened her grip on my arm and I gave her my attention. 'You have to meet some people I know,' she said. 'It is a question of employment.'

'Great,' I said. 'What people?'

The man in the dark suit came up behind her.

'Me for one, squire,' he said. He smiled at me genially, one hand still holding the napkin, the other resting on Mercedes's shoulder. She took her hand away from my arm, but she didn't look round at him.

'British, aren't you?' he said. He had a small moustache, like half a Brillo pad, and a regimental or old school tie, I didn't know which. He was about forty-five. He reached out his hand, put the napkin down on the table, and aimed the fingers in my direction.

'Thought so, squire,' he said complacently. 'My name's Bratling, George Bratling. No need to introduce me to the lady, we've met before.'

'Is this one of the people you wanted me to meet?' I asked her.

'Of course I am,' said Bratling. Yancy was absolutely right, he did talk as though he had a ping-pong ball in his mouth. Upper-crust, no, but perhaps it's hard for Americans to draw these fine distinctions. If I'd tried to place him, I'd have said he'd talked his way into the boardroom from the out-of-town sales force.

'You're Dr Yeoman, aren't you?' he said. Before I could

answer, he leaned across the table and went on, 'Between you and me, squire, I think we should get out of this hole. Some undesirable elements around. Word to the wise, eh?' He stood upright again and looked down at Mercedes. 'Word to the wise, eh?' he said again. 'I'm sure you take my meaning.' I couldn't tell whether she minded all this or not. Clearly he wouldn't have noticed one way or the other, in any case.

'The boys from Paris?' I said.

He frowned slightly. 'Not sure I follow you there, squire,' he said. 'You're among friends here, you can take my word for that.' I loved it. I was among friends.

'If you'll excuse me a minute,' I said. I stood up. Mercedes still hadn't acknowledged his presence.

'Not rushing away, are you?' he said.

'I'll be right back,' I told them. They watched me all the way across the room, until I'd pushed my way into the small passageway leading to the cloakroom and let the door swing to behind me.

Inside the cloakroom there was a shower stall and a row of hooks along a stretch of tiled wall. I looked around for a way out. I wasn't sure that I wanted to use it right now, but just in case. I could have saved myself the trouble; whatever the way out was when the place caught fire, it wasn't through here. The only other exit was a ten-by-five-inch slit in one corner with a painted grille over it.

I started to wash my hands. The way things had gone so far, I was totally unsurprised when the missing two faces from Yancy's portrait gallery walked in, particularly after Bratling's little chat about undesirable elements. I could see what had made Jissock so twitchy in Paris, and now it looked as though I was about to be elected as Jissock's replacement.

One of them was a thin man with protruding eyes. In Yancy's photograph he'd been walking down the steps of something like the Stock Exchange, wearing a lightweight raincoat and a Robin Hood hat. Now he was wearing a lightweight blue suit, open-knit tie and moccasins. He leaned against the door as though it had been a rough day, very rough, and he'd had about as much of it as he could stand. His partner was shorter, slight, with a pale-grey jacket cut too loose across the shoulders and hipster trousers; he rose and fell on the balls of his feet, twisting his body slightly to and fro. For him the day had barely started. It probably started when he swallowed the first pill or popped the first vein. He grinned when he saw me and turned to the leaning man.

'Does he know?' he said. 'You think he knows?'

The leaning man sighed and slid down a fraction of an inch.

'I guess so,' he said. They had identical Common-market accents and the dialogue came from the dubbing rooms in Cinecittà, except that they meant it. The boy in the tight hipsters grinned at me again, a pleasant open grin. A grin you could fall into and get all chewed up trying to fight your way out again. His smell started to reach me. Sweat and greenhouses and ten different sorts of aftershave with no baths in between. He was a lovely little fellow.

'Well then,' he said. He flicked his head around again like a bird and looked at the pop-eyed man. 'He was looking for the way out, is what I think,' he said.

'Possible, possible,' said the pop-eyed man. 'Only there isn't any way out.'

'You're wrong,' I said. 'I'm just going to use it.'

I took a couple of steps towards them. The pop-eyed man detached himself from the door and lifted a hand towards me, fingers splayed. The little queen flipped something out of his breast pocket and dangled it, swinging, from between the thumb and first finger of his hand. There was a gentle metallic sliding sound and five inches of switchblade slid out of the polished handle. He pinched his finger and thumb together and there was a click. Then he dropped the handle into the palm of his hand and pointed the blade at me.

'Not yet, dear,' he said.

'Won't keep you a moment,' said the pop-eyed man. 'We got something to say. Everybody relax.' He reached out a finger, delicately, and pushed the blade of the knife downwards until it pointed at my shoes instead of my throat. 'Relax,' he said. Nobody relaxed. Not me and not little stinker, nobody. I don't like knives, I don't like guns either but I like knives even less. I've sewn up too many knife wounds, and most of them go septic. A gunshot is at least sterile. The broken end of a bottle, of course, still takes top marks in the superficial damage stakes. You can never get the edges of the wound together and a high proportion of them are three-cornered or worse, but a knife wound comes a close second.

The door swung open, catching the pop-eyed man on the shoulder. Bratling came in with a small automatic in his hand. Before the pop-eyed man could get himself untired and unrelaxed Bratling hit him, hard, on the side of the neck and he staggered against the wall.

Both of them seemed to know Bratling. Happy Families.

'Drop the knife on the floor,' said Bratling. The little lad in the hipsters didn't even look at him.

'Tell Gloria to put it down, Marris,' said Bratling to the pop-eyed man. 'Otherwise Gloria is liable to cut a titty off with it by mistake. Sorry about this, squire,' he went on conversationally, 'But I did say so, didn't I? Tell him to drop the bloody thing, Marris, I'm not joking.'

The pop-eyed man coughed. He had difficulty speaking and held one hand to the side of his neck where Bratling had hit him.

'Put it down,' he said.

'If you say so,' said the boy. He flipped the knife upwards quickly and the blade slid back into the handle. He started to put it inside his jacket.

'On the floor, Gloria,' said Bratling.

'Oh, all right then,' he said. 'I didn't want to break it, that's all.' He put it down carefully on the floor and straightened up again like a ballet dancer overdoing it. Bratling nodded at me briskly.

'Okay then, squire,' he said. 'Now if you'd just like to go back in there and talk to the lady, I'll make sure you get out in one piece.'

I walked past pretty-boy and Marris. Close up, pretty-boy smelled worse than ever.

'Is his name Braun?' I asked Bratling.

'Full marks,' said Bratling. 'Gloria Braun, we call him, and a nice little lad he is too. Don't keep the lady waiting, squire, if you don't mind.'

As the door breathed shut behind me I heard Bratling say 'Now then, chaps,' like a Territorial Captain pepping up the awkward squad at the drill-hall. I pushed out of the short passage and into the clubroom. After the bright cream paint and tiles of the lavatory I couldn't see a thing across the floor, but I oriented myself by the stage, where a man in a sleeveless Spanish jacket and elasticated trousers was now standing on his hands on a pair of wine-bottles and preparing to pick up a cup and saucer with his teeth. I hoped I wouldn't upset his concentration by kicking over a table as I felt my way across the room and sat down by Mercedes.

If she knew what Bratling was doing she gave no sign of it. She inclined her head at me neutrally, finished her drink and rose to go.

'Don't you think we'd better wait?' I asked.

'No, I don't think so. Perhaps you would get my coat.'

As we left the room I think the man on stage succeeded in whatever he was doing. He got more applause than the stripper. I didn't see the end of his act myself, because I was too busy watching to see who was going to come out of the passage to the cloakroom and when. I don't know what I expected; Bratling blowing smoke from the barrel of his gun, perhaps? Bratling with an arm around the shoulders of both Marris and Braun? Mercedes pushed her way through the curtained entrance doorway ahead of me, so I never found out. It was nice, though, to be able to put names to all those photographed faces, there was that about it.

TWELVE

THE HOTEL – hers, not mine – was modern, smooth outside and in, and felt very slightly pressurized by air-conditioning, as though we were six feet under water. Roughcast walls and small modern reliefs here and there which made you wonder if the ones in the next room would turn out to be different or exactly the same. I sat in an inverted basketwork coolie hat mounted on a black iron tripod and Mercedes sat on the bed.

'Our offer stands,' she was saying. 'Although I admit you seem to be somewhat . . .' she held her head on one side.

'Stupid?' I said. 'What offer? The offer of lucrative employment, that one?'

'Yes. And of course I do not mean "stupid". Nothing of the kind. I know who you are, so I could hardly think you stupid. It's just that you have a difficult way of going about things. Is that fair?'

I tried to sit up. The chair made it impossible.

'Who am I?' I asked.

'A colleague of Captain Brightwell.'

'I'm nothing of the sort,' I said. 'I've been a friend of Captain Brightwell's for a long time but so what?'

She nodded her head gravely and I could see that I was wasting my time; however long I spent explaining that I was just a friend of Yancy's, she'd listen politely and then come right back with her offer of employment as soon as I shut my mouth. I wondered how long I was going to keep it up before being overcome by irritation. I fought my way out of the chair and went over to the window.

'I'm here on holiday,' I said. 'If you choose not to believe me, that's your affair. Tomorrow I'm going mountain climbing and I am not open to offers of employment. Is that clear?'

There was a knock at the door and George Bratling came in.

'Ah there, squire,' he said. He was wearing a camel-hair coat, one of those that are designed to make you aware that the wearer was highly placed in some military career before entering upon their present occupation. He peeled it off carefully and laid it obsessionally across the seat of a blue leather chair.

'What was all that hoo-ha in the bog, then?' he asked. 'Tried to tell you, of course, didn't I, but no, you wouldn't be told. Nod as good as a wink, that's about the form. Oh well. Lucky I was there to take care of things, I expect.'

'Thank you.'

'Not at all, squire. Well now.' He traversed his head from Mercedes to me and back again, like a tank turret. 'Merk been putting any naughty suggestions to you yet?'

Mercedes looked at him steadily. 'Don't call me that,' she said. It was impossible to fathom the relationship between them; tolerant dislike on her part, based on the fact that they had to work together? Presumption of familiarity on his, leading to jolly, open pinches on the backside in bars where the company was just sufficiently well-known to prevent her doing anything about it? It was hard for me to feel anything but the vaguest distaste for Bratling, but I recalled that, weeks ago now and in a different city, Jissock had been terrified of these two. Was it merely because Bratling carried a gun and Jissock was nervous of guns?

'Whatever you say, my dear,' said Bratling.

'Dr Yeoman is here on holiday,' she said.

'Is that a fact, squire? On holiday. Wouldn't have thought it was quite the best part of the year for it, myself.'

'He is going to climb mountains,' said Mercedes.

Bratling lowered himself, carefully, into the coolie-hat chair and patted himself all over for cigarettes.

'Brightwell's not dead,' he said. I couldn't tell whether he was asking or announcing. He lit his cigarette with a miniature butane flamethrower and cocked his head towards me. I said nothing.

'Ah for God's sake come off it,' he said finally. 'Mountain bloody climbing. All you've got to do is say yes or no and I personally,' he winked at Mercedes or it might have been at me, 'haven't got all night. We can push the odd dollar in your direction, you can give us a bit of an assist. If not, no hard feelings. Though of course,' he snapped the butane lighter on again and thumbed the flame into a blue roar, 'there's always Marris and Sweet Gloria Braun.'

'You mean they might be bidding against you,' I said.

'Not quite what I had in mind, actually,' said Bratling. 'What I meant was, they might thump you, squire. They'd have thumped you half an hour ago if I hadn't come along. Should have thought that might make us friends, not to mention Mercedes here who's a very friendly girl, as no doubt you've found out. Or maybe you haven't had time yet.' Mercedes looked at him neutrally. 'Anyway,' he went on, 'either we can do a bit of trade or I'll trot along for a spot of zizz, so make up your mind and stop nattering on about bloody mountains.' He turned to Mercedes. 'Tell you what,' he said. 'I suppose this *is* the right chappie, you haven't gone and picked up some poor sod who hasn't a clue what we're on about, have you!' He didn't sound worried.

Mercedes spread her fingers along her knee. She wasn't going to answer, but in any case Bratling went right on.

'That's right. Forgot. Knew who M. and B. were, called them the boys from Paris. And he does know who *we* are? I only ask because he seems a bit thick, if you'll excuse me, squire.' He didn't want to be excused, by me or anybody else.

'You killed Jissock,' I said.

Bratling leaned back as far as the chair would allow without pivoting on one tripod leg and crashing to the ground. He smiled.

'Thank you for putting my mind at ease,' he said. 'We're on the same wavelength then. Didn't really want to, of course, but needs must when the devil drives.' He stared at the ceiling, swivelling the chair around on its rearmost leg. 'LMF anyway,' he said thoughtfully.

'I beg your pardon?'

'Jissock. Low Moral Fibre. Odd chappie, bright of course, have to give him that, but any loud noise and he'd wet his knickers. You knew him, though, I take it, so I don't have to tell you. Or perhaps you didn't know him, I'm not a hundred per cent sure where you fit into all this, squire. Not that it matters.'

'Jissock was with the Resistance,' said Mercedes.

'Don't go on about the Resistance, darling,' said Bratling equably. 'Do you know anybody who set foot in France between forty-one and forty-five who wasn't with the bloody Resistance? Unless they were German of course. Some of them must have been on the other side, one gathers. Anyway probably that was something the silly bleeder told you in bed, I'll bet he talked all night and did damn little else. I don't give a monkey's knee if he was with the Resistance or the Mafia or the Daughters of the American Revolution. Chicken from here to Christmas, though *de mortuis* and all that of course. Main thing, the squire here's taken over from him—'

'No,' I said.

'To some extent, squire, to some extent. What extent I don't know, but that's what we want to hear among other things. If we can just stop going round in circles.'

I was still standing up, and I was beginning to feel tired of going round in circles myself. I was, as usual, on totally unfamiliar ground, though nobody seemed to be aware of this except myself.

'You're wrong, but I don't see how I can convince you,' I said. 'Just what had you in mind?'

He relaxed all at once and stood up, with a smile a yard wide and as genuine as an open-lot car dealer's.

'You come and work for us. One, we need information, of the sort you might have been chatting about with your friend Captain Brightwell. Two, we need a spot of advice and assistance, mostly scientific.'

'Who doesn't?' I said. I couldn't think of anybody I'd met recently who didn't. Some might be prepared to pay a bit more than others, but the cry for scientific assistance seemed to me to be arising from all sides.

'Three,' Bratling went on, 'this gets a bit tricky, squire, but just supposing you had A Certain Object,' he spoke in capitals, 'to sell us, if you catch my drift, well that wouldn't come amiss. If we were to say a thousand a week – sterling of course – for your valuable help and five, six stretching it a bit, thousand for that object, might we be operating in the same negotiable area?'

'How many weeks?' I asked. I didn't know what the hell I was doing, except that dimly at the back of my mind was some nebulous idea of finding out what the going rate for defecting scientists was these days.

'Minimum of ten weeks, starting now. Maximum probably up to you more than us but we would guarantee you two years if you wanted.'

'As a replacement for Jissock?'

'More or less.'

'Jissock, deceased,' I said.

Nobody answered. It began to look as though there might be two minutes silence for Jissock, deceased, but perhaps my imagination was stretching things out rather. Bratling seemed to be practising words in his mind, words to explain the unfortunate circumstances around the end of Jissock's employment (at least nobody had jumped up to deny that they'd been employing Jissock, I'd achieved that much). Just as I thought he was going to open his mouth and produce some jovial reassurance, Mercedes took over from him.

'Jissock was a fool,' she said.

'I know that,' I told her. 'A fool with Low Moral Fibre, and this is where you tell me that I'm no fool and that *my* moral fibre is terrific. All right. Just so long as we know. I'll think it over.'

Bratling marched across and picked up his coat. He fitted himself into it efficiently. Now that we were on the same wavelength, not to mention operating in the same negotiable area, it was surprising how much of the sales-conference air he'd suddenly sloughed off, though he hadn't got rid of it all.

'Good,' he said. 'But not for too long, eh?' He left most of the buttons on the coat undone and surveyed both of us, nodding what a good show it all was, and left the room. Mercedes leaned backwards on the bed until her head bumped gently against the wall.

'Twelve hours,' she said.

'Very well. Twelve hours ought to be long enough for any intelligent man to make up his mind,' I said.

'More than enough.'

I was still standing by the window. I pulled the curtain across, closing out the glowing geometrical city below, and came towards the bed. She watched me with eyes as expressionless as a pair of welders' goggles.

'I'd like to get the next bit over fairly quickly because I need some sleep,' I told her. 'I expect you do, too. Take off your blouse.'

'Or else what?'

'Or else I scream for the manager. What do you mean, "or else"?' I said.

She sat forward on the edge of the bed and looked up at me.

'Very well,' she said.

She undid the buttons of the white blouse and stood up, shaking it off her shoulders. She reached for the zip at the side of her skirt with both hands, awkwardly, the way women always do.

'Don't bother with the skirt,' I told her. 'I have peculiarities.'

'What do you mean?'

'You don't know about men with peculiarities?' I said. 'I have a thing about looking at women fully dressed except for their blouses, sweaters or the top halves of their dresses, whichever applies at the time. It's something to do with arrested development,' I went on, but I could see all I needed. The zip was on the left-hand side of her skirt, and her right arm was angled far enough across her body to show me the large, flat bruise under her rib-cage. It was faintly bluish now, and would look worse tomorrow. I reached forward from where I stood and gently touched the raised flesh.

'I'm sorry I hit you so hard,' I said. 'But at the time I thought you were a man. It was a natural mistake in the circumstances, and anyway you took a lot of skin off the back of my hand with that torch.'

I thought she might be going to slap my face, and I knew she packed quite a lot of power for a girl. But instead she smiled briefly and faintly, like a clear eddy in a sea-mist.

'I was trying to save trouble,' she said. 'But now I think, perhaps, it's better this way.'

'You mean, now that I'm coming to work for you and jolly George Bratling?'

'Yes.' She looked at me calmly; the smile might never have been there 'Now you get five thousand pounds for it.'

'Six thousand.'

'Six thousand, then. But at the time I thought it would be easier just to take it back from you, if I could find it.'

'You might have been right at the time, and wrong now. Suppose I decide against working for you?'

'I hope you won't do that,' she said. 'If you don't join us, George will take the crystal in any case. You know that. It's ours, after all.' She slid the zip downwards and stepped out of her skirt. 'And even if George doesn't get it, then

Marris and Braun will try to take it from you also, and they are . . . unpleasant men.' She had kicked off her shoes. She walked over to the blue chair and folded her skirt and blouse neatly on the seat. A muscle in her flank tightened as the bruise I'd given her caught against the movement of her body. She looks like a waitress setting a table, I thought. She turned. 'In the morning we shall go and see George and everything will be all right,' she said. 'But that will be in the morning. Now I want to hear about these peculiarities you say you have.'

I went across to the door.

'Another time,' I said.

She stood still, looking at me. There was no sign in her of humour or anger.

'You are not going to stay with me? Really?'

'No.'

'You have no interest?'

'Oh yes. But you see I know where George is,' I told her.

'Where?'

'Over in my hotel room, going through my luggage for A Certain Object,' I said. 'And that's where I'm going now. If he's there when I get there I'm going to kick his teeth in, because I don't like being called squire. So if you want to avoid some more trouble, and I'm sure you'd like to think we were going to get on well together as future workmates, I should try to get him on the phone.' I opened the door. 'If you're lonely,' I told her, 'George probably likes his girls slightly bruised.'

Just as I closed the door behind me, I could see her standing in the middle of the room, taking a clip out of her hair. About fifteen per cent of me wanted to go back into the room, but one smile in an evening didn't seem much of a basis for anything, and I kicked the door shut and walked along the corridor to the lift.

THIRTEEN

I SAT IN a cab because I'd left my street map in my hotel room and it was a little late to walk around Munich asking for directions.

I knew I was right. George Bratling would be searching my room, but I also knew that it wouldn't take him very long because my rucksack was in the Taunus I'd hired earlier in the day so there would be nothing for him to search. He'd probably found out by now that I'd paid my bill and checked out, but so long as I didn't bump into him by accident on his way back to Mercedes everything would be fine, just as she'd said.

I paid the cab off and walked the fifty yards to the Taunus with quite unnecessary caution, but no shots rang out, no knives thudded into my back and nobody threw any rocks, so I drove off.

I left the autobahn at Wangen and the main road at Starnberg, and drove along the western margin of the Starnbergersee, past lakeside cafés with darkened water-lapped terraces and moored collections of nudging dinghies; through Tutzing and Bernried and Seeshaupt, and off into the low forests which are the last washes of green in the school atlases before the Alps kick skyward in rows of cracked escarpments and subside again, a hundred miles to the south, in Italy.

The Taunus wallowed and yawed over mud-slicked pine-roots and the road got worse and worse. I arm-wrestled the wheel, dividing my attention between the darkness ahead and the pencil marks on the map Higsbee had given me. Once I stopped and seriously considered getting my ex-Army prismatic out of the rucksack, until I got a good look around and saw there wasn't anything to take bearings on except trees. It took me five minutes of wheelspin to get moving again, during which I missed a fork somewhere. After I'd driven for what seemed like hours and covered about seven more miles the headlamps picked out a black expanse of water ahead, fringed with reeds, and I realized I'd reached the end of the track. I backed the car carefully among the trees, switched off the lights, and put my boots on while I waited for my eyes to become dark-adapted. Then I got out and tramped around in the thin mud trying to work out where I ought to be going from here.

About ten yards from the end of the track there was a battered boathouse, and a path of sorts led past it around the margin of the lake. I hoped it was the Donnersee because that's where I was supposed to be. I heaved the rucksack out of the back of the car, hunted around on the floor until I found the flashlight, and set off. Assuming this was the Donnersee, I seemed to have struck it at the wrong place and there was no telling how far I'd have to walk to find Mikulicz in his schloss.

Despite its impressive name the Donnersee was, more or less, a biggish pond. Big enough to have a couple of rowing boats on it, perhaps, if you weren't going anywhere except round in circles. Like many of the bits of water hereabouts it was buried deep in pine forest and generously surrounded by marsh.

I looked at my watch. Half past two in the morning; an unusual time to be calling on Mikulicz, but then according to Higsbee he was an unusual man, and in any case I was still concerned with getting away fast. Away from Seeker if they'd started to look for me, away from Munich, away from Mercedes, George Bratling, Marris and Braun or any possible combination of them.

I didn't know what Bratling had in mind for me. He could have agreed to exchange me for a map of Novaya Zemlya and promised to deliver me on the hoof for all I knew. Maybe he and the Marris-Braun axis had by now agreed to divide me down the middle. Whatever way I looked at it, I needed to put a lot of distance between myself and Munich, and waiting until morning to call on Mikulicz wasn't the way to do it.

By about three AM I was soaking wet from the waist down and my boots were waterlogged, but I could see the schloss half a mile away and the path appeared to curve inland from the lake and then lead straight to it. A big old country house like a birthday cake, that's how Higsbee had described it, but I couldn't believe he'd actually been there. It certainly seemed to have a tower of sorts, and perhaps possession of a tower is what distinguishes a schloss from just any ordinary house, but the nearer I got to it the more dilapidated it looked. Somebody's one-time fishing lodge, I guessed, from the days when Ludwig of Bavaria was having fantasies about the Swan King and everybody else was dashing about translating his dreams into stone and timber and plaster.

I emerged from the lakeside path on to an area which looked like a forecourt and I could see the end of the track I should have come in on, if I hadn't lost my way. It didn't look any better but it would have saved me the walk. Water slowly trickled from the lace-holes in my boots as I squelched across to a pair of huge wooden doors, one of which was half-open and hung askew from its hinges. The stars were out overhead, but there was no moon. It was difficult to see where I was going, and practically impossible once I'd got around the half-open door and into some sort of deep archway. I shone the flashlight around. Ancient bell-pull in twisted iron. I pulled. It didn't come away in my hand but it didn't produce any sound that I could hear either.

'Anybody here?' I said. I tried again a bit louder, and the echoes of my voice were sucked up by sodden wood and damp stones. Supposing he'd gone away on holiday, or died quietly in the night? Was there a housekeeper?

Somewhere ahead of me a glow of light appeared, bobbing to and fro. I stood still.

'Hello?' I called. I hoped I was making clear that I was trying to be friendly, because if I lived in a schloss on the Donnersee and somebody came around shouting the odds at three in the morning I'd be carrying a shotgun as well as a torch. I couldn't see who was approaching and wasn't going to annoy them by shining my own torch in their direction.

Footsteps crunched towards me and a voice spoke gently from above the dipping circle of the flashlight lens.

'Who are you?' he asked. But he said it in English, and I was quite certain, somehow, that this was Mikulicz himself.

'How is my old friend Higsbee?' asked Mikulicz.

'He looked fighting fit the last time I saw him,' I said. 'He's in a little trouble for letting me get away to Germany instead of escorting me to a meeting in London, but I think he'll talk his way out of it.'

'I am sure he will. Higsbee is not the sort of man to take unquestioningly to authority, would you say? Nor, for the matter of that, are you, it seems. You had better have another drink.'

Mikulicz stood up and trudged across the room. Like myself, he lived at the top of his house. To be exact, as I could tell from the windows all around us, he lived in the tower. The furniture was nineteen-hundred health resort in style, in heavy mahogany and basket-work, and the room was full of bats.

'You do not object to them?' Mikulicz decanted water from a crystal jug into tall, narrow glasses already containing two inches of brandy. 'Some people do, you know.' He said it in a tone of tolerant surprise for the world's foibles. A huge tortoiseshell cat, gross from over-indulgence, was draped over several cushions on the fireside sofa. Every now and again it opened one eye and flicked an ear at me in idle hostility, but it had clearly given up, years ago, any attempt to do anything about these squadrons of flying mice. The bats swooped and chittered, flicking in and out of the dim murals of light cast by the oil lamps, slotting themselves effortlessly between the bars of the shutters which held out the damp lakeside night and weaving intricate angular flight-patterns around the beams overhead. Mikulicz swirled the glasses to mix the brandy and water and came over to the fire.

'I don't mind them,' I said.

'Of course not. They are my friends. If I say they are the only friends I have left, would you consider me sentimental?'

'Probably I would,' I said. 'What about Higsbee?'

'Ah yes, you are of course right. I was talking to him earlier this evening, but it isn't quite the same. A man needs friends he can see and touch, and I haven't seen him for more than a year.'

It saved me the trouble of asking how Mikulicz had known who I was. I couldn't see the telephone, but perhaps it was downstairs, somewhere in the warren of disused rooms, stone-flagged passages and spiral stairways we'd traversed on the way up here. In any case I was hardly curious; I had reached the point where either I had to accept him, complete with his schloss, tower and bats, or start asking questions which would, in this context, sound stupid even to myself.

'Radio,' said Mikulicz, pointing. I turned my head and saw the stacked grey cabinets against the wall. An efficient rig, even though the external speaker was a coiled and lacquered brass horn standing by itself on a side table. It seemed obvious, really. Higsbee and Mikulicz, both electronics experts, both eccentrics. One lived on a converted Dutch barge and the other in a derelict Bavarian fishing lodge and of course they talked to each other, probably every night.

I swallowed brandy and water. Mikulicz was an old man but a very tough old man. Maybe about seventy, eighty, it was hard to tell. Indestructible and wise. That mad old sod in Bavaria, according to Higsbee's affectionate way of putting it. I liked him, bats and all, and some day I would come back and talk to him for days on end, but not now.

'There is the question of the Doppler effect,' said Mikulicz.

'What?'

My mind was on the direction-finding set I'd come here to pick up. I couldn't see what the Doppler effect had to do with direction-finding.

'The Doppler effect has been insufficiently considered by most students,' Mikulicz went on. 'It is known that bats locate both obstacles and their prey by means of echoes similar to the sonar used by submarines. The mechanisms have been adequately studied, but so far one comes across no mention of the Doppler effect. Now bats move at high speeds.' He looked up and so did I. There were the bats, moving at high speeds. 'More than this,' he went on, 'they accelerate and decelerate rapidly. I would expect these sudden changes in velocity to produce the Doppler effect and this Doppler effect in turn must alter the echo-location patterns perceived by the bat.'

'I hadn't considered it,' I said truthfully, 'but I should think you're right. Look, just at this moment—'

'I know what they must say of me,' he said firmly. 'It is inevitable. Ill. Sick, in the head, sick, is what they say. They are of course quite incorrect.' He watched me, old, the way an old grey blackbird will watch you in the garden. 'Well?' he said.

'I have heard it put forward,' I said cautiously.

'But with deference.' He smiled.

'Oh yes,' I said.

'Very well. Now, my earthquake detector, my small listener to Vulcan's footfalls. Eh? You are here on behalf of your country's Secret Service, that I understand.'

'It's a little less official than that,' I told him, 'but that's the general idea, yes. I have to find one of your devices and examine it.'

'This you are competent to do.' It was hardly a question. He would be too courteous for that. I nodded. 'Which one?' he asked.

'It's in Yugoslavia, in the northern mountains.' He probably knew already.

'Yes,' he said. 'It broke transmission recently. It has almost certainly been tampered with; Higsbee agrees with me.'

'You've discussed it with him?' I asked. I couldn't have cared less, but I wondered if McKellar and Driver knew.

'Discreetly,' said Mikulicz. 'Oh, you Intelligence people need have no concern that the operation, what is the name of it—'

'Rock Baby.'

He framed the words once or twice with his mouth, silently.

'They have these names,' I said.

'I know. From the war. Rock Baby. Rock Baby. Well, well.'

'You were saying that you hadn't discussed the operation openly over the air,' I said, trying not to appear hurried.

'Yes. So you need not be anxious in British Intelligence.'

'I'm not really in British Intelligence,' I said. It wasn't true. I had better stop saying it at every conceivable opportunity. I was the only person it mattered to, in any case. Mikulicz got up.

'Excuse me,' he said. He left the room. So far as I could tell there was only one way out; a door in one of the angles of the octagonal tower which led directly on to a narrow stone staircase. I heard his footsteps grate on the dusty, wedge-shaped steps.

I got out of my chair and went to one of the shuttered windows. The cat opened both its eyes and followed me with baleful suspicion and the bats swooped past my head, bouncing their tiny high-pitched sonar echoes off me. Outside the window was a sheer drop of eighty feet to the bank of the Donnersee. Wind creased the water surface and drove ripples in formation among the reeds. It would soon be dawn, and I wanted to get away. Mikulicz was an interesting old man. He was what I might turn into if I lived that long; an old man with a badly-arranged filing system of a mind, stuffed with a huge accumulation of knowledge and with problems – such as the possible use of the Doppler effect by bats – which would never be solved before death solved all problems. But I still had to get away, because men with guns and girls with bruised ribs were coming after me.

Mikulicz came back. I was glad to see he was carrying what must be the DF set. It was about the size of three cigarette packets and he had a circle of polished wire, the directional aerial itself, looped over his wrist. He was breathing evenly and slowly after his climb up the stairway and in his left hand he held a gun.

He came across to me and gave me the DF set and the aerial, showed me the sockets for the loop and the tiny signal-strength meter on the side of the black-japanned casing, and left me holding the gun while he searched in the drawers around his ham radio outfit for a pair of lightweight earphones.

The gun was old and well-oiled, one of the ancient stiff Lugers made before they started cutting the weight down with alloy.

Mikulicz came back with the earphones, and with another small radio set. It was about the same size as the DF set and had an extending rod aerial instead of the loop. I gave the Luger back to him.

'Ah. You have one,' he said.

'I haven't, and I don't want one.'

'Is that true? It is your affair of course.' He handed me the second radio. 'This is an ordinary transmitter-receiver,' he said. 'You will need it to speak to the Shackleton.'

'Thank you,' I said. 'But I'm not sure they'll be speaking to me.'

'Really? You will not of course transmit for long because of possible homing on your position by other parties. By the way they will almost certainly have booby-trapped the seismograph when you find it, you know that? Rock Baby.' He laughed. 'But there is no reason why I should tell you this. I think they will have made the self-destroying mechanism much more sensitive, to the slightest touch perhaps, and there is plenty of room in the casing for enough explosive to blow your head off. That would be the simplest way, it seems to me. So be careful you don't get bitten. Now that is that. You are in a hurry to leave.'

'I'm sorry,' I said. 'I hoped it wasn't obvious.'

'Not at all. You have been very patient. I am an old man and old men are stupid and talk too much. Stupid because I should have seen that you would not have called on me in the middle of the night if you could have afforded to wait until morning, and stupid because there must be men following you, just as there were men following Jissock. So you will please forgive me, and come back to talk with me another time.'

I packed the DF set, the loop aerial, and the little transceiver into my rucksack. I tightened down the straps before I turned back to Mikulicz.

'Higsbee told you about Jissock, did he?' I asked.

'Higsbee? No.'

I straightened up and came back to my chair. I was in a hurry, but not so much of a hurry that I couldn't afford a little time out. I felt, as I was beginning to become accustomed to feel, as though I were trying to catch a thrown egg in a tablespoon.

'Then how do you know about Jissock?' I asked.

'He was looking for me, about a month ago, maybe a bit longer. You knew that, I thought.'

'I didn't know anything of the kind,' I said.

'There are no men following you, then?'

'There are men following me all right,' I said. I could see

that we were going to get ourselves up to the necks in a mass of 'I thought you knews' if we weren't careful, but I had to sift things through. I couldn't see why Jissock would have been looking for Mikulicz at any time. If Higsbee hadn't discussed Jissock with Mikulicz over the air during their late-night radio sessions – and I wasn't even sure that Higsbee knew that the body Seeker had been playing around with, in and out of deep-freezes, was Jissock's – then I didn't see any necessary connexion between Jissock and Mikulicz at all, let alone why Jissock should have been looking for the old man just before he was killed. Had Higsbee talked about 'a body' or 'Jissock's body' or what? I couldn't remember, which showed how bad I'd be at any sort of real Intelligence work.

'Where is Jissock?' asked Mikulicz.

'In the mortuary,' I told him. 'He got killed trying to get across the Channel from France last month.'

'Ah.' He was neutral. No sign of whether he thought it was a pity, or a surprise.

'Did he find you?' I asked.

'Excuse me?'

'You said he was looking for you a month ago,' I said. 'Did he find you?'

'No. I was in Salzburg.' Mikulicz sat down opposite me, by the cat. He ruffled its neck and it leaned its ear against his hand. 'There appears to be some difficulty in your mind, Dr Yeoman,' he said. 'Is there some way I can help you?'

'Yes there is. You could tell me why Jissock wanted to get hold of you.'

'Certainly. At least, I can tell you part of the reason why. He was trying to purchase a piece of scientific equipment from a French firm which manufactures such things. Rather an unusual piece of equipment, not part of a normal manufacturing run. The company is called Lectronique. I own, and used to manage, Lectronique and Jissock knew this, so he tried to contact me. I understand he intended to come down here to see me, but as I say I was in Salzburg and it wasn't possible. As I told him, Lectronique has offices in Paris, so in the end he dealt directly with them.'

I knew that I ought to leave it there. If I didn't, I'd have to expose myself far more than was wise. But if I left it there, then I had two coincidences involving Jissock on my hands. Coincidences and plausible explanations.

I was over here to find Rock Baby, but all the time I kept finding Jissock's dead hand reaching out and tapping me on the shoulder, pointing out some unknown connexion between Rock Baby and the whole carnival parade which involved Yancy Brightwell, Bratling-Mercedes-Marris-Braun and the laser crystal in my rucksack.

'I'm sorry,' I said. 'I don't see why Jissock would have wanted to contact you personally. He was in Paris at the time, wasn't he?'

'Precisely.'

'Why didn't he just go straight to this company, Lectronique? Why should he bother to try to contact you in Bavaria, even if he knew you were in control of Lectronique?'

Mikulicz hauled the cat effortlessly across from its cushions and on to his knee, holding it by the scruff of the neck. Its body dangled like a sack of meal but it seemed perfectly happy with the arrangement.

'In particular,' I went on, 'what did you mean when you said that there were men following him?'

He leaned back.

'I have known Jissock for many years,' he said. 'I will not say, as a friend, because it would not be precisely true, but at any rate we knew each other. Jissock was over in France with the Resistance during the war. I have an old man's memory and I cannot even tell you which year, but that is how I met him. I think that perhaps Jissock saw me, if you will allow a phrase which has lost much of its meaning and all of its value in these days of psychology, as a father. I listened to him, you see, and few people listen to each other any more. Children do not listen to their fathers, that is certain, but here and there one can discover a father who listens to his children, and so perhaps, as I say, that is how Jissock regarded me.' He stopped.

'You were with the Resistance too?' I asked.

'Dr Yeoman, you are a young man. I do not think you know how old I am. I was born in eighteen-eighty-six. I was ten years older than the boys who killed each other in the mud at Ypres and Passchendaele. In nineteen-forty-one I was fifty-five. I cannot truthfully say I was with the Resistance, though they used to borrow my bicycle and I had some small skill in repairing and building radio sets. The Resistance was for heroes,' he cocked his head at me, the old wise blackbird again, 'and at fifty-five one is too old to be a hero.'

Faint light was just beginning to show in horizontal lines between the shutter slats. I looked up, and the bats had stopped their flickering dance and were hanging in half-seen leathery pouches, like wrinkled tropical fruit, along the beams. Every now and again one of the pouches would shift slightly, with a faint whiskery scratching sound.

'All right,' I said. 'They brought you your slippers and pipe and you sat and mended their radio sets. What about Jissock?'

'Jissock was not a brave man,' he said. 'And I do not mean merely that he broke out in a sweat at the thought of doing something dangerous and that later, when the dangerous thing came along, he went and did it without looking back. That's the normal way, for all of us who have any imagination at all. But Jissock had too much imagination altogether; he saw, I think, all the time the bullet that would strike him or the Nazi who would question him, or the grenade that would roll towards him and that he would watch for the endless two seconds before it blew him to pieces. You must understand that the Resistance did many courageous things, but it was no place for a man such as Jissock to find himself. In some units perhaps he would have been helped, but as it happened he was sent out from England to perform one task, just one, and he arrived among a group of . . .' he thought it over for a moment, 'young tigers. I do not know how to explain this to you. Men who would go out and shoot a sentry at night just because he was a sentry and a German. I do not blame them too much. I am of course a Jew and,' he smiled faintly, 'for a Jew it was not necessary to be a sentry to be killed. So. But for Jissock. He had been sent over in connexion with a bridge that must be destroyed. I expect you have seen many cinema films where bridges are blown up but believe me it is not always easy. A bridge is a bridge, and a stick of dynamite or a pound of *plastique* is just that and not some all-powerful destroying force.'

I nodded.

'This was a question of engineering and of geology, of rock formations and the manner in which the piers of the bridge were keyed into the rock, do you understand me?' said Mikulicz. 'This was not a question of many tons of explosive, but of putting a certain quantity in a certain place. Not of *boom, boom*, like in the cinema.' He gestured '*boom, boom*', with his arms and the cat opened its eyes again for an instant. 'So a scientist had to come and look and this scientist was Jissock, and he found himself an over-imaginative coward among the tigers.'

I could hear Bratling's voice saying the same sort of thing about Jissock in different words, and I could imagine how it must have been for him. How many George Bratlings had there been in the Resistance?

'He was over in France for about ten days, if I remember,' Mikulicz went on. He stopped again. 'Listen,' he said. The cat was purring but I couldn't hear anything else. 'I am sorry,' he said after a minute. 'It is nearly morning and you must go, but there is time for me to tell you about Jissock. He was in France for ten days. There was, as I have said, a bridge. Jissock was to make drawings, perform certain calculations, and tell them where to place their explosives. They took him out one night, down by the river; they sat for two hours while the men guarding the bridge came and went. The other men in the group watched the guards and sometimes they watched Jissock. He had come over from some quiet job in a laboratory in England, and at first he tried to hide the fact that he was afraid, but then after a while he could not or didn't bother. When they got him down beside the bridge and the rocks his hands were shaking and he was sick They were annoyed because of the noise he made vomiting. He did his drawings all wrong and made hardly any notes at all, because you see he wanted to get back out of that place. They could see he was useless. One of them tried to calm him down, but in the end they had to come away, and Jissock tried to pretend that he had got all the information he needed, but they knew he hadn't. They were angry and who can blame them? They swore at him and left him alone back at the farm where they were hiding for the rest of the night.'

I knew that Mikulicz himself had been there, down by the bridge. He wasn't just the old man who mended the radio sets, but he didn't say so. Not because he was falsely modest but because it was not part of the story, the one he wanted to tell.

'The bridge didn't get blown?' I asked.

'Oh yes. Jissock came to me the next morning. He was still afraid, you understand, but he talked to me about the bridge and the rock and the way the rock was set. Well, I am a scientist, you see. I made a list,' Mikulicz drew parallel lines in the air with his thumbnail, 'a list of the specific questions that needed to be answered, and we went back.'

'Jissock went back?'

'Yes. With me. The water was running down his face with fear and he was sick again, but he could answer questions that I asked him and slowly he was able to do more than just answer questions. We made an analysis, and I took it to the young tigers because Jissock was ashamed to talk to them again, and the next night they blew the bridge and the night after that Jissock went back to England. I saw him five, six times between the war and now. Usually on matters of equipment. I made money and I do not know exactly what happened to him, but these last two years I think something not too good. So that is why, I think, he tried to see me a few weeks ago. But I could not.'

'Why not?'

Mikulicz stood up and dumped the cat on the floor in front of the dead fire.

'I didn't wish to. It would have been an impossible situation,' he said. 'And now I think you ought to go.'

He stood still, listening, and looked up as though he were counting the little leather bags which were the sleeping bats.

'Of course,' I said.

'You're ready? It would be best to leave quickly. Because I believe that your enemies are nearly here. You have not told me in so many words, but they are dangerous, and I would guess that they are a mile away, maybe less.' He moved his head from side to side, still looking up, and I began to have the senseless feeling that at any moment now he would raise his arms in a gesture and the bats would unfold and drop away from the beams, and flutter out into the dawn to search and confirm that what he said was true. I reached out for my rucksack and slung it over one shoulder.

'I'm ready,' I said.

'Then I will show you the way.' His face swung down until he was looking directly at me. 'You will have to take the boat. They have a car and they control the approach to the landward.'

He strode off towards the door, an old man with a young man's walk. I followed. Instead of going down the spiral stairway he turned sharply and vanished in a narrow embrasure. I felt my way after him, and saw that he'd started to climb a steep wooden ladder. After I'd hauled the rucksack up about twenty rungs I heard the creak of an opening trap, and a few moments later we emerged on to the roof of the tower. It was a flat area, boarded in wood and surrounded by toy battlements. Mikulicz pointed.

'Over there,' he said. 'Two cars. I heard them some time ago, but the road is bad and it was important that you should know about Jissock. He is dead and we are alive, and if the living do not understand the living they must understand the dead.'

Across the lake an early-rising bird had started to call. I looked where he was pointing, and I thought I could see something that might have been the glow of a car's lights deep in the trees, or two cars if that's what he insisted, but I couldn't be sure.

Mikulicz walked around half the tower's circumference and beckoned me across. I looked over the edge and there, sure enough, were the top rungs of a bar ladder, set into the stones of the tower itself. Below them the water of the lake lapped methodically against the bank, almost but not quite invisible in the spreading, metallic dullness of the dawn. There was no mist; it was going to be a cold day, not bitterly cold but cold enough to make the top rung bite into my hand as I swung myself over to begin the long descent.

Mikulicz leaned over me.

'The boat is to your left, if you face outwards when you reach the bottom,' he said. 'It is about five yards away. Row across the lake, straight across, so that you keep the house always between yourself and the roadway.'

'What about you?' I asked.

'I? I am an old man who makes friends with bats. Don't trouble yourself about me.' He laughed.

I thought about the ancient, oiled Luger. His hand wouldn't shake. I started down the iron rungs, moving slowly and cautiously because I didn't know how firmly they were set. When I was about ten rungs down I heard his voice for the last time.

'I should have helped Jissock,' he said. 'Individuals are more important than groups. If we have not learned that, we have learned nothing. I knew he was in trouble, and I should have helped him.' His head and shoulders vanished behind the parapet and I went on climbing down for what seemed like a century or two. There was a drop of about ten feet from the last rung of the ladder, and I landed in grassy mud. As I struggled to my feet I heard the sound of a car engine in low gear on the other side of the schloss. I wanted to stay and see what happened, but I couldn't, of course. It was unlikely that I could have been much help, in any case.

Instead I walked along the bank, leaning against the wall in places for balance, until I found the small flat-bottomed boat hidden among the reeds. It contained a pair of oars, one of which had been broken a long time ago and mended with two pieces of board. I climbed in and pushed away from the mud and reeds with one of the oars until I could begin rowing. There was too much water in the boat for me to be able to put the rucksack down, and I kept it on my back, which made the whole thing about four times as difficult as it need have been. There was no sign of life anywhere in the schloss and the car on the other side had cut its engine. I pulled steadily away from the bank, hoping that whoever was in the car wouldn't get to a point of vantage and spot me.

It took longer than I'd estimated to cross the lake. The

farther I got from the schloss, the more it looked as though it was about to collapse into the water, like the House of Usher. From a distance the walls became a camouflage pattern of light and dark grey, the top half of the pattern standing out against the sky and the lower half merging with the trees behind. The water of the Donnersee clucked under the slapping bow of the boat and dripped like treacle from the ends of the oar-blades. The events of the night seemed unreal, as though I might have to search about in the rucksack for the hard, angular shapes of the two radio sets and the clear circle of the DF aerial in order to convince myself that the old man and his bats had ever existed. Of course, I hadn't slept.

I was nearly at the far bank when I heard faint shouting and then the sound of a shot. I pulled too hard on the broken oar and it snapped, so I had to paddle the last few yards to shore. I ran the boat in among more reeds, pulling myself along by the stems, and climbed out. For once I seemed to be on reasonably firm ground. I looked across at the schloss again. There was a figure on top of the tower, but the light was still bad and I could make out very little about it. There was the sound of another shot. Unless the figure on the tower had a rifle I couldn't believe the shot had anything to do with me, not at that range.

I strained my eyes, trying to make out what was happening, and as I did so there was the unmistakable sharp stammer of an automatic weapon and I saw the figure on the tower half-turn and lean towards me, then topple very slowly over the parapet and fall just as slowly, it seemed, all the way down the side of the tower. I waited to hear some sort of thump or splash, but the early morning wind was beginning to move the branches of the pines around me and I could hear nothing. It still seemed, at that distance, to have nothing to do with me; I turned away and plunged in among the trees, hoping that I hadn't been watching the death of Mikulicz but afraid that I had been doing just exactly that.

FOURTEEN

I DON'T KNOW what they were all doing in London and Munich during the next week because I spent it walking across Austria, or across most of Austria anyway.

I knew very little about surveillance procedure or the various arts of having people followed, but I was fairly certain that one of the best ways to make certain that nobody knew where I was headed would be to walk.

I found the Donnersee again on Higsbee's map and wove my way through several kilometres of forest until I struck the Walchensee. I kept off the road down the western bank which forms part of the German Alpine Route, and then crosssed it and walked east along the tollroad to Niedernach. After breakfast I climbed southward again over the ridge to Vorderriss on an easy path and then started to slog up the road which slopes upward and across the Austro-German border to Hinteriss. I had no difficulty at all at the customs post, which is hardly surprising since, as a rule, there isn't anywhere much to go on the Austrian side of the border except Hinteriss and Eng. I exchanged greetings with three precise and cheerful officers and got my passport stamped. I didn't want to enter Austria illegally, though I had every intention of leaving it without benefit of rubber endorsements. Nobody wanted to look inside my rucksack, which perhaps was just as well.

On the second day I climbed south-east out of Eng, ate sandwiches at the Lamsenjoch Hütte feeling sore in every joint, and then descended past the Stallenhütte and caught a train in Stans in the comfortable knowledge that anybody who'd even tried to follow me by car would have driven a hundred kilometres and been forced into a whole lot of fancy guesswork in Garmisch and Innsbruck, to say the least.

I changed trains in Jenbach, feeling stupidly conspicuous, just the same. The local train to Zell-am-Ziller was a small toast-rack affair which clacked its way past allotments and tiny wooden halts, and the bus which took me up to Gerlos ground its way up the hairpin mountain road in first gear, the driver manhandling the steering wheel as though opening and closing some mighty sluice-gate. I stayed overnight in Gerlos and thumbed a lift in a Haflinger the next morning to Krimml. Mid-morning saw me starting southward again, up the Habach river, past the Alpenrose Wirtshaus and up the deep gorge at the head of the Habachtal to the Thuringer Hütte. I was no longer quite as stiff and sore, so I was getting something out of all this walking. Next day I climbed eastward across the Labmkogl ridge and down across a glacial valley to the Neue Further Hütte, a procedure which the *Wanderkart* describes as 'Four Hours, Easy', meaning that you need most of a day, a guide and a constitution of iron.

The Neue Further Hütte, at seven thousand feet, looks out westward over the Kratzenberg See. I sat and contemplated the huge bowl with the lake held in it like water in a cupped hand, and thought about Driver and Dylan. Dylan believed that for simple-minded scientists truth was truth and no mucking about. For political types it was different, apparently, and truth came in slices and the slices changed from day to day. In a way I could see what he meant though it was hard for me to agree with him. I thought of the slices of truth about Jissock I was collecting, from Driver and Yancy, from Bratling and from Mikulicz, and wondered if I would eventually collect enough slices to form the whole truth about him, clear and round and shiny like an apple. I knew Jissock was important, and I wished that I could work out exactly how and why. I adjusted the laces in my boots, carefully taking in a millimetre here and there until they were comfortable, and set off southward for the three hours to Innergschloss.

After lunch I went on down to Matrei and Huben and the hard walking was over. Two days later, having travelled another forty kilometres or so on foot and taken the *Postauto* for the rest of the way, I was somewhere to the south-east of Villach with nothing between me and Yugoslavia but the six-thousand-foot sweep of the Karawanken range which is the southern border of Carinthia. It was all clever stuff and it did me no good at all as things turned out, except that I got to see quite a bit of scenery, one way and another.

Two

Yugoslavia, Albania

FIFTEEN

I HUNCHED MY shoulders against the rock.

I was getting colder and colder, but it was marginally better to have rock against my anorak than to leave a space for the mountain wind to funnel through. My shoulder-joint – the one I had used to illustrate my philosophical and useless protest to Andy Dylan – was aching steadily. I was trying to get some sense out of the radio operator in the Shackleton; what I really wanted was for him to belt up and let me get on with the job, but I hadn't got through to him yet because I wasn't using correct procedure. Doubtless if I'd stayed for my briefing in London I'd have known all about correct procedure.

His disembodied voice crackled through the headset, superimposed on a hail of static like dried peas being poured into a tin bowl.

'Berlanco Berlanco,' his voice said. 'We have your signal Delta on vector zero five erwunner . . .' he sank without trace beneath the static ocean for about ten seconds and then surfaced, '. . . request your signal repeat, Berlanco Berlanco,' and then stopped. I held the tiny transceiver to my mouth and tried for about the tenth time to get not merely my signal (I assumed that I was Berlanco Berlanco) but a sentence of actual chat through to him. I'd have ignored the Shackleton, except that I could see they had some reason for anxiety about me and they must have been flying around in circles for at least a week. Where were they? Somewhere over the Adriatic, I guessed. At least they were warm.

I was cold because I was about five thousand feet above sea-level and it was four in the morning. Summer wasn't far enough along to have burned the snow off, let alone provide mild nights. I was in Yugoslavia, at least I was fairly certain I was, though I hadn't stopped anyone and asked. But I was on the southward-facing slopes of the Karawanken, and the Austro-Yugoslav border runs along the summit of the range, so I must have crossed it.

In principle it's fairly easy to cross a mountainous border, provided the mountains are neither too high, which means rock-and-ice work, nor too low which makes for easy surveillance. I could have crossed from Germany into Austria quite easily without going through passport control, but I didn't want to. In the skiing season, plenty of people cross various borders between France, Italy and Switzerland quite unintentionally during snowstorms, when they can't see the route-markers.

The borders of Yugoslavia are a different matter, of course, since arrivals in Yugoslavia with incorrectly-endorsed passports are liable to be regarded with suspicion, even though no visas are needed now for visits of less than three days. I was probably going to be here more than three days, but on the other hand I had no intention of going any where near a village, so nobody was going to look at my passport.

The passes are officially closed, most of them, and the paths through them guarded. But the rocks were there long before men came and drew artificial borders along them, and it is not absolutely necessary to travel by the paths, though skill and care are needed to diverge from them. To police the twenty-five kilometres of mountain border between Villach and the Rosenberg car-train tunnel – the section of border somewhere along which I'd crossed – would take far more men than could be spared by any government, and in any case, what would be the point? Anybody who crosses the border is presumably going to turn up sooner or later in a town or a village, and the matter of his passport can be taken up there. The entry of persons who intend to contact nobody whatever during their stay is not, except in wartime, allowed for. I hoped that on this account I would get by.

I would rather have been deeper in Yugoslavia, and my fingers were numb.

I didn't think anybody would get a fix on my transmissions this early in the game, and being near the border didn't make it any more likely that they would, so I was being unreasonable. But the nearer I was to Rock Baby before they even heard me, the more chance I stood of getting away.

In any case I was at a good altitude and I might never be in a better position to get a fix on Rock Baby, so I went on talking to the Shackleton until I finally got some sense through to them. I told them I was fine, just fine, and they gave me a message from Driver. Stripped of transmission procedure, Driver wanted to know where I was and what the hell I was doing. I didn't blame him. I gave the Shackleton people a short and pithy message to pass on to Bayswater and Whitehall, got a time-check to correct my watch, and signed off.

I moved on, to the difficult bit. Higsbee's schedule of transmission times told me that Rock Baby would be coming on the air in six minutes and I knew that it would transmit for five minutes after that. Then there would be dead silence for (I consulted the schedule again, shining the torch on the figures and hoping the paper wouldn't be torn out of my hand by a gust of wind) twenty-two hours and forty-three minutes.

I worked out my own rough position. It looked as though Rock Baby couldn't lie on a bearing of less than a hundred and ten degrees from where I was, nor more than two hundred and sixty, unless I was dead out of luck and Driver's areas of maximum probability were hopelessly inaccurate. This still left me with a sector of a hundred and fifty degrees to cover but it was better than every damned point on the compass. I set up the loop of the DF set and plugged in the headset.

When the signal came – a confused, high-pitched warble which I had no interest in decoding for the present – I got a clear null a little west of due south. My fingers had almost seized up with cold by the time I'd checked and rechecked the signal, but at least the position of smallest strength seemed to be sharp, constant, and accurate within about a degree and a half either side.

I unclamped the loop, packed the set away and blew on my nails until they started to send pulses of agony up my arms. To the south was the dark outline of Triglav, the highest mountain in Yugoslavia. The really tricky thing would be if they'd dropped Rock Baby slap on its summit, in which case

I'd do a smart about-turn and head for home. But Triglav was about fifteen kilometres away and there was a lot of territory in between; despite the accurate bearing I'd got from my first cast, I wasn't stupid enough to hope that if I just marched a little west of south I'd trip over Rock Baby in due course. I unsoldered my knee-joints and started downhill.

My only anxious moments came when I'd dropped down to two thousand feet and had to cross a minor road, a railway line and a small river, all running together along the valley floor. I was in open ground for about a thousand yards or so and the only bridge carried the railway tracks across both the river and the road. I could have avoided getting my feet wet by a twenty-minute detour but it would have been very silly indeed to take the risk.

The river was much deeper than it looked and I didn't dare wait until daylight came and I could see what I was doing. The sixty-five-pound pack didn't help much either. I stood on the far bank while tiny torrents of ice-water poured out of my sleeves, wondering if anyone would be curious enough to investigate all that splashing, but the only sign of life was a half-minute *obbligato* of barking, torn apart by the rising wind and drowned by the thrash of the stream. I stumbled uphill across short grass, dropped into a gully, and was under cover behind the toe of an outcrop a few yards later.

By sunrise I'd dug myself into a crack at the foot of a rock chimney, invisible, I hoped, unless some freak of chance brought a shepherd near enough to fall over my feet. I drank a third of a canteen of water, fought down most of a packet of dates, and went to sleep.

It took me three more bearings to pin down Rock Baby. The first two were cross-bearings based on what I thought was my accurate position on each occasion. But either I was getting signals slightly deflected by rock or my map-reading wasn't so good, because I spent a fruitless and nerve-wracking two hours casting about the point where the bearings crossed in ever increasing circles and with no results whatever.

My third bearing showed me that I'd missed by a quarter of a mile, which is a long, long distance when you're halfway up a mountain searching about five acres of rocks, grass-tufts and occasional clumps of bushes. When I finally picked it up in the fading evening light, sighting my binoculars across the notch of the compass, only its spherical regularity distinguished it from any of a dozen similar rounded boulders. I could almost have kicked it over by accident if I'd gone on walking around long enough, I thought. Remembering Mikulicz's comments on its probable sensitivity and possible explosive power, I was glad I hadn't.

I made camp without going over to look at it more closely. It had been here for a year and it would still be here in the morning. I brewed a mug of strong, scalding tea over my solid-fuel tin burner, dripped brandy into it with the reckless abandon of a Madison Avenue bartender showing the vermouth bottle to a Martini, and went to sleep with my head on my boots and my feet wrapped in a spare shirt. In my dreams I followed Rasmussen and Binnie Abrams down an endless alley, until they both turned to face me and Binnie said, 'Drunk again, I see,' and Rasmussen tapped me on the chest. 'Predestination,' he said and his fingers pressed harder and harder into my ribs. I woke up and dug out the sharp stone I'd shifted on to in my sleep. Thin light was knifing around the mountain edges above me, and a little late snow fell and melted, flake by flake, on the cover of my sleeping-bag. I was a sneak-thief in a strange land. An unguessable distance away a wild cat started to cry, sobbing out that forlorn and angry howl which is one of the loneliest sounds in the world.

SIXTEEN

I'D ALWAYS known that the time would come when I'd be sorry I hadn't brought along Conrad's bomb-disposal man from DI 6, and the time was right now.

I lay on my stomach in the hot morning sun, surveying Rock Baby carefully from twenty yards away through the binoculars. I was about half a mile from my semi-permanent camp. I don't say it was impossible to spot, but I'd done my best and, short of an overhead pass by a very low-flying helicopter, I thought it would pass muster.

My tent and flysheet are made from a lightweight and nearly indestructible French plastic material and I'd covered them with artistic smears of the meagre, greyish soil which was scattered in between the rocks. I'd found a small scooped-out cave to cook in. I'd broken up the rectangular outline of the tent itself by sticking rocks around it and dragging over a few small mountain myrtle bushes to conceal both it and the cave mouth.

I was working in the middle of a large amphitheatre, a glacial valley whose sides were two of the outlying arms of Triglav itself. I'd climbed up to the crests of both side ridges and the encampment was invisible from either of them. The back of the amphitheatre shelved skyward in successive steep ridges to a summit glacier, five thousand feet above my present position, and the north-facing open end of the valley dropped over a lip and concealed me from below. Perhaps it would have been ideal to have been operating in the middle of a forest, but for open terrain this was good enough. I felt no unease about my domestic arrangements. I couldn't say the same about Rock Baby.

The little seismograph itself appeared almost to have constructed its own camouflage. Through the glasses I could see about two-thirds of its spherical body, dull grey like the rocks around it and with one or two small patches of lichen here and there on its surface. The low tripod legs which, I knew, supported the sphere were entirely hidden by pebbles and tufts of grass, and part of the sphere itself was concealed by the twigs of some unidentifiable shrub.

I began to see what Higsbee had meant by saying that you could scatter these things around the country like confetti without anybody finding them. Even now I occasionally swept the field of the binoculars across Rock Baby without seeing it at once.

I focused again and went on looking at it until I could no longer delude myself that I was achieving anything useful, and then I got up and walked the intervening twenty yards until I was close enough to reach out and lay a hand on it if I wanted to. I didn't want to.

If you want to make an object explode, sound a whistle, puff out a cloud of pink smoke or play Rule Britannia when disturbed, you can use one of several mechanisms whose collective name is the trembler circuit.

In its simpler forms this circuit is found on those car-thief alarms which cause such amusement among the children in the streets where such cars are parked. You suspend a pendulum between two contacts, the pendulum itself being electrically live. Anything which rocks the supports of the pendulum enough to make it swing against either contact closes a relay and either rings an alarm bell or sounds the horn. Neither of these events attracts any attention from passers-by, who have heard the things go off twenty times already that morning, but the principle is sound.

In wartime, this device is used to trigger anti-personnel bombs and, occasionally, to discourage enemy Naval experts whose hobby is the defusing of mines. I knew that the self-destructive mechanism inside Rock Baby worked on much the same principle, except that since Rock Baby carried sophisticated power supplies to drive the seismographic pick-ups, the 'pendulum' consisted of a wire coil held between the poles of a magnet. If the coil moved relative to the magnet, a current was generated in the coil itself and this current was what activated the 'destroy' mechanism.

Among other things, this meant – as Mikulicz had suggested

– that the system could easily be tuned to any degree of sensitivity. What I had better assume, even if it turned out not to be true, was that it had been set for maximum sensitivity, that the mechanism would operate if I breathed heavily on Rock Baby, and that behind the tin alloy casing, three feet away from me as I squatted beside it, there'd be sufficient gelignite to blast a biggish crater in the valley and leave nothing much of me except my boots.

I grew tired of squatting and sat down instead.

Then there was the other fuse inside, as I remembered from the blueprints they'd showed me in Whitehall. I didn't want even to begin thinking about that one, since it involved pressurizing the interior of the sphere very slightly with compressed gas, and having a barometric fuse in the casing set to blow if the gas was released, like for instance by some earnest truth-seeker with a brace and bit or a set of Allen keys.

That made two sorts of fuse I knew were inside. If Driver, McKellar, Higsbee and Mikulicz were right and other people had taken the thing to bits and reassembled it slightly differently, then of course there were various other possible fuses that could have been rigged instead, or in addition. Magnetic fuses, though I didn't think it likely – there were too many stray magnetic fields around inside Rock Baby to start with, what with the seismographic pick-ups themselves and the magnetic storage discs for recording and relaying the information obtained from the pick-ups.

Scrub out magnetic fuses. What was left? Light-sensitive fuses? It was presumably dark in there, and breaching the sphere would mean letting in light. The cell out of somebody's light-meter and a few bits of wire would do to make a fuse that would blow if that happened. Keep light-sensitive fuses on the list. Then you could make a fuse sensitive to sound, or to body heat. You could make a fuse sensitive to great big drops of sweat falling off the investigator's brow, though presumably you wouldn't catch a real live bomb-disposal man that way because they probably didn't sweat at all.

That seemed to be enough sorts of fuse to be going on with. Plus of course all the sorts I hadn't thought of. 'Ah yes, how cunning,' I would say to myself in the tenth of a second between realizing I'd have to add another fuse to the list and falling in lots of little bits all over the scenery.

I became sharply aware, as upon many previous occasions in my life, of the distinction between theory and practice.

After lunch I went for a short walk and set some rabbit-snares. Dehydrated vegetables and chicken soup were all very well, but if I was going to be here for more than a day or so I'd need fresh meat.

Around five in the afternoon I took the Allen keys and a small pair of snipe-nosed pliers and sat down by Rock Baby again. I don't really know why I took them. Perhaps I was trying to remind myself that sooner or later I'd have to stop theorizing and open Rock Baby up, come what may. I'd travelled a long way to do it. But I knew I wasn't going to do it this evening.

Electrical fuses, of whatever type, have one thing in common. They involve the closing of a circuit. Somewhere in that circuit are a source of electricity, and a detonator.

All such fuses, therefore, are open to two areas of attack. If you cut the wires – those leading to the detonator itself, for instance – then you're home and dry. Such wires, however, are likely to be virtually inaccessible because the setter of the fuse has thought of that one first.

The other approach is to ground the live side of the circuit, usually at the triggering mechanism itself. If you succeed in doing this then you have by-passed the trigger, whatever sort it is; electric current flows in the circuit you have created and not in the original circuit which includes the detonator, which is therefore rendered harmless.

There is, of course, the small matter of finding the right place to attach your grounding wire, and then attaching it, and achieving all this without tripping the fuse circuit first. All of which involves clarity of thought, steadiness of hand, and the sort of temperament which leads men to play Russian Roulette, none of which qualities I possessed.

The sun eased itself down behind the western wall of my playground and I began to feel cold. What would happen if I just packed up, went back to London, and told them that I'd found Rock Baby but I was too chicken to open it up?

If Conrad's DI6 man were here, what would he be doing? Listening to it through stethoscopes? Applying subtle devices, discussed only in secret enclaves of Bomb Disposal experts, which enabled one to take the top off a pressurized sphere and still keep the barometric fuse it contained from blowing?

What would happen if I climbed the back wall of the valley and rolled a damned great rock down on top of Rock Baby and *then* packed up and went back to London? I could always say my hand slipped.

The sky was cloudless, and the temperature dropped quickly. I took a last, long look at Rock Baby in the fading light, as though if I looked long and hard enough the key to what I ought to be doing might appear, magically etched on the smooth metal. Open This End. Something like that.

There was a sudden soft click, so soft that I would never have heard it except on a silent evening such as this and with ears tuned by solitude, and then a gentle, whirring hum. For a terrible instant, although I had made no move, I thought the thing had tripped. I had forgotten the transmitting schedule; Rock Baby, whether I was there or not, had a timetable to keep to, information to send. Unconsciously, now that I'd found it, I had begun to think of it simply as an unexploded bomb. Now, inside and invisible to me, the small magnetic discs were turning, releasing their stored message. True or false? I had no means of knowing, not this evening. The Shackleton would be somewhere in the sky, fifty miles away, a hundred perhaps. I felt a sudden urge to talk to the radio operator in the Shackleton. I waited until the humming stopped, listened to more insect-like clicks as the relays set themselves and transistorized circuits fell into new patterns, and went back to camp. By the time I reached the tent I no longer wanted to contact the aircraft circling in the still air, over to the west and out of my world. I had been by myself for too long, perhaps. Tomorrow I would do what I had come here to do, and then leave. Maybe they'd even give me my job back if I did it well enough.

I went the rounds of my four rabbit-snares, to no profit. I ate mint-cake and drank a mugful of boiling soup, took off my boots and washed in a spring which fed – eventually – the river in the valley a thousand feet below me, and lay on my back in the still-warm tent with my hands behind my head.

Perhaps the wind did come after all, without my noticing it. Otherwise I would have heard a stone slide or the faint crackle of trodden earth. But I heard nothing at all until there was a faint scratching on the flysheet of the tent; a woman's voice said, 'Is this yours? I nearly got caught in it,' and Miss Amanda Grayle, last seen in room thirty-four at the Institute taking down notes on the thermionic valve, ducked her head down and looked in at me.

'It's supposed to catch rabbits,' I said. And then, because I had indeed been by myself for too long and could think of nothing more sensible, I added, 'Maybe I can make you a cup of tea?'

SEVENTEEN

IT WAS nearly pitch dark by the time I'd made the tea and she'd drunk it. I could hardly see her. I sat cross-legged at the back of the tent and she leaned against my rolled-up sleeping bag in the tent mouth. Her knees were drawn up and occasionally she turned her head to look over her shoulder at me.

'We'll take it in order,' I said. 'First of all, where is all your gear?'

'What sort of gear?'

'Come on,' I said, 'You didn't just hike all the way up from Bled in that sweater and with your make-up case in the pocket of your jeans.'

'Oh, I see. I have a bivouac over there.' She pointed. 'In

the next valley to this one. I've been here some time, you know.'

'How long?'

'About a week, I suppose. There are very few rabbits, you know. Did you know that? And I don't think you set your snares in the right places.'

I leaned over and offered her the brandy flask, but she shook her head.

'I think I set them in just exactly the right places,' I told her. 'Look what I caught, for a start.' I was beginning to get accustomed to the darkness and I could see her smile. It was exactly the smile I recalled from the days when I was teaching her electronics, an occupation which I now thought might have been a great waste of time. 'Sorry I took so long getting here,' I said. 'But all sorts of things cropped up along the way. Did you say your bivouac was just the other side of that ridge?'

'Yes.'

I closed one eye and squinted past the profile of her forehead. Now I could see one or two stars in the sky, beyond her and above the far rocks. The moon must have been rising, too, because I could pick out the planes of light and shadow shifting across those high cheekbones of hers. I poured a few drops of brandy into my cupped palm and licked at them thoughtfully.

'I didn't see you,' I said. 'And I climbed that ridge yesterday.'

'I know. You're supposed to be careful about skylines.'

'I was careful. Apparently not careful enough, though. You could have picked me off like a cardboard Indian, I expect. It's a good thing you're on my side, loosely speaking that is.'

She straightened out her legs and then curled them underneath her. They looked even longer than I remembered, or perhaps it was just the jeans she was wearing now. 'You do know about me, then,' she said.

'Oh yes. I know about you. You're Conrad's man from Defence Intelligence Six, aren't you?'

'Man?'

'Well, I can't remember exactly how it was put. I must have been jumping to conclusions. You're Conrad's beautiful Field Intelligence Operative from DI6, then. I'm sure you have some rank or label. I don't suppose you've got a number because DI6 must be getting pretty tired of all those jokes by now. I expect you're a hard-working girl with a boring job to do just like everyone else. Right?'

'That's it,' she said. 'Black Belt, of course, and I can shoot the pips out of the six of diamonds at any range you care to mention. Does that make it more interesting?'

'No. All I'm interested in is your ability to take the machinery out of the insides of bombs, torpedoes, landmines and Jack-in-the-boxes. If you can do that, then you're very welcome. If you can't, then I suggest you shove off back to DI6, and now would be a good time to do it.'

'You're goddam prickly,' she said.

'Also half-witted,' I agreed. 'You're going to fall apart laughing about this, but do you know it never occurred to me that you'd come straight here and wait around until I found Rock Baby, can you beat that?'

She shifted round until she was facing me.

'You're not half-witted. You're a man who got trapped into doing something he didn't want to do, with no aptitude and no training for it,' she said. 'I think they did a lousy stinking thing to you, but you aren't obliged to believe I mean it. I can open Rock Baby up for you, yes.'

The odd thing was that I did believe she meant it. Even though I knew what she was and where she'd come from – though she hadn't admitted it yet – and therefore what sort of person she was likely to be, I still believed her. As I was meant to, no doubt.

'It would have been a bigger laugh still if I'd had a go at Rock Baby myself, this evening,' I said.

'I know. I watched you,' she said seriously. 'I was very worried, as a matter of fact, but I was too far away to stop you if you'd tried. I'm glad you didn't. It's a very tricky job.'

'I realize that it's an all-fired, ever-loving, bloody tricky job, thank you.'

'There's no need to get angry.'

'I'm not angry,' I said. She smiled at me again and I tried hard not to be angry. 'Maybe it's the thought of all those pleasant hours I spent teaching you electronics,' I said. 'What beats me is why I'm here at all. You can open the thing up, and I'm reasonably sure you can take the recording mechanism to bits all by yourself and find out whether it's been tampered with. Can't you?'

'Oh no. No. Look, you're right of course. About teaching me electronics at the Institute, I mean. I do know a bit about it, but not nearly enough to work out the circuitry of Rock Baby. You've got to do that.' She watched me. I said nothing. 'If it hadn't been a one-shot thing we might have been able to do it that way, the way you said. We thought about it, I admit that. But we couldn't afford any sort of mistake, because this is the only one we know about so far. And supposing I thought I knew what I was doing and then did something silly like, I don't know, leaving the erase head switched on and wiping out the signal before I'd had a chance to read it off and examine it? Something like that. Do you see? We've only got one chance, so I've got to defuse it and you've got to examine it.'

Well, it was plausible. I'd say that for it. I still thought that they – Conrad, McKellar, whoever it was – could have taught her enough in about six weeks or so to dismantle the recording apparatus inside Rock Baby, on a simple step-by-step basis. But there is a difference between messing about with your own television set and making an expensive mistake with somebody else's. I could see that.

'You *are* a genuine, twenty-nine carat bomb-disposal expert, though?' I asked her.

'Yes.'

Very well. So she was. As I looked at her, unable to make out anything of her face now that she had her back to the light, I began to realize what was making me so uneasy about her.

'How old are you?' I asked.

'Twenty-two.'

'*Twenty-two*. Oh my God.'

She said, 'Some people grow up quicker than others,' but I was barely listening. A twenty-two-year-old bomb-disposal expert? I needed a twenty-two-year-old bomb-disposal expert like I needed four more thumbs and a teen-age brain surgeon. Of course it needn't be true, she might be any age, but somehow I had a terrible feeling that she meant exactly what she'd said.

'Listen to me,' I said. 'I'll try to put this in some way that won't sound too naïve. How long exactly does it take to become a bomb-disposal expert? And don't tell me that you learn by your mistakes because I'm not in the mood for sick jokes.'

'I spent eight months. Two months in Birmingham and the rest in Scotland,' she said. I was going to speak, but she didn't give me a chance. 'Be quiet and listen,' she went on. 'Do you know what Captain Bryce told us? There were four of us and he was the man who taught us, all the time, start to finish. He said that BD people were all the same age, because age didn't mean how long you'd been alive but how long you had left. He was forty-five.' She stopped.

I said, 'Which meant he was really good. A forty-five-year-old BD man is a good BD man.' She nodded.

'You don't have to trust my ability,' she said. 'In fact I'm not going to let you trust it. You are going to stay right here and when I've opened the casing you can come and take over. But I'm good at it, or you can bet I wouldn't be here.'

I couldn't make her out. She switched to and fro so easily, between the naïve speech of a child and her brisk, tough grown woman's manner. No, not a woman's manner, the manner of a BD man, all clipped orders and keeping the civilians out of the line of blast. What was she, tough on the outside and crying for mother underneath? That would be too flip a judgement, far too flip.

'I know you wouldn't be here,' I said. 'Not that Conrad gives a damn about you, but he'd hate Rock Baby to go up before we'd had a look at it, wouldn't he?'

'I think you're misjudging Mr Conrad. You don't know him very well.' She spoke with quiet reproof, which made me madder than anything so far.

'I don't have to know a wasp very well if I'm caught on the stinging end. I'll bet he's a big, huggable old darling, doing what he has to do because it's there to be done. The older men are his battle-scarred comrades-in-arms and the young ones idealize him. You are his children. If you ask him for bread, will he give you a stone? It makes me brush aside an unmanly tear, thinking of all the good times I've missed with not being in DI6,' I said.

'Okay.'

'Too much okay.'

'Let's skip it, shall we?' She was very slightly contemptuous but unconcerned, as though she'd found out I didn't care for Oscar Peterson.

'It wasn't kind old Uncle Conrad's idea, for instance, that cute trick with the dead body?' I asked. I was waiting for her to ask, 'What body?' but she didn't.

'Not specifically,' she said.

'Whose idea was it?'

'I don't know. It just grew out of a whole lot of discussion.'

'Discussion in which you took part?'

'Yes.'

'A sort of committee for opportunism.'

'I'm not sure what you mean.' She seemed to soften a little, though it was hard to be sure. 'You'd have had to come and work for us anyway, well, not *us*, McKellar I mean.'

'After getting thrown out of my job,' I said.

'Yes. As a matter of fact the body was just a piece of luck for McKellar. But he'd have got you anyway.' I still couldn't see her face very well, but her voice was cool. 'I'll tell you why I was at the Institute,' she went on. 'I was supposed to accuse you of trying to rape me, and I expect you know that accusations of attempted rape are very difficult things either to prove or disprove. Life would have been rather difficult for you.' She was clinically disinterested, as though she were discussing the possibility of having me framed for nicking half a dollar from her handbag. They probably got like that very early on, in Conrad's department.

'Most unpleasant,' I said. 'I wish I'd known. Then I might at least have tried to rape you. The other way – you know, with Jissock's boring corpse in my bed – was no fun at all.'

She laughed. The laugh chilled me, though there was nothing very sinister about it.

'You can make up for lost opportunity now,' she said. She worked her way gracefully backwards towards the tent mouth. 'I'm going to have to move in with you tonight.'

'Nice,' I said.

'We'll have to start early in the morning. And I'm not going to waste three-quarters of an hour climbing back over the ridge. Besides it might make me out of breath, and Captain Bryce told us not to get out of breath before taking on a piece of work.'

'I don't think you'd get breathless,' I told her. 'I don't think anything would make you breathless, even for a moment. Move in. The hell I care.'

'My sleeping things are outside,' she said.

She slept quietly, without moving, her back turned towards me in her quilted sleeping-bag. In the middle of the night I thought it would be a good idea to reach gently across and remove the leather folder, about the size of a passport or a little larger, that I'd seen her slip under her air-pillow. I just wanted to find out exactly who she was, and if possible whether she was twenty-two, as she said, or thirty.

Two inches of the folder protruded from beneath the pillow and none of the weight of her sleeping head was resting on it, so I stretched out my hand. It may have been a good idea but it didn't work. I didn't touch her or disturb her in any way at all, but she rolled over quickly, so quickly that I had no time even to react, and faced me with her eyes wide open and a tiny toy gun in her hand pointing directly at the bridge of my nose.

'Don't do that,' she said.

I gripped her wrist. I don't like having guns pointed at me, for good reasons or bad.

I intended to push her hand firmly aside, so that if the gun went off it would make a neat little hole in the tent instead of in me. I am no giant and I don't tear telephone directories in half with my teeth, but I have always thought of myself as being fairly strong. The wrist I held was about as soft and feminine as a sawn three-inch vanadium-steel bar and the gun didn't move. It was one of those little gold-framed Replica Derringers you see in American mail-order catalogues, usually called the Ladies Gun. .22 Long Rifle cartridges and strictly for laughs at anything over ten feet, but since I was only six inches from the muzzle I hoped she wouldn't pull the trigger. I also knew that if I turned this into a wrestling match she might. I relaxed.

'That makes twice,' I said.

'Twice what?' Her voice was crisp and the gun still didn't move.

'Twice I've lost already, fighting with girls,' I said.

When I woke in the morning she wasn't there. I dressed and crawled out of the tent, reflecting that I'd seen altogether too much of the dawn over the last ten days or so. The canteen had been filled with water and rested neatly alongside the little alcohol stove. Overnight, it seemed, the cave had become a woman's kitchen.

I must have been quiet over getting up, because she hadn't noticed me. She was fifty yards away, standing with her feet in the gravel pool of the spring with her back towards me. She wore a neat, sensible pair of brief pants and nothing else. She bent and splashed water about, and I could see that she was correctly dressed. She was washing her hair.

I went back into the tent and knocked a few things over while I hunted among the food supplies for coffee, sugar and powdered milk, and when I emerged again a few minutes later she was striding briskly towards me in jeans and a check shirt. Her dark hair was still damp and she was carrying a small bundle of damp clothes.

'Good morning,' she said.

'Hello,' I answered. 'Isn't that one of my spare shirts you've been using to dry your hair?'

'Sorry. Yes it is. But I washed it through for you anyway, and it needed it.'

'Yes, well,' I said. 'You'd better come and have some breakfast.'

It was much lighter when I went to wash. The spring-water was below freezing point, or felt that way. I took a long time over washing, because I could see I was caught in a minor trap of my own devising, and it was an old and extremely stupid one. I didn't want to be there while she opened Rock Baby, but I was damned if I would be left behind. She didn't want me there either, and had told me so. No useful purpose would be served if I sat and watched her. But I was tied to her by her age, by being totally unwilling to sit in the tent while a twenty-two-year-old girl, even a girl as cold as dry ice, fiddled with a potentially lethal machine. Logic told me that I was being childish, that there was no point whatever in two people getting killed where one would be enough, but logic wasn't adequate, not in this situation.

When I got back to the tent, she wasn't there. Instead there was a note, fastened to the tent flap with a safety-pin. The note read: 'Please leave me alone for half an hour,' and I looked out over the valley and there she was, hunkered down alongside Rock Baby and just looking at it, so far as I could tell. After about a minute she turned and saw me. She waved a hand casually and then turned away again.

I stood with the note in my hand. It seemed that to go down there would be to make a really stupid issue of the whole thing, so I stayed where I was.

It was still very early and the sun hadn't risen. I went into the tent. Lying neatly on the head-pocket of my sleeping-bag was the leather folder I'd tried, with such lack of success, to steal last night. It was now open, like a book, and across it lay an airmail envelope.

I sat down on her sleeping-bag and reached across for the folder. According to her passport she'd been lying about her age: she wasn't even twenty-two, not by a couple of months yet. There was no means of telling where the passport had come from, of course, and it might have been straight out of DI6's fiction department.

The envelope was thick and heavy. I opened the flap and shook out about twenty photographs.

I laid them out in a wide fan on the sleeping-bag and went through them one by one. They were all of Amanda Grayle. In only two of them was she wearing anything and then it was the black brassière and pants so often favoured in what are called, in some circles, lingerie poses. In another two of them she'd shaved her body hair, and in three she appeared with another girl, blonde and shorter than herself, so far as could be told that is. All the prints were badly processed, the way dirty postcards always are.

Pictures such as these usually only make me laugh, which I supposed deprives me of one of the minor and more dubious pleasures in life. For one thing the whole affair is linked in my mind with images of those gentlemen in flower-pot hats who are supposed to sidle up to you in the warmer Middle-Eastern ports saying 'Psst. Effendi . . .' or whatever the correct words of approach are. For another, I cannot really visualize any woman as being able to work herself into the state of passion implied by the postures in pictures such as these, purely for the benefit of somebody who is going to fire off the hundredth flashbulb in her face. I have a certain admiration for the young men who appear less frequently and whose powers of sustained virility in similar trying circumstances I cannot understand either, but that is as far as it goes.

It was impossible not to see that she had a splendid figure. I already knew this. None of the pictures contained guns, whips, handcuffs or men, so I suppose they were a fairly mild lot. I sorted through them again. Some of them had been taken out of doors, on a beach somewhere, and in one of these she appeared to be smiling at the camera with genuine pleasure. Most had been taken in a rather colourless bedroom, with the bottom two of a flight of china ducks on the wall appearing in shot now and again. Nearly all of the bedroom poses were silly. Silly in a sort of look-at-me-what-I'm-doing way; not even her magnificent presence could rescue them from crude banality. The three in which she was paired with the other girl were athletic but just as stupid; I wondered, from the absence of expression in her eyes, if she had been three parts drunk or drugged at the time, but it was pure speculation. She had perfect breasts.

I ran through them again for the last time and tried to find them amusing, but I couldn't. I didn't want to connect them with the girl outside in the valley. I didn't particularly like her but she was intelligent and beautiful. Cold beauty, perhaps, but I had no taste for iced beauty with hot fudge sauce. I thought of dozens of other prints, the twins of these, dog-eared and thumb-marked. I packed them together, squared the edges, and put them back in the envelope.

Outside the tent the sun hadn't yet climbed over the eastern ridge but was promising to do so. She was sitting on a boulder by the spring, so I walked across to her.

'All right,' I said.

She looked down at the edge of the pool, where the water spilled over a miniature weir of rocks.

'My great-grandmother was an Arapaho Indian,' she said. 'You don't know anything about the Arapaho and I know very little, far less than I ought to. I even have an Indian name. The Arapaho were High Plains Indians from what are now Montana and North Dakota.' She said it as though they'd been renamed last year. 'Two of my grandparents are French Canadian. They've lived in Quebec all their lives and in Quebec that means something. The Arapaho raided as far south as Mexico, and that's a long way to send a war party. They did the Ghost Dance to drive away the white men and bring back the buffalo and before that they were doing the Sun Dance. That was when they used to thread strips of leather through the flesh of the young men's chests and tie the other ends of the strips to a stake in the ground. The men danced until they tore the leather strips out of their bodies, through the skin and through the muscle underneath. They fought the Comanche and the Kiowa and the Crow and they'd have beaten pure hell out of the white man in any kind of fair fight.'

'All right,' I said again, irritably. I was angry about the photographs and because I was softening towards her and didn't want to. I didn't want to listen to her any more either. She looked up when she started to speak again. Her voice didn't alter by a fraction, but tears were running down the channels each side of her nose and spilling over the corners of her mouth, the way a child's tears do. 'Well they bloody well would have, you know,' she said.

'Simmer down. Captain Bryce wouldn't approve of all this,' I said.

'No. He wouldn't, would he?'

'I don't know about the Arapaho,' I said. 'I've been to too many Westerns to get a fair picture, but I'll believe the white man took away the buffalo and gave them whisky, syphilis and planned living, and none of it did them any good.'

She smiled, and for the first time I liked it. She went straight back to her cool bomb-disposal style, but it didn't seem quite the same now.

'When I was sixteen I was in France with my parents and my grandfather,' she said. 'I used to sunbathe without any clothes. I don't know. I like it. Perhaps that means it was all my own fault. I still do it.'

'I can imagine. I saw you washing your hair.'

'I know you did. I didn't mind. I knew you were watching me.'

'That's not what I said. I said I saw you, and there's a difference.'

She stood up and put her feet in the water of the pool. She was wearing soft leather moccasins, I noticed for the first time. I remembered the fact that I hadn't heard her coming up to the tent last night, too, and I wondered what her great-grandmother looked like and whether the Arapaho would have any natural aptitude for taking bombs to pieces. It seemed likely.

'I used to have my own beach,' she went on. 'Then one day I was coming out of the water and I saw somebody duck down behind some rocks. I grabbed a towel and went for him. His name was Alain, he had fair hair. He'd taken a whole lot of pictures of me and I was really mad, but he was about twenty and good-looking, so of course like a fool I fell in love with him. We had a whole summer together and it was terrific, I have to remember that. Whatever else happened, I have to remember that.

'Then one day he came and said somebody else had got hold of the pictures, not just the ones he'd taken of me when I didn't know, but from afterwards as well. I was just coming up to seventeen and I'd wanted him to take more photographs of me. He had a thing, you know, a self-timer, on the camera and there were pictures of the two of us together as well. It was all very stupid,' she said reflectively. She stepped out of the pool and scuffled the wet moccasins in the pebbles.

'Anyway that was it. This other man had the pictures, he'd stolen them, Alain said. He was threatening to show them to our parents. If.'

'If you didn't let him take a whole lot more pictures,' I said.

'That's about what it came to,' she agreed. 'If I'd been as old as I am now I'd have told him to go and screw himself, but I wasn't. And my family, you know, and Alain's family. Very stupid. So I did. I hated it of course, but he said they were just for himself and he was a sculptor, and he gave me the negatives.'

'After making copy negatives. Or so many prints that it didn't matter.'

She shrugged. 'I don't know about that,' she said. 'All I know is that a whole year later, when I was back in London, I got prints of all the pictures, Alain's, this other man's, the lot, through the post. And a telephone call later suggesting that I might be interested in making myself a little money in the evenings. If not then photographs of me would start turning up in Canada and London and France. I was in my first year at university. The first man, in France, had given me a whole lot of rubbish about artistry and the structure of the female body, but this time they didn't even bother with that. Alain was there. Dear sensitive Alain had been in on the whole thing from start to finish. Actually I very nearly killed him,' she said in the same precise manner she'd used about myself and attempted rape. 'But it didn't do me any good. I was going to be an engineer. Structural engineering in architecture, and I wanted to do it like hell. Looking back on it, I expect the university would have helped me but I thought they would just kick me out on top of the whole family bit.

So the whole horrible business started all over again, after I'd stalled and stalled for months. In the end I could see that it was just going to be more and better dirty pictures, and probably a little call-girl work on the side, and I tried to commit suicide, pretty inefficiently.'

'And then?'

'Oh, then Andy Dylan came along with a handy solution to the whole business.'

'Andy Dylan?'

'Yes, why not?'

'I don't see why not,' I conceded. 'His answer was what? Join DI6 and see the world, and anybody who tried to twist your arm about dirty pictures would have to answer to Driver and Conrad? I didn't know they were as matey with each other as all that.'

'Well, I was a scientist,' she said. 'Or at least I was training to be one, of sorts, so that's how it happened that Seeker Section wanted me in the first place. But several things happened – not important things – and it didn't look as though I was going to qualify as anything, let alone an engineer. So I ended up with Conrad.'

'And me.'

'Yes. And you. You mustn't misunderstand anything I've said. I'm not complaining, at least not really. Sometimes I wonder what the hell I'm doing, but a lot of the time I think, what would have happened if I'd just been a structural engineer? Maybe I'd have been bored. I don't know. I like what I'm doing. You don't, I know that. All I'm saying is, if you were dragged into this, so was I. That's all.'

And a whole lot more, I thought. I'd never get a handsomer apology. I knew it didn't mean she'd refrain from kicking me in the guts if it suited her purpose, because anybody in Conrad's department would do that without thinking twice. And the whole thing could have been deliberately aimed at disarming me. It could have. But I wasn't ready to start thinking like one of Conrad's men yet, and I hoped that I never would be, even if I got damaged through refusal to make the effort.

She started back towards the camp, her moccasined feet

leaving damp footprints which the sun would soon dry off. She pulled out her rucksack from the back of the cave and started to drag things out of it.

'What about your family?' I asked her.

'They think I'm personal assistant to the technical manager of a light engineering company. I have to do a lot of travelling. I even sent them a postcard from Italy.'

'Yes. Last thing,' I said. 'How did you get here?'

'Illegally,' she said briefly. I didn't pursue it. She squinted around. 'The sun's up.'

'Time to take the top off the egg.'

'Yes, I think so.'

I started to collect together what I thought I'd need. Then something else occurred to me. Most likely nothing would come of it, but it was worth a try. I dug down to the bottom of my rucksack and found the chocolate-covered laser rod.

'What's that?' I asked, handing it to her. She turned it over once or twice and tore off the wrapper.

'A chocolate bar,' she said. 'With something inside it. It's too heavy.'

I took it back from her and cracked away the chocolate and Rice Krispies from one end. She watched me, and I tried to read something from her face. I showed her the end of the crystal, its jewel-smooth concentric rings picking up the morning sunlight. 'Do you know what it is now?' I asked.

'No. Am I supposed to?'

'That's something I couldn't possibly tell you without having a long talk with your Mr Conrad,' I told her. 'I don't know if you're telling the truth and I have no way of finding out, but just the same I'll ask you again. Have you ever seen this, or anything like it? Or heard about it, or read anything about it in the minutes of one of your department's general discussions over the tea and toast?'

'No. I told you, I don't even recognize what it is. You could always enlighten me, couldn't you?'

'It's a laser crystal,' I said. 'I believe it's for use in some sort of exceptionally high-powered equipment, but after that I'm as lost as you are.'

'Like a death ray?' she said brightly.

She was still kneeling down, packing her stuff into a small canvas bag. I reached over and patted the top of her head.

'Full marks,' I said. 'That's probably just what it is.' It occurred to me what a good thing it would be if she went back and told Conrad about death rays. It's funny what a hankering people have after death rays, ever since Wells and Oppenheim no doubt. There isn't going to be a laser death ray. There isn't going to be a death ray at all unless somebody finds a way to beam neutrons without having to build the necessary gear into an oversize railway truck, which I suppose might eventually happen. Since platoons of soldiers no longer climb out of trenches and charge across open ground very much these days, I can't think that the death ray will in any case become a decisive weapon in modern warfare. But I was sure that Driver and Conrad between them could work up some sort of Intelligence frenzy about the development of death rays, and maybe it would keep them off my back.

'Forget it,' I said. 'You go on down and start whatever you've got to start, and I'll be down to join you in a few minutes.'

She looked at me speculatively.

'You're not going to stay here?' she asked. It wasn't, this time, an order.

'Not if you can bear to have me looking over your shoulder. The way things seem to be going, a man never knows when he might need a lesson in elementary bomb disposal.'

'Okay.' She swung the canvas bag over her shoulder and started to pick her way down among the stones towards Rock Baby. I waited until she was a quarter of a mile away and then buried the laser crystal under a thin layer of soil. I laid a couple of smallish rocks over the spot, and then lugged my own burden of Allen keys, signal meter, read-out probes and battery-powered pen-recorder down the slope after her.

EIGHTEEN

BY ELEVEN O'CLOCK I'd stopped having a coronary every time she laid her hands on the thing.

She'd cleared away the bush alongside it with scissors, and she hadn't let me lift any of the rocks in case I should drop one while I was doing it. Now both of us were lying on our stomachs looking at it, squatting malignantly on its three legs in front of our noses. She'd attached a small drill-guide to the surface of the sphere with suction discs, moving swiftly and accurately while I watched her in nervous admiration, the sweat growing in my armpits. Once she'd asked me to steady the sphere, while she applied the suction pads; it was surprisingly easy, but I'd left damp marks on the metal where my palms had touched it. For most of the time I'd just watched and thought.

Under Rock Baby and between the tripod legs I could see the sensing probe, thrusting downwards and connecting the little seismograph to Yugoslavia like a metallic umbilical cord. The probe extended downwards for somewhere between six inches and a yard, I knew, depending upon how far it had been able to drill before striking rock.

The legs themselves rested on neoprene cushions, so that the tiny tremors it was designed to record would move the probe and not the spherical body itself. The probe converted these tremors into electrical signals and it was these signals that Rock Baby recorded and retransmitted, helping to build up a pattern of earth movements, major and minor, occurring over Europe and – so far – about half of Russia.

That was the idea, if somebody hadn't moved in on the operation. And from what I'd seen so far, I didn't think they had.

Amanda wriggled cautiously backwards and rested her head on her arms.

'That's it,' she said. 'Next thing, I start making holes.'

'I'm glad to hear it,' I said. 'How are you going to stop the gas leaking out?'

'No problem. I've got a gadget with a collar and a pressure gauge to take care of that. Afterwards I'm not so sure. What do you think, Giles?'

I turned on my side and stared at her. 'I have no opinions,' I said. 'I stopped having them as soon as you turned up, and I'm not going to start again until you tell me I can move in.'

'I didn't mean that exactly,' she said. 'I meant, if you had to bet which way this thing would turn out, what would you say? Has somebody been messing about with it or not? After all that's what we're here to find out. I just wondered if you'd made a guess.'

I turned on my back.

'That I have been thinking about,' I said. 'I don't know if I've got very far. There are four possibilities, aren't there? One: this thing is a false alarm. Rock Baby quit by accident and started again by accident. It happens. Nobody even knows it's here, and so long as we don't kick it about too much we can go back and tell Driver, McKellar and Conrad not to worry. That's where my money goes, as it happens.'

'It's not where *their* money goes.'

'I know that. It's still what I think, and I'll tell you why. Their minds are far too complicated. They see little men with nasty ideas behind every lamp-post down Whitehall. I'm simple-minded and as far as I'm concerned all the other possibilities are too complex by half.'

'You'd better go on with the other possibilities just the same,' she said. 'In case it makes a difference to what I do next.' She was still lying with her cheek on her sleeve. She was calm and relaxed, the way I expect the Arapaho were while they waited for the cavalry to come through the pass.

'Okay. That's possibility one. The other three all include the supposition that little men with nasty ideas do exist and that they *have* dismantled this thing and put it together again so that it sends out false information. I can see the point of that, particularly if they could get at several more of them. Then they could explode bombs all over the place and still have these gadgets send back word that nothing was stirring, not even a mouse. So, possibility two: they have fixed this one and have taken the destructive mechanism out and left it out, which would make things nice and easy for us. Possibility three: they've put back the destructive mechanism exactly the way it was to start with, as a sort of insurance. In which case it's not quite so easy for us but at least we have no additional problems, or you don't anyway.'

'Or they've put in explosive devices of their own. Different ones or additional ones. Which is what everybody back in England thinks.'

'All right, that's possibility four. I admit that if I'm wrong and they're right, it's the next most likely bet. Extra booby-traps. Because that way, any clever bastard like me who came out here and tried to find out what had happened wouldn't stay alive to carry the news back home. As far as Rock Baby was concerned, the only thing anybody could say for certain would be that it had stopped transmitting and blown up. Other guesses might be made, but not proved, which would leave us all back at Square One. But that's not the way my bet goes. I'm not so confident that I'll start unscrewing things, but if you ask me the whole set-up is a product of Driver's corkscrew mind. I'll tell you for sure when you find out if there's still pressurized gas inside the casing.'

I felt pleased with myself. It must have showed in my face.

'What's that got to do with it?' she asked.

'Well, I'll tell you. The barometric fuse is the most difficult one to cope with as far as opening the casing goes, isn't it?'

'Yes. All right.'

'Well then,' I went on. 'If somebody is feeding false signals through Rock Baby, then they have to keep on doing it. Before we started our twenty-four-hour schedule, Rock Baby was sending off its signals about once a week or so. That means the recording discs hold about a week's worth of information at a time. So once a week at least, somebody has to come along and open Rock Baby up and feed the false signals on to the recording discs, and you can't tell me that whoever has that little chore wants to have his life complicated by being forced to run circles round the barometric fuse every time he opens it.'

'No. I suppose you're right,' she said.

'In fact, if it were me,' I went on, 'I'd have put in some sort of external plug and socket so that I could feed signals in without having to open the casing at all. But we've been looking at this thing pretty closely for the last three or four hours, and I don't see any socket. Do you?'

She shook her head.

'That's another good reason why I think Conrad and McKellar and Driver are all having fevered dreams. No external socket. If you find there's still gas pressure inside as well, then I'll be ninety per cent certain that it's the same gas that Rock Baby started life with.'

She fitted a little pressure gauge to the drill-guide, drilled her hole and withdrew the drill in its rubber-sealed collar. The needle on the gauge flicked across at once, to nine psi.

'Right,' I said. 'That's it then.'

She hardly paid me any attention. 'Be quiet,' she said. 'I need some time to think.'

At ten minutes to twelve she straightened up suddenly.

'Give me your Allen keys.' She held out her hand.

'Now wait a minute.'

'Come on. You're right, of course you're right,' she said. 'Give me the keys.'

'Hold it,' I said. 'I'll admit I'm clever but that doesn't mean I'm right. You're just going to take the top of the casing off, is that it? Just like that?'

She still held her hand out, impatiently. 'Yes, that's what we'll do. Now look, I can do this one of two ways. I can neutralize the barometric fuse, which will take me about five hours. I shall have to cut a section out of the casing itself and keep it sealed with a transparent plastic window. Then I shall have to work through the plastic – it's self-sealing – and keep the gas pressure topped up to replace any gas which leaks out while I'm by-passing the fuse itself.'

'That sounds fine,' I said. 'I like that. I'm in no hurry.'

'Or,' she went on, 'I can assume you're correct and that the only fuses inside are the original ones. In which case we're dealing with a fairly slow reaction, a smoke cartridge and a thermite bomb. I can loosen the socket screws without releasing the pressure, until the top cover's free.'

'And then what?' I had a nasty feeling I knew what, but I wanted to hear.

'Well, then you lift the cover off quickly. That releases the pressure and probably trips the tremblers at the same time. The smoke cartridge will fire but that doesn't matter. I shall have lots of time to deal with the thermite bomb because you'll remember it's not supposed to injure anyone and it's got a five-second delay on it. I can get to the leads between the delay switch and the igniter in that time. How does it sound?'

This was what you got if you drew an embryonic BD expert instead of a middle-aged one, I realized.

'I can imagine what Captain Bryce would say about it,' I said.

'Oh sure. But we won't tell him, will we?'

'I'm not even going to answer that,' I said.

'No, but seriously. And the marvellous thing is that we can forget about the trembler circuits as well, at least when I've got the socket screws undone.'

I projected all Higsbee's colour slides, in quick succession, on a mental screen. Nothing had actually been said about a five-second delay but she was probably right. Higsbee, in the slide sequence, had clearly pushed the thing over and he'd had time to get out of the way before it started to burn. The question was still whether Rock Baby now contained the original mechanism, or an instantaneous fuse and several pounds of explosive. The terrible thing was that I'd talked myself right into this and I could see nothing wrong with my reasoning. Not yet.

'I've got an even better idea,' I said. 'All we have to do is wait around another few days and see if anybody comes to do anything about it. If they don't then we can be a hundred per cent sure.' But I could see the faulty reasoning there right away. Because Rock Baby had an approximately five-day-long gap in between transmissions – in normal service – it didn't necessarily follow that the recording discs only had five days or a week's capacity. Probably not, in fact. Three, four weeks maximum I thought was fair. The argument about the difficulty of resetting and circumventing the barometric fuse each time still held, but we couldn't hang about for three or four weeks. And the recording capacity could be still longer. I didn't know. It was just the sort of question I should have asked, at the briefing I didn't go to.

'Okay,' I said.

For an instant which lasted a couple of centuries I thought I'd bungled it, that I'd released the internal gas pressure without getting the top casing off cleanly. I counted, very slowly, to three. I choked on a lungful of coloured smoke because I was downwind, and I hoped none of it had got in her eyes.

'You can put it down now,' she said, and I dropped the half shell on the ground. She was kneeling by the side of Rock Baby with the wire-cutters in her hand. She showed me the cut ends of the igniter leads and blinked at me smugly, like a kitten in a sunbeam.

'Very crafty,' I said. I got out my instruments and went to work, but it was obvious what I'd find. I traced the faulty connexion which had put Rock Baby off the air, probably due to contraction in a spell of low temperature, and had then cut back in, intermittently and badly, to produce the suspect recordings. I wished that Captain Bryce were here, because he would undoubtedly find words to describe the idiotic performance we'd just been through and I couldn't pick just the right ones.

We took the thing to bits and hid the bits in various places. Amanda thought that I ought to repair it and she ought to reset the trembler fuses, but I hadn't contracted to do anything of the sort and told her so.

'You don't have to swear,' she said.

'Oh yes I do. You have no idea,' I told her, and in the end she saw it my way.

We were packing away the tent when the helicopter arrived, representing Possibility Five, the one which Driver must have been considering all the time. Amanda shaded her eyes and stared at it, and for a while I thought that she'd been expecting it, that this was the way we were supposed to get out of the country. But as it came closer I recognized it, and I couldn't really believe that Conrad's department had the used of an Aeroflot MI2, even with their undoubtedly extensive Kremlin connexions.

There was no place we could go to, so we stood and waited while it threshed its way to a landing in the exact centre of the valley. Two men in green uniforms got out. They climbed all the way up the scree slope, sure-footed as only mountain-trained soldiers are, their carbine barrels rising and dipping with every step but never enough to encourage any action on our part. We picked up our packs in response to their gestures, and went down with them.

Inside the cabin of the helicopter was Bratling, in whipcord trousers and a Glen Urquhart hacking jacket.

'Ah there, squire,' he said genially. 'Welcome aboard. Cast your bread upon the waters, and what happens? You get it back' – he looked at Amanda Grayle – 'with butter on it. I must say that's rather good. The best butter too.'

NINETEEN

WE FLEW approximately southwards for longer than I would have thought likely. I say 'approximately' because the helicopter followed a jinking course, along valleys and over flat, deserted stretches of plain, and I was in no position to watch the compass. I sat next to Amanda on an uncomfortable seat made of canvas and alloy tubing, and Bratling perched opposite us, chain-smoking and thinking what a brilliant lad he was. The two soldiers leaned against the rear bulkhead. One of them was compact and wiry, with dark curls sprouting around the edge of his beret. He watched us unblinkingly with both hands on his carbine. The other was an enormous, balding man with the end of a harmonica pushing up the flap of his battledress pocket; he looked out of the window, clenching his jaws to some internal rhythm, his eyes incurious.

Some time during the afternoon Bratling got up and went forward to the pilot.

'Crossing the border, chaps,' he said, battling his way back to his seat.

'What border?' I asked him. 'Albania?'

'Full marks for navigation. Give the man a coconut. Albania it is.'

'I thought the Albanians were a bit paranoid about people crossing their border from Yugoslavia,' I said. 'Or am I out of date?'

He prodded me in the chest, expansively. 'Ah,' he said. 'Very astute of you, old boy. Very astute indeed. Only as it happens we're popular here, well, I say popular, perhaps that's stretching it a bit. But we're not going to get shot down, that I can say with a fair degree of confidence.'

The pilot turned round. 'Please do not talk, Mr Bratling,' he said. It was his only line during the whole flight, from take-off in Yugoslavia to our landing on what I at first took to be a tennis court chiselled out of the side of a mountain.

As we all got out of the helicopter the larger of the two soldiers pointed upwards towards the mountain face with his carbine and said 'Vishnica Drila', but I couldn't tell whether it was the name of the place we'd arrived at, or just an order to move the feet. The smaller soldier stood aside while the pilot climbed down. He wore silvered glasses and a dark-green leather coat complete with turned up fur collar and heavy-gauge zip. An elegant, ageing ton-up boy. He nodded to Amanda and flashed his metal eyes in my direction.

'I am Milo Drakon,' he said. 'I think we can help each other.' He stared past me and lifted a hand in greeting to somebody behind my back. I turned. It was no surprise to see Mercedes coming across the court towards us, but she had Braun with her, the fancy little lad from Bei-Willi, and the sight of him made me apprehensive. I tapped Bratling on the shoulder.

'Don't look now,' I told him, 'but I think the undesirable elements have sneaked up on us.' He nodded but didn't say anything. 'What about Marris?' I asked.

'He got himself shot,' said Bratling.

'And the old man?' I hoped that Marris had been the only casualty, that it had after all been Marris tumbling down the side of the tower.

'What old man is this, squire? Who are we talking about?' He frowned slightly, as though dealing with an imbecile.

'Forget it,' I said. It was quite likely that Mikulicz had vanished into the walls, taking the cat with him, perhaps. Even the bats, come to that. We all moved off towards a long flight of steps cut into the rock face of the mountain itself. I hoped that whatever else happened we'd get a good meal.

TWENTY

'THE VIEWS are superb,' said Drakon. 'Of course this place was one of the casualties in the struggle against Revisionism, but that cannot be helped. It suits our purposes, which is all that matters.'

I stood beside him and looked out of the window. Two hundred feet of almost sheer drop separated us from the small asphalt landing platform on which the helicopter stood. To right and left the walls of the building curved slightly back, producing an effect as though we were in an observation gallery set in the mountainside itself. It was hard to tell what the building had set out to be; a luxury hotel, perhaps, though most of the hotels would be on the Adriatic coast, I knew.

He looked at me sideways. We'd had dinner and Drakon had lectured us non-stop on the subject of Revisionism. I almost understood what it was by the time coffee arrived, though I couldn't grasp whether he was for it or against it, or indeed if he cared a damn one way or the other. I'd come close to asking a couple of times, but I lacked the nerve.

'Yes, of course,' I said.

'An awkward time for the whole country,' he said. I waited for him to go on. 'The Palace of Culture has not, even now, been completed.' He looked at me again. Without the metalled sunglasses and the ton-up jacket he seemed correct, courteous, and a size smaller. A man you would meet at a conference somewhere and forget immediately afterwards. The others had stayed behind in the dining-room, but Drakon wanted to make sure I understood about the effects of the fight against Revisionism.

'Yes,' he said. 'An awkward time. When the Russians withdrew in the summer of 1961' – he dabbled tidily at the air with his fingertips – 'chaos. The drills and the cement mixers stopped all over Albania. Peking will start them again eventually, but one has to ask when? The East Germans went home from the copper plant at Kurbneshi. The Czechoslovakians suddenly lost interest in refining chromium and nickel. The Ukrainians stopped sending their wives and families to swim in the sea at Durazzo and all the winter courses at the University of Tirana had to be cancelled. An unhappy, unhappy time.' He sounded dramatically unhappy. 'Shall I tell you who was made happy by all this?' he asked. I nodded. 'The United States Sixth Fleet. Do you want to know why? Because the Russians also withdrew their submarine flotilla from its base at Valona and left the Mediterranean.'

'It's nice to think somebody got a prize out of the tub,' I said.

'It is not our concern to make the Americans happy,' said Drakon severely. He looked out of the window again. It was getting dark, and low, ragged clouds streamed like pennants from the sharp peaks of hills across the gorge in front of us. I tried to remember in detail what the front of the building looked like. There hadn't been much time to take it in while we'd walked across the helicopter pad, and the long, zigzag flight of steps was cut into the rock so tightly below the place that I couldn't see it from where I now stood, unless I were to open the window and lean out.

A jump from this window would land you on the steps themselves, I realized, if you fell close enough in against the building. Three feet farther out, and you'd go all the way down to the landing platform. Thirty feet to the left and you'd miss that, too, and bounce from rock to rock for another hundred feet or so until you ended up somewhere in the bottom of the gorge. Above us? I couldn't picture it. The building was three storeys high, or was it four? It was built on a natural rock ledge, reinforced with concrete. So far as I'd been able to tell, the back of it must nearly, if not actually, touch the bare surface of the mountain. A few centuries earlier the place would have been a fortress, and perhaps it once had been. Perhaps, even more to the point, it still was.

'You'll have to forgive me for asking this,' I said, 'but are you Albanian?'

'Contractually speaking and for the purposes of our discussion, yes,' he said. I must have looked baffled, because he added, 'I am under contract to raise the standard of living in Albania.'

It sounded a vaguely worded contract to me. I tried to picture Drakon signing a contract with Enver Hoxha to raise the Albanian standard of living, and couldn't. Nor could I determine whether he'd contracted to explain the course of the struggle against Revisionism to visiting firemen, or whether that was something he was doing on his own account.

'Now I understand,' said Drakon, 'that Mr Bratling has laid certain proposals before you, concerning the possibility of your working for us, and that you have declined. One minute.' He raised his hand. 'Mr Bratling is an annoying man though of course perfectly competent in his own field. I can well believe that you found it difficult to reach an understanding.'

'Oh, I think we managed that part of it quite well,' I said.

'I will be frank with you. We need help here and I believe, from your obvious competence with equipment such as the Yugoslavian seismograph, that you are capable of giving us the sort of help we need. Our situation is very difficult, very difficult indeed. I doubt, you see, if we can find the level of competence we must have, not here in Albania.'

He reached in front of me and pushed open the window. The frame had warped and he had a brief struggle with it. He rubbed his hands on a handkerchief and turned back to me. 'It's going to rain, heavily I think,' he said. 'It causes difficulty with the plumbing. I do not want in any way to force your hand, though the circumstances in which we found you today were unfortunate, to say the least.' He waited for me to comment, but since he was right I couldn't think of anything useful to say.

'I don't want to mention payment except to say that there is likely to be no difficulty there,' he went on. 'There is another inducement, which would not have occurred to Mr Bratling but which does occur to me, having made your acquaintance. We are engaged, Dr Yeoman, on research here which is quite fundamental, entirely new in concept. Nothing comparable, to my knowledge, is being done anywhere else in the world. It is work, therefore, which any scientist with imagination must find fascinating and, although I do not know you very well, I am quite certain that you would find it as fascinating as I do myself.'

'No, thank you,' I said. Some sort of wheel had turned full circle, I thought to myself. From saying no in London to saying no in Albania. Probably with about as much effect.

'I assure you that there is nothing illegal in what we are attempting,' said Drakon.

'Maybe not,' I said. 'What is it? Antigravity? Death rays?' He looked at me as though he couldn't be sure if I were joking.

'Nothing like that, Dr Yeoman. This is a serious matter.'

'I'm sure it is. But I'm not interested.'

He leaned against the window-sill. 'Would you mind telling me why not?' he asked.

'Of course I wouldn't mind. First of all you've brought me here against my will,' I said. 'I'll pass over that because, as you so rightly observe, we were in unusual circumstances when you picked us up.' He pursed his lips judicially. Perhaps he really did believe he was a simple subcontractor. 'Also,' I went on, 'I can't pass judgement on the legality of what you're doing, because I don't know what it is. But what I do know is that at least two men have been killed in the pursuit of whatever it is, and that doesn't exactly fill me with confidence. I suppose you do know that two men have been killed?'

'Yes,' he said. 'I have been meaning to speak to Mr

Bratling about that. Miss Van Erhlenmeyer too, of course.' He sounded as though he might dictate a memorandum about it when I'd gone.

'Do it now,' I told him. 'Before they get entirely out of parental control.'

He pulled himself away from the sill and closed the window against the first heavy spots of rain. I saw his shoulders shake, and when he faced me again he was laughing quietly. It didn't make me feel any better.

'Thirdly,' I said patiently, 'both Miss Grayle and myself are in a country with which Her Majesty's Government has severed diplomatic relations. This must sound very old-fashioned to you, I know, but I don't think the Foreign Office would approve of my accepting your offer.'

'You cannot be certain they would disapprove.' It was impossible to discourage him. 'After all Major Driver personally, and Seeker Section in general, have extensive connexions with the Foreign Office.' He said it with the air of a man laying out the ace-king of trumps, but it didn't impress me very much. I was about to say, 'So what?' but Drakon was determined that I should hear the whole thing anyway.

'You see we have been monitoring the Yugoslavian device for some time now,' he said. 'Speaking loosely, it is a piece of scientific intelligence equipment, and we have known for many years that Seeker Section is responsible for such matters. I would of course be happy, by the way, to know some more details about the device, in particular how many more of them are in existence and where, but I must assume that you aren't going to tell me. I will not press it.'

'That's a surprising line of approach,' I said.

'My dear fellow. What did you imagine? I have neither the time nor the inclination to string people up by their thumbs, and particularly not Major Driver's associates.'

I was glad to hear that there were some advantages to being connected with Seeker. One of the more distressing things about Driver, I reflected, was not so much that he forced me into things like this but that I was getting labelled as one of his associates, a fact which everybody seemed ready to accept but me.

'I am what I say I am.' Drakon was going on inexorably. 'I have undertaken to perform certain services and I am performing them to the best of my ability. If you will not assist me, I understand that. As for the device in Yugoslavia, I am interested in it just as anyone in my business would be interested in it. I will admit,' he started walking away from me towards the door, 'I used the fact of its existence to get hold of you, or somebody like you. I hoped to be able to persuade you to give me some of your time. But if I cannot do so, then that is that. We had better be getting back to the others.'

When I caught up with him he said, 'However.' We both stopped in the doorway.

'What?' I asked.

'There is another matter about which I am more entitled to be insistent.' He reached his hand into his coat and brought out a folded piece of yellow paper. 'You have something that belongs to us. There is no question about it. *You* are illegally in possession of my property, for which,' he waved the yellow slip at me, 'I have a receipt.'

'Okay,' I said. 'Let's see the receipt.'

'Certainly.' He unfolded the slip in front of my eyes, holding it by the top and bottom margins as though I were a Customs officer and he was trying to convince me. 'You see I am so sure that you have it that I am prepared to let you examine my title to it.'

The slip was a ruled invoice form. The itemization read: PROJET UNIQUE 1: 52/RLaSaph./11136/AJ and the price quoted was fourteen thousand dollars US, which made Bratling's offer for it about fair, I supposed. Some phrases were added underneath in English, or rather mixed English and cryptic numerals, but among them were the words 'Angstrom' and 'Pulse Durn. 15 nanosecs' which more or less confirmed that it was a receipt for laser equipment and not somebody's mink coat he was showing me.

He folded the slip neatly and put it back in his pocket. We went back to the dining-room, a long panelled barn of a place with half-finished murals depicting Achievement Through Sweat, and Drakon led the way across it to where Bratling, Mercedes and Amanda Grayle were sitting by the electric fire. The fire, as in the capitalist world, came complete with flickering imitation logs. At least Braun wasn't around, and the coffee was still hot. Drakon poured out two cups of it, handed one to me, and said, 'So there it is. You return that thing tomorrow, or tell me where it is. If not I shall hand you over to the Albanian authorities and you can try to explain what you are doing here.'

'I should have thought they'd give us medals,' I said.

'What for, squire?' Bratling thumbed open a packet of cigarettes and made a lightning pantomime of offering them around.

'Being in Yugoslavia illegally. An enemy of the Revisionists is a friend of Hoxha, or did I get it all wrong?' I said.

'Not very funny, old boy,' said Bratling.

TWENTY-ONE

HE CAME marching into my room later that night, so much later that I took several seconds to swim up into consciousness. When I saw him I was sorry I hadn't stayed asleep.

'Wakey-wakey,' he said. 'Stand by your beds.'

'Push off.'

'On your feet, squire. Got to have a little talk.' One of the other two men came past him and hauled me upright. It was the smaller of the soldiers, complete with carbine as always. I looked at my watch. I was probably never going to get a clear night's sleep again.

'You always kip in your clothes, do you, squire?' asked Bratling.

'Only when I think I may be going somewhere.'

'Not a hope,' he said. I knew that perfectly well. There weren't likely to be many ways out of this place and all of them would be difficult. They'd locked the door and there wasn't a window, which spoiled the hotel-room atmosphere a little, but in any case, where could I go to? I found my shoes.

'That's the ticket,' said Bratling. The other man with him

was Braun, Gloria Braun. He stood by, simpering, ready to jump to attention whenever Bratling told him to. I wondered how much he was getting paid, and what conceivable use he was to the outfit.

We walked along several miles of passage, or that's what it felt like. I tried to work out where I was in relation to the ground plan of the building, but I couldn't manage it. I was short of sleep and my head felt packed tight with cotton waste. Bratling pulled open a plywood door, unpainted, in the side of the passage and we all trooped through into another corridor. There was something different about this one. Fresh cream paint and a sensation of weight and solidity. Ten yards farther on there was a steel-studded bulkhead door, oval, like those found in submarines. It was dogged shut with a heavy swinging latch, and Braun fought it open as though it were the entrance to a bank-vault. Beyond it the passage continued in a straight line for fifty feet or so and then kinked right and left. The slam of the steel door behind us echoed briefly and was absorbed into silence, and the air was hot and slightly oppressive. I knew where we were now: heading straight into the mountain.

Round the kink in the passage was a third door. Beyond that, we were in a room also painted cream and so roughly-shaped that it must, I could see, be a cavern in the rock, cemented and plastered. It seemed a great place for a firing squad.

Mercedes was sitting near the wall in a candy-striped upright deck-chair, and glanced up as the four of us marched in, Bratling in the lead, the small soldier with his gun in my back and Braun bringing up the rear. I half-expected Bratling to make a motion towards whipping off my cap except that I didn't have one. Braun closed the door and went over to the deck-chair, propping himself against the wall. I was wide awake now because I could see roughly what was coming. There was little I could do about it, but I would have liked to see Drakon there.

'Right then,' said Bratling. 'All secure, chaps, all very nice and quiet. You're a clown, squire, as I'm afraid we're going to have to make clear to you.'

I looked around. Boxes and crates of all sizes were stacked in tidy rows and pyramids. There was another door, exactly like the one we'd come in by, on the opposite side of the room. Two heavy planked tables, end to end, supported blue enamelled-steel apparatus which I couldn't identify. Four ventilation grids were set high up in the walls, where they would have met the ceiling of the room if it hadn't been irregularly dome-shaped. I guessed it was some kind of underground storage chamber. It seemed reasonable, given the site of the building itself. Perhaps it had been a wine cellar. I looked at the stencilled marks on the crates. Behind Mercedes's chair, Braun took out his flick-knife and tapped it softly against his cheek.

'Bright chap, old Milo, in his own way. But too complicated up here.' Bratling laid a finger against his temple. 'Not my style. Situation report. You have our laser crystal and we need it. Don't ask me why. Would have been glad to have you along with us, but you aren't going to play. Right. Makes things easy.' He pulled out his cigarettes and stuffed them back into his pocket again. 'Bad show,' he said. 'No smoking here.'

Braun boosted himself away from the wall for a moment. 'Don't forget about the *thing*,' he said. 'Don't forget that, George.'

'Yes, as Gloria says in his own inimitable way, the gadget up in the Yugoslav hills. Vital to know a certain amount about that too. You with me so far, squire? Keep the issues simple.'

He went across and opened the second door. I caught a glimpse of still more cream-painted passageway, shading off after a few yards into bare rock with washes of cement here and there. But I didn't get the chance to see much because the doorway was mostly filled by the larger of the two soldiers. He was wearing a sweatshirt and blue drill trousers, like a grossly overweight PTI. I hadn't really taken him in before, but now I could see that he was well over eighteen stone and not all of it was fat. He came into the rock chamber and stood patiently, looking at me from under heavy eyebrows. His balding head gleamed.

'Koniec,' said Bratling. The man in the doorway nodded in his direction and then turned back to me. He pushed his foot backward and swung the door shut. It was all very stupid.

'So I cooperate or I get bent by him?' I said.

'Not quite. Sorry, squire. Wrong this time. This is just where we throw the big doggies a piece of meat.'

He inclined his head at the big man. As Koniec started towards me, the last clear picture I caught of anything other than him was the pink-and-white deck-chair canvas under Mercedes's forearm. Out of place, I thought, and after that I only watched Koniec.

He came towards me steadily. I backed into a stack of crates. It would be nice if I could leap nimbly out of his way, apply some subtle grip unbreakable even by the strongest opponent, and end up facing the audience with a confident smile, but that wasn't how it was going to end up. I was as fit as I'd ever be, but when I saw the professional way he moved I could predict almost exactly what would happen. If a fit man weighing a hundred and fifty-odd pounds goes in against a fit and practised man weighing two hundred and fifty, what happens is that he gets beaten to bits, no matter what the books or pictures say.

I knew what I wanted and it was quite straightforward. I wanted to be laid out before any permanent, crippling damage was done. I didn't want my kidneys ruptured, my crotch kicked, or my shot and repaired shoulder torn open again, and if he wanted to do any of these things particularly he could probably do them.

He held out his hand towards me, palm down and fingers spread, standing off about four feet. I did nothing. There was no real way I could get him off balance. He waited for me to make a move, and I liked that less than anything else. He was in no hurry; nobody was going to call time, no bells would clang. I moved sideways, away from the crates. He faced me all the way, his hand still held out. I hoped for some boost of adrenalin to flood me and make me lose my temper, but nothing happened. I edged past the tables and searched them, gropingly and with little hope of success, for a spanner or even a loose piece of apparatus to clout him with, but I didn't dare take my eyes off him and I got no help anyway. In the end I turned my right shoulder inward and slammed towards him in farcical desperation. I hit him low in the chest and he rocked backwards, grunting. He wrapped a pair of ferro-concrete arms around me and squeezed. I cupped my hands under his chin and tried to force his head up, and when that didn't work I drove my knuckles into his windpipe. He unwrapped his right arm and put his fingertips against my bottom rib; when he snapped the heel of his hand down it was like being hit with a club. The fight had been on for about twenty seconds. I don't know how much longer it lasted, but as far as any real effort on my part was concerned it ended right then. At one point I found myself held in the leg scissors which looks so amusingly painful on the television screen but which I knew was one sure way for me to end up in a wheelchair. I dug my thumbs into the nerve at the side of his knee and flailed my way out desperately as his calf muscles relaxed, which I suppose was the nearest I came to any sort of success. Every time he got in close to me he snapped another short punch into my ribs like the first one, levering on his fingertips, and after a while I just got plain tired and rolled down a pile of boxes and lay still. Bratling came and stood over me. His voice buzzed down at me, keeping me angrily away from unconsciousness.

'Threaten a chappie with a bit of a pounding,' his voice said, 'first thing he does is make up a whole lot of lies. No good. Wastes time. I'm a simple soldier, don't understand all this psychological stuff. What your chappie needs is a good pounding first, then a bit of a break, then more pounding. Doesn't matter much how it's done. Pretty soon he gets worn out. Can't really be bothered to think up any fairytales. It's the tiredness that does it. Expect you know all about that, squire, don't you?'

I didn't answer. He was right, I could see that. I tumbled towards sleep. I felt him kick me but there was no real force in it. A gesture, I thought, and big doors of shadow folded in on me, closing me gently into the humming dark.

I pitched into the world again, confused because I thought I'd be lying down and I wasn't. Somebody was holding the back of my neck, painfully, and I was being sick into a wash-basin. Both taps were gushing and the ceramic edge of the basin solidified against my fingers. I leaned forward and rested my head against the mirror and wondered what the damage would be when I opened my eyes to take stock. Amanda pulled me back upright and steered me across to the bed.

'Half an hour,' I muttered. 'I want half an hour.'

'All right,' she said.

I woke up and it was just beginning to get light. Amanda Grayle sat opposite the bed, and I couldn't tell for the moment whether they'd brought her to my room or taken me to hers.

'What's your name?' I asked her. She told me and I said, 'No, the real one.'

'Oh. It comes from the time I was born. Falling Shadow,' and it fitted into the night so perfectly that I went to sleep again.

The third time it was morning. I sat up too quickly, thinking there was something I had to do. My ribs hurt like hell but I could feel that I was all right. She watched me as I got off the bed and went to the mirror above the wash-basin. Every time Koniec had hit me with the heel of his hand he'd left a bruise, and the bruises ran together and patterned my lower ribs like a Rorschach ink-blot. I stretched cautiously and pressed here and there with my hands, waiting for the short, grinding pain of broken bone-ends, but nothing happened, or not very much anyway.

'It was worth it,' I told my reflection.

'Did you tell them anything?' said Amanda. I counted slowly, remembering that probably that sort of thing was quite important in Conrad's department.

'I didn't get asked,' I said. 'Not this time round. Next time maybe.'

'What do you mean, it was worth it?' she asked.

'Because I know what this whole thing is about now,' I

said. 'I know why they have to have that laser crystal, and I know why they're interested in Rock Baby.'

And most of all, I thought to myself, I know why Jissock has kept on sticking his dead hand into the course of affairs, why he keeps turning up as a factor in two totally different and seemingly unconnected missions, and the coincidences are over.

'Falling Shadow,' I said. I saw her face change in the mirror.

'Don't call me that,' she said.

'Okay.'

'I'm sorry, Giles. I didn't mean to sound like that.'

I did up the buttons on my shirt. I was fine. I hoped I wouldn't get a cough and I would sell my soul cheerfully for a hot bath, but I was on my feet. For the moment.

'You didn't have to tell me,' I said.

'I know. I can't tell whether I'm sorry about it or not. What *is* this whole thing about?'

I came back to the bed and sat down. 'The trouble with both of us,' I said, 'is that neither of us knows when to keep quiet.'

TWENTY-TWO

THE SUN streamed into the dining-room, turning the rectangles of the window-panes into parallelograms and laying them out like tiles on the dusty floor. Drakon, annoyed and with good reason, paced up and down between two of the windows like a sentry while the rest of us sat in shiny cafeteria chairs. It was ten in the morning, and if breakfast had been served then I'd missed it.

'I cannot believe,' said Drakon, 'I simply cannot believe that anyone could be so stupid.' He didn't mean me, he meant Bratling, who had his feet on one of the deal tables and his eyes half closed. I hugged my ribs and looked at Amanda, who appeared to have spent the hour and a half since I'd been briskly marched out of her room and back to my own in ironing her jeans and giving herself a shampoo-and-set, even though I knew she couldn't have done anything of the sort. All I'd been able to manage was a rapid and inefficient shave with Bratling's razor. They'd taken all my blades away, but I knew Bratling would lend me one if I asked him. He couldn't stand anybody being idle on parade, even if all he had in mind for me was another toughening-up session behind barracks.

Drakon finally came to rest and pulled a chair over to mine.

'So now you know,' he said. 'Isn't that true, Dr Yeoman?'

'Yes,' I said. I was still dog-tired and there wasn't much point in pretending to be dense, though I knew what was likely to happen to clever people around here.

'I ought to hear your conclusions,' said Drakon. 'I owe it to you. You seem to have been correct in your estimation of Mr Bratling and Miss Van Erhlenmeyer. One cannot always pick the associates one would like.'

'They were only trying to help,' I told him. 'In their own little way.' Across the room, Mercedes shifted impatiently in her seat.

'Milo,' she said. 'We haven't the time to wait while you work through your nice logical arguments with Dr Yeoman.'

'Thank you,' said Drakon, and then, with surprising venom, 'you stupid bitch, why couldn't you have done it in here anyway?'

'We were afraid you might hear something and disapprove, dear,' she said.

'So you took him, in order to avoid my disapproval, to the one place in this whole building which – once he'd seen it – would enable him to make a reasonable guess at what we are trying to do. Just in order that you could indulge yourselves by watching Koniec beat him senseless? It doesn't seem possible.'

'You're doing them an injustice,' I told Drakon. 'They aren't just a bunch of sadistic cretins. I'm not saying they aren't that as well, but what they probably wanted was to force your hand.'

Bratling swung his legs off the table and stood up. 'You know, squire,' he said pleasantly, 'you aren't half as daft as I thought. Don't know if it'll do you much good of course, that depends, but still, credit where credit's due. If you could just rake together enough brains before we have to knock them out of your head, perhaps we could still dodge round a lot of trouble. Like to see that happen.'

Drakon moved his chair half an inch to the rear and resettled himself, looking at me and being sorry about Bratling.

'Well, Dr Yeoman. And you conclude what?' he asked me.

I took in the rest of the room. The small soldier was over by the door. Braun had moved to the table recently vacated by Bratling's suède boots and was perched elegantly on it, swinging his legs gently. He hadn't spoken, but then nobody who spent much of their time around Bratling would have many opinions to voice.

'It took quite a time before I got around to believing it, what with this bunch of leftovers from Fred Karno's Army,' I told Drakon. 'But it's the only explanation which fits all the information I've collected up to now. You're trying to build yourselves a thermonuclear bomb.'

They shut us up politely but firmly in Amanda's room while they all thought out what to do next. Perhaps there were microphones. I didn't much care.

'It's why they were so worked up about Rock Baby,' I said. 'They're south of it, you see. Even supposing that Rock Baby could only do half of what it's designed to, an explosion to the south of it instead of north or north-east would stick out like a sore thumb. And a couple more in operational trim could nail the source of any shock-waves down quite easily.' I leaned back against the wall and Amanda came and sat on the bed by me. 'Not that I suppose I'm telling you anything you didn't know already,' I said.

'I didn't know. I can't answer for anybody back in London but as far as I'm concerned I don't even think I believe you. You must admit it's pretty improbable, Giles. Come on now. Are you sure?'

I put my feet up and folded my hands behind my head. My

left shoulder protested, but not nearly as much as the muscles around my chest.

'Fairly sure. I don't suppose they've got very far, or half the Albanian security force would be tramping around the corridors,' I said. 'In fact I can't believe they've got very far anyway, not unless they've got a mad genius locked away in a cellar somewhere. Mind you I think they *had* a mad genius, but what's left of him is in a deep-freeze in McKellar's garage, or wherever they keep the meat back there.'

I was becoming more and more certain that I was right. Nobody had admitted anything in the dining-room before they put us in storage, but Jissock was the cornerstone upon which the whole lunatic enterprise was built.

'What did you see in there?' she asked. 'Lead boxes full of uranium or plutonium or whatever? Is that how you worked it out?'

I reached out and took her hand. I was glad that Captain Bryce hadn't yet started a course on atomic weapons as part of what every young BD expert should know.

'No uranium or plutonium,' I said. 'A thermonuclear bomb is what they're trying to put together. That means a fusion bomb, an H-bomb, whatever the household word for it is nowadays. They're trying to explode a tiny one, just like everybody else. It's a difficult target to aim for. You can't make a tiny fission bomb, fission bombs being what they were exploding between 1945 and 1950. You have to have ten pounds of uranium 235 or plutonium 239 per explosion for those, and less won't do.'

She frowned. 'What about tactical atomic bombs, then?' she said. 'I thought they were supposed to be small?'

'It's only the explosion that's small; if you want to you can arrange for not all of the ten pounds to explode, but you have to have it in the warhead to begin with,' I said. 'If you don't have ten pounds there, you don't have critical mass, and if you don't have critical mass you don't get any bang. The difference between a tactical weapon and a strategic one is that the tactical weapon is shut inside a weaker casing. It blows apart easier, and in fact it blows apart so quickly that most of the fissionable stuff gets no time to absorb neutrons and explode, it just gets spread all over the countryside. But you have to start with the same old ten pounds of junk.'

'Well then,' she said.

'But we aren't talking about uranium or plutonium. What we're talking about is deuterium – heavy hydrogen – and tritium, and various other things such as lithium hydride and lithium deuteride, which are what fusion bombs are made of. There's no question of critical mass with a fusion bomb. You can make it any size you want, large or small, in theory anyway. In practice you can't, not so far anyway, because like most other bright schemes there's a built-in snag. You can't get a fusion reaction to start without heating things up a great deal. I forget how hot you have to get a thermonuclear warhead inside before it explodes but it's a good deal more than a million degrees, so it's a bit more complicated than lighting the blue touchpaper and retiring immediately. Right now the only way to get things hot enough is to explode an ordinary fission bomb as a sort of trigger, so naturally your fusion bomb can't be any smaller than its fission trigger. So far.'

I stopped. She didn't say she couldn't understand and would I mind going over it again, nor did I expect her to.

'All right,' I went on. 'Now this means that there's a small prize waiting for anybody who can invent a method of triggering a fusion reaction *without* using a fission bomb to do it with. Firstly because fission bombs are hard to get hold of and damned heavy to handle. Secondly because fission bombs are what cause all that nasty floating radiation, mainly anyway. Nobody's suddenly turning humane about radiation, though the PR boys like to think so. Personally I don't have much of a preference, one way or the other, about dying of radiation or dying of burns, so all the people who are making noises about clean bombs in the name of humanity are just rehashing the old arguments about whether it was okay to use dum-dum bullets on the Fuzzy-wuzzies. On the other hand you have to admit that if you're going to bombard a place and occupy it later then it's a help if you don't all have to wear lead suits because the scenery is glowing at night, so the military are still in the market for nice clean fusion bombs. The prize is still there for anybody who can think up a quick, easy, reliable, cheap, non-radioactive and preferably lightweight way of making a fire hot enough to start a fusion reaction, and you can bet your boots they're working on it from Los Alamos to Sinkiang.'

Amanda got up off the bed and went over to the basin. After a bit she saw me watching her make faces at herself in the mirror and stopped doing it.

She said, 'And you mean to tell me that these people here have beaten everybody else to it?'

'No.'

'I should damned well think not.'

'What I'm telling you,' I said patiently, 'is that a man called Jissock thought he could beat everybody else to it. He believed it so strongly that he tried to tell the Scientific Advisers to the Cabinet about it, and when they wouldn't listen he tried to tell the Americans and they turned him down too. But eventually he found somebody who listened.'

'Milo Drakon.'

'Yes.'

She turned around and leaned against the edge of the wash-basin. 'How did he think he was going to do it?' she asked.

'With a laser. More accurately, with a Q-switched giant-pulse laser, one of the components of which I've shown you, and which Drakon, somewhat naturally, wants back. And the hell of it is,' I said, 'I don't know enough to be able to swear that it can't be done.'

TWENTY-THREE

I DIDN'T KNOW enough, but I got asked just the same. Drakon gave me black coffee and a Turkish cigarette in the room overlooking the gorge, and talked endlessly about the benefits to Albania of nuclear energy. I tried to make up my mind if he really knew nothing at all about nuclear energy or if it was an elaborate pose on his part.

'I take it that you think the scheme impractical,' he said.

'I don't think one way or the other. What I really don't understand is how you came to let Jissock loose in Paris in the first place.'

'It was an error of judgement. He had been working here for many months without any sort of break, and although he was quite happy he clearly needed a rest. He persuaded me that he needed to go to France to obtain a vital piece of apparatus whose specification and performance he alone could check. I refer to the laser rod which I hope you will find convenient to return to us. We had very little alternative but to let him go, accompanied of course. There was also the question of the seismograph. He said he wished to confer with a man whom I believe you have met, Professor Mikulicz. Since Professor Mikulicz is known to myself and my associates, for reasons I won't trouble you with, I agreed. Cautiously, but I agreed.' He looked down at his knees. 'One is very much in the hands of the scientists these days,' he finished, almost to himself.

'So you sent him off to Paris with Bratling and Mercedes Van Erhlenmeyer.'

'There were other factors,' he said.

'I suppose it could have been a pleasant trip. Only he ran away and Miss Van Erhlenmeyer, or possibly Bratling, threw bombs at him. One phosphorus grenade and one fragmentation.' As I'd about given up the idea of protesting about Driver, I thought I might as well go the whole hog.

'Yes,' said Drakon. After a moment he said 'Yes' again. I waited. He drummed his fingers on the side of his knee. 'Jissock maintained that a power of five million billion watts per square centimetre would be sufficient to produce nuclear fusion temperature,' he said, squinting up at me.

'It may be possible. I don't know,' I said. 'Jissock was mentally unbalanced, you most likely know that. It doesn't necessarily mean he was wrong of course, but it's something that ought to be kept in mind.'

Drakon thought this over. 'I would like you to believe that I am sorry for what happend to you last night,' he said finally.

'You'd probably have got around to telling me all your

troubles anyway,' I said. 'So we'd have ended up in the same situation.'

He took me by the arm and we went over to the door. He pulled it open and called 'Joseph', and the small soldier led me away. Drakon shouted down the corridor after me, 'The situation is not yet desperate.' I was glad he didn't think so.

'What you've got to get into your head is that it doesn't matter how unlikely I think it is,' I told Amanda. 'It's what Drakon believes that counts.'

'I'm getting tired of this room,' she said. 'At least you've got somebody to talk to. All I can do is yell when I want to wash my hands or something, and I can't keep on doing it. *Do* you think it's likely? That they've got anywhere, I mean?'

'No. But the only real reason I've got for saying so is that the British, the Americans, the Russians and the Chinese must have thought of roughly the same idea, and if none of them has got anywhere with it then I don't think the shot's on the board. Of course if they have got somewhere with it they might not say so.'

'But surely the British Government would have, I don't know, kept hold of Jissock somehow. If they thought he was working along the right lines? I mean they wouldn't just let him walk out of the country, for goodness' sake.'

'Yes, all right,' I admitted. 'You can't just lock somebody up simply because they're in an inconvenient line of research, but in principle you're right, I suppose. The Government or its advisers must have thought he wasn't worth bothering their heads about. On the other hand if I had a shilling for every time the British Government had been wrong when people have come along with bright ideas I'd be nearly as rich as the Americans have got on the inventions we've thumbed down.'

I sat and thought about a few of the Evaluation Committees I'd sat on. There are few imaginative committees and virtually no radical ones, which is inevitable because imaginative and radical thinkers have no time for committee work, even if by some chance they should be asked to undertake it. I was still considering the probable interchanges between Jissock and his Evaluation Committee, if he'd got that far, when the door opened and I was taken away again.

Koniec did the taking away this time. He was neither friendly nor unfriendly. He'd hammered me to bits last night and, if Bratling's view of the world prevailed, he'd do it again tonight, but right now I was just something he had to deliver. I didn't give him any trouble. Joseph passed us going the other way, carrying a tray which I hoped was for Amanda. He grinned at Koniec and hurried on. The gun was slung across his back so as not to interfere with the tray.

In the dining-room, Mercedes was with Drakon. They wanted to talk about the disruption of nuclear binding forces by laser power, and I wanted to know about Jissock.

'We had just paid him a large sum of money,' said Drakon. 'Everything was agreed, everything was understood. Jissock believed in the need for world-wide cooperation in the field of nuclear physics.'

'That's what he said he believed in,' I pointed out.

'No, no. You do not understand. In matters of what a man believes, I know what I am talking about. He believed; you can take my word for it. A country such as Britain is too cynical for such men.' I stared at him in amazement. 'He was a man who had been rejected and we gave him recognition. He had no home and we gave him one, here.' Drakon pointed to the floor between us. 'Nobody in England or America would give him a penny to follow up his research. We gave him a laboratory, all the equipment he asked for.'

'Yes, that's another thing,' I said. 'What equipment *did* he ask for?'

Drakon considered me. 'A mass spectrograph,' he said. 'A bubble chamber. Things like that.'

'You bought him a mass spectrograph, just like that? Who maintained it?'

Mercedes said, 'Three technicians and myself. The men have returned to Tirana for the moment, since we have no need for their services at the moment. They will be brought back when we are ready for them.'

She didn't look to me as though she could tell a mass

spectrograph from a hair-dryer, but I reminded myself that Amanda wasn't everybody's idea of a bomb-disposal man.

'You gave him everything he'd ever need,' I said. 'Fine. You took him in and repaired his self-esteem and bought him a whole lot of toys, and he worked in the cause of international cooperation in nuclear physics. I'll do my best to believe it. How much did you pay him just before he went to Paris?'

'That is none of your affair,' said Drakon.

'This whole madhouse is none of my affair.'

He tilted his chair backwards. 'We paid him seventeen thousand pounds,' he said.

'Then that's where you made your mistake,' I told him. 'If you want one solid piece of advice, I'd say what you ought to do is get going, and the sooner the better. Before Enver Hoxha begins to wonder when he's going to see a return on his outlay.'

Drakon let his chair fall forward with a thump.

'I see,' he said. 'That's your advice. Thank you.'

'Did they give you anything to eat?' asked Amanda. 'I saved you some bread and cheese, just in case.'

'It looks a bit dusty, doesn't it?' I said.

'You don't sound very grateful.'

'I am. It was a generous thought. Though as a matter of fact they did feed me, thank you very much,' I said.

'Because they still think you're going to be a valuable addition to the group, I suppose.'

'I don't know about that. If they do think it, I have a feeling they're going to stop doing so any minute now.'

She wrapped the bread and cheese up in her handkerchief again and put it back under the bed. 'Waste not, want not,' she said.

'I imagine all that's going to happen is that some revolutionary-conscious mouse will get it,' I said, 'but it's up to you of course.' She straightened up and pushed her hair back.

'What are you going to do?' she asked.

'I don't know,' I admitted. 'What do you think we should do?'

'I've been thinking. If you were to, well, play along with

them for a bit, we could penetrate this operation, couldn't we?' She slapped dust from her palms against the sides of her jeans.

'Great. There speaks Uncle Conrad's little girl,' I said. 'Penetrate? Operation? What operation, for God's sake?'

'There's no need to raise your voice. You asked me what ideas I had and I'm telling you.'

'Will you get it into your head that there isn't any operation?' I said. 'If you want to make out a report for Conrad, fine, but don't let's start living in a fantasy world right now. What we have here is a poxed-up, paralytic bunch of morons trying to let off a bigger and better firework in the back yard, not a branch of the Chief Directorate of the KGB. They're technically incompetent, which doesn't surprise me, and they're pretty useless in almost every other field except for doing the odd casual murder here and there.'

'Well then, that's all right,' she said. 'If they're incompetent then they can't do it.'

'No, it isn't all right. Because any second now they are going to have me beaten up again, which I don't want, or alternatively they are going to get around to thinking it would be better fun to beat you up, which I don't want either. In fact that's why they've left us together so much. What I want is to get out of here, and I don't know how.'

'What we need is to get hold of somebody's gun,' she said.

'Yes,' I said, 'that would be terrific. I suppose that since I'm marginally bigger and stronger than you are, it ought to be me that tries to get it. If I come charging along the corridor and shoot the lock off your door, will you try to be ready to move out? Or alternatively if you hear a whole lot of shooting, and I don't come charging along the corridor because I have a large hole in my belly, will you move out anyway if you can?'

'Don't worry,' she said. 'I'll be ready. I'd rather we tried as soon as they come in here next time, though.'

'No,' I said.

'Because you don't want me in the way when you try to get somebody's gun.'

'That's it.'

'Okay,' she said. 'Do it your way.'

Around eight o'clock in the evening I was with Drakon again. His summary of the position was concise and accurate.

'You are not going to work for us here,' he said.

'No, I'm not.'

'I am sorry to hear it.'

'Don't feel too badly about it. You don't need me anyway. What you need is a magician.'

He smiled briefly and offered me a cigarette. 'An alchemist would be more appropriate, don't you think? We are concerned after all with the transmuting of elements. I accept your decision with reluctance. I still need the laser crystal and, less urgently I admit, I need information about the Yugoslavian seismograph. If you refuse me these things I shall either have you shot or possibly thrown off the roof. Miss Grayle too, of course. I offer you the traditional twelve hours to consider the matter. You will not be troubled by Mr Bratling tonight, on that you have my assurance.'

Joseph took me back to my room. If he'd put a hand on me I might have fought him for his carbine, but he either knew or sensed that I was under provisional sentence of death and he took no chances. He marched me all the way at gunpoint, staying six feet behind me. If I scratched my ear I knew he'd kill me.

My room contained the same furniture as Amanda's. A large chair, too heavy to pick up and swing. An iron-sprung bed, one of the sides of which might have made a good battering-ram except that I had nothing to undo the retaining bolts with but my fingers. The bolts were rusted solid. Two blankets, which a foolhardy hero could have dropped over an armed man's head, hoping he got it right first time and that there wasn't another armed man behind in the corridor. A wash-basin cemented into the wall and with several feet of piping available to anybody with a hacksaw and a lot of time, but not to me.

I could break the mirror with the heel of my shoe, manufacture a crude but efficient knife from a splinter of glass wrapped in a handkerchief, and hurl myself into the attack with it, but on balance I thought I'd prefer the blankets. The electric light was behind an armoured grille, and in any case, so what? There was nothing in the room which I could believe would give me a better chance than my bare hands. I didn't do anything with the blankets except lie on top of them and think about the best way of taking a carbine off Koniec bare-handed.

I must, despite everything, have gone to sleep. Perhaps it wasn't surprising. The first scrape of the key in the lock brought me upright.

The door swung open a few inches, slowly, and then Amanda's voice said, 'Don't do anything,' very softly, and she pushed it all the way open and came in. She carried a square, heavy automatic in her hand and there was a raw pink flare across her cheek and the side of her neck. She looked pleased and sly, like a cat which has dropped a bird somewhere out of sight.

'There you are,' she said, handing me the automatic. 'It was too good an opportunity to miss.'

I examined the gun to make sure I knew where the safety was.

'There's no hurry,' she went on. 'We can take things slowly and quietly. Have you any idea which way we ought to go?'

I pointed. 'Up,' I said.

'You're sure?'

'A reasonable chance,' I said. 'They were going to throw us off the roof, unless he was just kidding. So there ought to be a way of getting on to it. Why isn't there any hurry?' But I knew why, already.

'My door's locked. I've got the key. That nasty little man is dead and Bratling's unconscious. He may be dead too,' she said in the departmental tone of voice I had come to recognize. 'Hang on a moment.'

She went and looked at herself in the mirror. Her shirt was torn, I noticed. I could assemble it, except perhaps for one detail.

'How did you kill Braun?' I asked her.

'That's his name, yes. Braun. I shot him. They started to play around with me, so I shot him.'

'With the little pistol.'

She pulled her hair down and forward, across the reddened side of her face.

'Damn, I need a safety-pin,' she said. 'But I don't expect you've got one. Men never do. Yes, that's right. Bratling hit me and then Braun got all excited and tore my shirt. I only had one round or I'd have killed both of them.'

I was going to ask where she'd hidden the Derringer, but I decided not to. 'Okay, I'm ready,' she said. 'I passed the stairs on the way here, if you can't remember.'

'You're quite sure Bratling's not going to come round and start shouting the odds, for a while anyway?' I said.

'Yes, quite sure. He didn't know I only had one round. I took his gun and made him turn round. I hit him fairly hard.'

I recalled grabbing hold of her wrist in the middle of the night back in Yugoslavia. Bratling was out. We walked along the passage and nobody shouted at us. It had clearly been a private little party, just Braun and Bratling and nobody else around to tell them when they had to stop. The Derringer would have made hardly any noise. We went up two floors and prowled quietly along dirty boarded floors until we found the emergency roof exit. It was locked, but the screws holding the lock were on our side. I took them out with the leading edge of the magazine from Bratling's gun.

Outside on the roof, it was a warmish, damp night. Roughened asphalt stretched in all directions, broken by chimneys and the slatted tops of ventilation shafts. The mountain, as I'd thought, adjoined the back wall of the building. It sloped steeply back from the roof edge itself, with a deep lead-lined channel between the bare rock and the parapet to carry away rainwater. I couldn't tell how far we might have to climb if we tried to go up the mountain.

A cast-iron fire-escape led down one side of the building, but it would have an echoing landing at each floor and I didn't want to risk being heard or seen. I looked over the front edge of the roof, and could just make out the shape of the helicopter on the landing pad, far below. There was very little light; clouds bellied across the sky like clippers under sail, obscuring the stars, and the wind flapped wetly against the parapet and the airshafts and misted our faces with droplets too small to be rain.

With the exception of the fire-escape, none of the possible ways down looked very promising. In the end I slid over the lip of the drainage channel and climbed down ten feet of iron pipe. Then I swung across on to the face of the mountain itself and beckoned Amanda to come down too. I knew I didn't have to worry about her falling; anywhere I could lead she could undoubtedly follow.

We edged around a curving shoulder of rock. It was an easy traverse, but I wouldn't have tried it in daylight since we were in plain view from the opposite side of the gorge all the way. After about thirty feet of crabbing sideways we were suddenly out of sight of the building itself and behind the granite shoulder, and I began to feel better. Water streamed down the rock and I was thankful the air was warm instead of freezing. Another twenty feet of traverse brought us to the top of a flake, and we edged down one side of it. I occasionally kicked loose small showers of stone, but Amanda never seemed to put a toe or a finger wrong; since I was underneath, I was grateful.

All the way down to the bottom of the gorge I waited for the first shouts from inside the building. Both of our doors were locked, but surely Joseph or Koniec would look inside one or other of our rooms soon? The rock shoulder flattened out below the level of the ledge on which the building stood, which made the going easier but left us exposed to anybody who happened to take a look out of the windows on this side.

I slid the last thirty feet or so to the floor of the gorge and looked at my watch while Amanda felt her way down quietly and daintily. I was surprised to see that it had only taken us twenty-five minutes or so. It seemed a long way, from down here. The walls of the gorge towered up on either side of us, and a brisk rill of water threaded its way importantly between stones and meagre tufts of grass at our feet. We walked downstream for a quarter of a mile, until we were no longer in sight of the building, and started to climb up a damp cleft on the far side. Amanda sat down after a while and took off her left shoe.

'We're going to have to walk a long way,' she said.

I sat down. Koniec had taken more out of me than I'd put in during my week of training in Austria, but it wasn't only that which made me feel tired out. We were free all right, but for how long? I began to realize why Drakon wasn't obsessional about guard duties. Amanda felt around inside her shoe, frowning.

'They'll come and look for us with the helicopter. I don't think it's stone, it's a nail. Damn.'

'The helicopter isn't what worries me,' I told her. 'We shan't be walking by day.' She nodded, accepting it.

'Where are we going?'

'I don't know. Here,' I said, 'you'd better give it to me.' She handed me the shoe and I found the nail-head. I put a stone inside the shoe and started to hammer at the sole with Bratling's gun. 'We can either walk to Greece, or back to Yugoslavia. Only don't ask me which is nearer, because I don't know where we are.'

'Yugoslavia would be north. You're making a frightful row with that,' she said. 'We haven't got a compass, we'd have to use the stars.' She narrowed her eyes. 'There aren't many stars to be seen right now, though, are there?'

I stopped hammering and passed the shoe back to her. At least I'd found a couple of uses for the automatic so it wasn't a total loss. The more I thought about it, the less hope I could see for us. Drakon and what was left of his crack-brained crew would come out after us whenever they felt like it, and if they didn't find us the Albanian security forces would. Suppose we could make ten miles in a night? How long would it take us to reach a border, and how would we cross it when we got there? Without a map, how would we even fix our position? What was the cruising speed of the helicopter? How far, and in what direction, had we flown after Bratling announced that we'd crossed the border from Yugoslavia? The best I could think of to do was to march east, rather than north, merely because Albania was narrower east-west; sooner or later, I supposed, we must reach Greece if we were now south of Lake Prespa or Yugoslavia if we were north of it. That just about exhausted my store of knowledge on the subject of Albanian geography.

Amanda moved a little closer to me.

'We had to get out of there,' she said.

'I know. Look,' I said, 'the best thing we can do is to get to the top of this side of the valley, and try to work out some idea of direction. We can do it now, and we may not have as good a chance later.'

We started to climb the gully again, and after twenty minutes or so I pulled myself out of the narrow mouth of it on to a flat hill-top studded with gigantic boulders. The wind had stopped carrying its burden of mist and there was about six-tenths cloud cover. We sat down to wait for a sight of the stars, but I thought it would turn out to be more of an intellectual exercise than anything else.

It was about half past two in the morning when we first heard the man moving among the rock pillars and patches of scrub over to our right. He seemed to be skirting the edge of the gorge and he was taking no particular trouble over being quiet. Amanda lay down flat and whispered 'Sigurimi'. She dropped her head and I saw his silhouette as he pushed himself away from a boulder and came steadily in our direction. 'What did you say?' I asked her. 'Security patrol,' she mouthed, and pulled my head down next to hers. 'Who else would be walking around at this time of night?'

'What about a smuggler or a shepherd?' I asked. She gave me a look straight from the imbeciles-only reserve bin, and went on checking the breech of the little Derringer. 'Just let him go away,' I suggested. But I could see as well as she could that he'd step on us if he carried on the way he was headed now, and it was too late for us to start crawling in any direction.

When he was about fifteen yards away he stopped and whistled, the low chirrup which is the international callsign for summoning a dog. He turned away from us, looking around. Amanda inched her right hand and arm into aiming position, resting it firmly on a granite slab in front of her. I didn't think she'd hit anything at that range myself, but I didn't want her to try. The man turned his head in our direction again and I reached across and tapped Amanda gently on the bridge of her nose.

'Don't shoot,' I said. 'It's Yancy Brightwell,' and the man whistled again softly and said, 'Hey there, goddam it. I know you're around some place.'

I got to my feet. 'Here,' I said.

Yancy made a flat gesture of welcome with his hand. 'Well, you aren't making much noise, are you?' he said. 'For a guy who was making like an avalanche an hour back.'

'Where's the rest of the platoon, Yancy?'

'Nobody here but me,' he said. 'On the other hand, I see you brought the artillery with you.' He came over to where Amanda was sitting up and took the Derringer delicately from her with his thumb and forefinger. I held my breath. 'A man could get himself a nasty scratch with a thing like that,' said Yancy.

'Don't fool yourself,' I told him. 'There's at least one man who knows differently.'

Yancy grinned all over his face. 'Well, any road,' he said. I looked at Amanda and saw that she was smiling too.

'What is it that you've got, Yancy, that I haven't?' I asked.

'Logistics,' he said. 'Bubble gum and salvation. You nice people follow me and we'll get this whole thing sorted out.'

TWENTY-FOUR

THREE AM.

Yancy unhitched the big night glasses and handed them to me. He rolled sideways, away from the narrow triangular embrasure formed by two rocks leaning against each other, and I took his place. His ribs were in better condition than mine right now, I could tell that.

'The big one is called Koniec,' I said. 'The man standing beside him is Drakon himself. I can't tell you who the third one is because I can't see far enough into the room.'

'Okay. They got a searchlight, do you think?'

'I doubt it. We were on the roof and I didn't see one. I should think the roof is where it would have been. Besides, why would they need one?' I asked him. Yancy made a series of thoughtful clicks with his tongue. 'How far is the border?' I asked.

'Seven, eight miles. That way.' He pointed. As it happens it wasn't the direction I'd have chosen.

'You walked here, Captain Brightwell?' Amanda was sitting against one wall of Yancy's natural dug-out, her face turned towards us and resting on her drawn-up knees. Lying beside her was a CETME assault rifle, five spare magazines stacked neatly against the stock. Yancy's pack was by my feet and I kicked it as I turned round and knelt upright again.

'No, honey, I did not. I came in by parachute, and like the joke says, I'm leaving the same way,' said Yancy. He took the glasses from me. 'They won't do anything,' he said. 'Not till daylight.'

'I just thought perhaps we ought to get moving,' said Amanda. 'Don't you think so, Giles?'

'I've stopped thinking again now the Americans are here,' I told her.

'Well, I haven't,' she snapped. She'd decided some time ago to stop smiling at Yancy. She hadn't exactly declared war on him yet, but things were tending that way. It was none of my business. They were both professionals and I wasn't. I was just a mangy, senile old sheep. Everybody had let me go right on thinking I was being brilliant and independent, but here I was in the pen just the same with the dogs hanging around looking pleased about it.

'That's her,' said Yancy. I couldn't think what he meant for a minute, but then I realized he'd got Mercedes in the field of the binoculars and that, of course, he'd seen her before.

'You two sound mad at me,' Yancy went on. 'You mad at me, Giles? I couldn't do anything with three busted ribs and pneumonia, now could I? Be reasonable. What did you say the name of the other guy was, the one with the way-out English accent?'

'Bratling. George Bratling.'

'Check. Haven't seen him around yet.'

'He's probably lying somewhere with his skull crushed in,' I said. 'Miss Grayle here hit him with the butt of his own gun.' Yancy squinted back over his shoulder and I showed him the automatic.

'Nice going,' he said. 'Listen, Giles, of course I knew all about this place. I was with Jissock for quite a while back there, you recall? He told me about home-made atom bombs and I thought he'd been chewing peyote, but I had to make sure. I gave you a better than sporting chance anyway; you didn't have to open the package. What's the other guy look like, Joseph?'

'Short. He'll be in the same uniform as Koniec, probably, if you can make it out,' I said.

'I got him. Right. You're sure that's all? Drakon, Koniec, Bratling if he's not a stretcher-case, the girl and Joseph? Braun got himself shot, didn't you say so, honey?'

'Yes,' said Amanda. 'I take it your plan is to steal the helicopter.'

'No such thing,' said Yancy. 'I'm still a sick man. My ribs are strapped.'

'But not strapped tight enough to stop you parachuting.'

'Just try not to fret,' said Yancy. 'We're all going home, one way or another. I want you to understand my situation, Giles. If Jissock had got around to telling me exactly where that gadget of yours was—'

'Rock Baby?'

'Rock Baby, right. If he'd told me exactly where it was, well then sure. Maybe I could have waited until I was on my feet again and then gone and taken a look at it myself. Though there mightn't have been time. But he didn't tell me where it was, and I figured it would be a sight easier to find *you* than to sit around twenty-four hours a day waiting for it to do its little squirt act. A man could grow old that way.'

Amanda considered him. 'I don't really see why it's any business of American Intelligence to stick their noses into British operations,' she said. Yancy swivelled right round and looked at her wonderingly. 'Well, I mean,' she said.

'She's very good at taking bombs to pieces,' I told Yancy.

'Sure, sure,' he said.

'And I don't think, in passing, that Major Driver or Mr Conrad would approve of all the information you've given Captain Brightwell,' she said to me.

'Or maybe,' Yancy said pleasantly, 'Giles and me ought to take you and toss you over the edge of this little old precipice here to stop you going around telling everybody what sinners we are. Of course I can't speak for Giles, but you better believe you're tiring me out, baby.' He turned to me. 'You seriously think that's what they're doing in there? Trying to fire a hydrogen bomb with a laser trigger?'

'Yes. In my opinion they haven't a hope, but they're trying.'

'I'm sorry,' said Amanda. 'I realize you didn't have to come here after us.'

'I didn't say I came here after you,' said Yancy.

'But you did, didn't you?'

'Well let's just say that you and the Doc here blew it and I'm trying to retrieve the situation.' He went back to studying the face of the building across the gorge through the night glasses.

'Acting on your own initiative,' I said.

'Yeah, yeah, I know. What between you and Jissock I could really wind up with my ass in a sling. At least I was in Yugoslavia as a bona fide tourist, looking at the mountain scenery around Bled and Jesenice. I don't know what in hell I'm doing here.'

'What it comes down to,' I told Amanda, 'is that while you were sitting around watching me, and I was fooling around with my little DF set trying to locate Rock Baby, he was watching both of us. So was Drakon. If Driver had really been thinking hard he could have sold tickets.'

That must have been just about the way it was. Both Yancy and Amanda knew approximately where Rock Baby was, but they had to wait for me to roll up because I had the DF set, which meant I was the only one who could pin it down precisely. Of course, back in Whitehall, they could have given Higsbee's DF set to Amanda once they found I'd gone rushing off on my own, but according to her account she needed me there anyway, to deal with the electronic side of things. (Among other things I could see that Higsbee must have told them I was going to collect the other set off Mikulicz, which was fair enough, I supposed. He hadn't made me any promises.)

Drakon knew where Rock Baby was exactly, but he wanted to get hold of me and his laser rod, so he had to wait around too. Enter Yeoman in false nose and flapping boots, to the cheers of all and sundry. The fact that I had spent a ludicrous week in shaking off all pursuit by traipsing about all over Austria merely heightened the general hilarity.

'Well, I can tell you one thing,' said Yancy. He was still looking out between the rocks and his voice sounded muffled. 'The Defence Department aren't going to like this.'

'I don't see why the Defence Department has to bother its head about it one way or the other,' I said.

'You're one hundred per cent sure they'll never make any sort of bang, then?'

'Pretty sure.'

'Not good enough. A hundred per cent sure is what I said.'

'Ask the boys at Los Alamos or Oak Ridge,' I said. 'They'll give you an opinion.'

'I don't have the time. I'm asking you.' Yancy wriggled back and sat up. 'Come on, Giles. No kidding. You are absolutely cast-iron certain they haven't found a new way to let off nuclear bombs which all the big boys haven't thought of yet. Yes or no?'

'I am not absolutely certain, no.'

'That's what I thought,' said Yancy.

'And?'

'Well, we have a situation here. I think we have to deal with it ourselves. That's why we didn't start walking a while back. I think we have to get inside that place again and spread a little havoc.'

'Yes, I think so too,' said Amanda quickly. I was just going to ask them if they were serious when I saw their faces. They were serious all right.

'What exactly do you propose?' I asked. Yancy at once

started drawing imaginary diagrams on the ground. He was wearing a blue ski-jacket and denim trousers and was seeing pictures of himself as a commando.

'You said there was a tunnel into the side of the mountain, right?' he said. 'Then a room, a rock chamber, that's how you described it, with a whole lot of boxes and crates and junk. Then another passage leading deeper into the mountain, and you think the machinery for this bomb is down there. Isn't that what you told us?' He glanced at me. 'Right,' he went on. 'Then I think somebody has to get in there,' he leaned over and pointed to where his invisible drawing ended, 'and destroy the machinery.'

'Shall I tell you what I think?' I said. 'It's about the most idiotic suggestion I've heard yet, and I've heard plenty just recently.' Yancy looked at me encouragingly. This was conference stuff, he loved it. 'Why should we do anything of the sort, and where would it get us?' I asked him.

'Look, Giles. This may be a nutty scheme or not. Maybe it is. Maybe. One of the principal nuts – Jissock – is dead and therefore he can't start the whole thing over. So far as we know the rest of the nuts are in there.' He jerked a thumb over his shoulder. 'So if there's an unofficial explosion, shall we say, who's going to shout? Nobody, that's how I see it. We're on the spot now. You can take it from me there's nothing around for miles except goats, and so far as we know all of us are here quite unofficially. In fact the only people who know we're here at all are, once again, inside that building. Whereas, just supposing we walk away and leave everything the way it is, and it turns out that it's not such a nutty scheme after all, why then there's going to be notes and interchanges and upsets in the balance of power and all kinds of uproar, and who wants that? Nobody.'

He sat back on his heels. I'd never seen him carry on like this in the Compass Committee or the International Flight Instrumentation Congress, though I suppose I'd known all along that he was capable of it.

'How are we going to set about all this proposed sabotage?' I asked. 'Do we take the powder out of all our cartridges and make crude but efficient demolition charges, or what?'

'Well now, I've been studying that problem a little,' said Yancy. 'Jissock can't have been intending just to shine his laser beam on a test-tube full of heavy water, can he? The way I understand it, you have to have a whole lot of pressure as well in the middle of your warhead, isn't that right?'

I opened my mouth and shut it again.

'That's the way it works,' persisted Yancy.

'Yes, it is,' I said. 'And of course you're quite right, the stuff in those boxes is most probably dynamite or gelignite. If he was going to get it to work at all he'd have to generate his extreme pressure by implosion, the way they did with the Nagasaki bomb.'

Amanda gripped my arm. 'Then that's it,' she said. She looked as though she were a small girl just opening the top of her Christmas stocking. 'I think you're both very clever,' she said breathlessly. I began to feel a sort of desperate acquiescence creep over me. Within the frame of reference they used, the frame which had now trapped me, they were right. A little local surgery now balanced against a whole lot of possible trouble later. I must have nodded agreement, or perhaps they merely sensed it, because Yancy edged across to his pack and started to take things out of it.

'Great,' he said. 'Well now, men, I think we've just about got time for a short war,' and I could also see, although no short straw had been drawn, who was going to try conclusions with all that explosive.

TWENTY-FIVE

I WALKED NORTH along the edge of the gorge for a few hundred yards, until I found the really easy way down. The most straightforward way of doing things would have been to back-track along the route we'd taken on the way out, but I thought it would take too long. I had to be on the roof of the building again at around the time they'd be getting ready to lift off in the helicopter, and if there were any question of getting there early or late, it had better be early. Once they got the helicopter into the air, picking off a man climbing across exposed rock or walking about on the roof would be so easy it didn't bear thinking about.

Yancy had started to explain why it had to be me and not him, but I wasn't disposed to listen. I knew where I was going and he didn't, for one thing. For another, he was a better shot than I was ever likely to be. I went back to them and said I'd picked my route.

'Fine,' said Yancy. He unwrapped things and started handing them to me. 'Pneumatic fuse,' he said. 'Ten to fifteen minutes, so don't stick around too long.' I rolled the little plastic tube across my palm. Did he keep one by his ballpoint pens all the time, or had he come here with the intention of carrying out a single-handed search-and-destroy mission? Amanda reached over and took it from me.

'My province,' she said.

'Your province is to sit right here and pass the ammunition,' I said, but without much real confidence. I could see that she'd fixed it with Yancy while I was out surveying. I thought of all the good sound arguments I could use and crossed them off one by one. She was a fast and tidy climber and she wouldn't, therefore, hold me up. She had both a natural and a cultivated bent for destruction. The real reason she wanted to come along I thought I knew. She had accounts to settle, and she was too young to settle them inside her head, which is what we mostly have to do. I didn't know how far along Bratling and Braun had got with whatever fun they'd had in mind for her, and she'd been deliberately over-casual in telling me about it; but given the facts of her recruitment into Conrad's group, any distance at all along that particular track would have been too far by a mile, and she wanted blood. More blood, I corrected myself. More blood. Well, all right.

'You going to take that thing?' Yancy pointed to Bratling's automatic.

'I don't think so,' I said. 'I've taken a couple of screws out of a door with it and used it as a hammer, but aside from that I can't see what good it's going to be.'

'Take it anyway,' he said. 'You might be able to scare somebody into a heart attack.'

About three-forty it was getting much lighter than I'd have liked. Amanda was crossing the stream in the bottom of the gorge ahead of me. We were out of sight of the building, upstream from it this time, but I thought I heard the first sounds of activity around the buttress of rock which hid it from view. I badly wanted to walk a few yards downstream to see what was happening, but I had no time. I looked back at the cogged crest of the gorge wall we'd just descended, but of course I couldn't see Yancy either.

Amanda had begun to climb the opposite wall of the gorge and she'd picked the wrong place to start. It was my fault for hanging around instead of getting on with the job in hand. I called to her softly, and she slithered easily across from the narrow crack she'd been clambering up and which I knew petered out twenty or thirty feet farther up, and followed me instead.

After twenty minutes I decided we'd gained enough height and that it was time to start moving sideways. The gorge face was cut into strata, which is always deceiving; on any long traverse you either end up higher or lower than you intended because the cracks and ledges slope.

We sidled outwards along the wall until I could just see the roof of the building, about thirty feet below and to our right. I'd brought us up too far. I flattened myself against the rock, because Joseph was on the roof, leaning against the miniature penthouse which contained the access door and smoking a cigarette. I was just beginning to think that Yancy couldn't see us when his first shot tore open the morning and bounced echoes up and down the gorge. Joseph dropped flat, but I knew that Yancy hadn't been trying to hit anything, he was just trying to make an assault rifle sound like somebody taking pot-shots with an automatic. Joseph elbowed himself backwards, lying prone, and pulled open the door; I heard the clatter of his footsteps as he bolted down out of sight, leaving the door swinging.

I edged round for another ten feet or so and slid over the

rim of the ledge I was standing on, feeling for the holds that would bring me down to the one below. Amanda followed me down neatly, holding herself well out from the rock, and I took the last fifteen feet of descent in too much of a hurry and missed my footing. The automatic ground into the front of my thigh as I slipped down on the gutter between the roof and the rock face, and I was sorrier than ever that I'd listened to Yancy and brought it with me. All it was doing was wearing holes in my pocket and threatening me every other minute with a truly laughable accident.

I lifted a hand in greeting for Yancy's benefit as Amanda dropped to the roof behind me. I couldn't even identify his position among the tumble of rocks on the far side of the gorge, and I hoped that the same went for the people underneath us. I went to the forward edge of the roof and peered cautiously over. As I stepped back there was a long, hammering burst of carbine fire from somewhere under my feet, and tiny puffs of rock-dust marched in an untidy row across the cliff top opposite us.

'They don't know what they're shooting at,' said Amanda contemptuously.

'No, but they will soon,' I pointed out. 'The next bit is run, run, all the way. Have you got that clear?'

'Yes, of course.'

As we went through the access door and started down the narrow stairway, the heavy slam of the assault rifle sounded again four or five times in succession. I heard, faintly, the explosive tinkle of breaking glass as Yancy began his diversionary campaign in earnest. Drakon had no way of knowing that he was dealing with anybody besides ourselves, but he'd work it out for himself any minute now.

The dust on the boards of the top floor had been scuffed by running feet and the main staircase door was open. Joseph must have been in a real hurry to find something to shoot at. I kept ahead of Amanda, down two more flights of stairs and along the half decorated hotel-like corridors, hoping I could remember where I was heading.

The outer wooden door to the tunnel into the mountain was closed and locked. I didn't know how to set about shooting the lock off, so I reversed Bratling's gun again and smashed it off instead, messily and at the cost of several skinned knuckles. More shots sounded off-stage as we ran down the cream-painted passage. There was no lock on the heavy steel door ten yards farther in, just the massive steel latch. I closed the door behind us, checking before I did so that the latch could be operated from both inside and out. From here on it was a question of how long Yancy could keep everyone's attention focused elsewhere, because the first person who came along the outside corridor would see the splintered wreck of the lock and I wanted it to be a long time before that happened. We raced along the tunnel past the right-and-left kink which was either a natural fault or a firebreak or both, and along to the third door which led into the chamber where Koniec had tried to pound common sense and the cooperative spirit into me. The candy-striped canvas chair was folded tidily against the wall, and the third of the boxes we opened contained dynamite.

Amanda took out several of the paper-wrapped sticks and sniffed at them professionally, while I pulled open the far door of the chamber and started down the passage from which Koniec had emerged to begin his Doctor Death act.

The paint on the walls ran out after five feet and the cement-work a bit beyond that, and then I was in a big cavern with a beaten earth floor. The lights were on, just as they had been all the way from the outside corridor. I don't know what I'd been thinking I'd find here, but there were no gleaming walls banked with computers, no flashing panels of signal lamps, no secret dream laboratory. The air smelled of damp soil and decay and rust. Rubber-covered cables snaked across the ground, leading to badly-finished junction boards from which more cables sprouted untidily. Metal-shaded flood-lamps poured yellow cones of light down from slotted-angle wall brackets and carved out a roughly circular working area beyond which the cave receded into blackness.

I tilted one of the lamps to follow the course of a cable which led out of the central complex of brick and cement tables, and traced it until it vanished into the mouth of a low rock tunnel shored up with baulks of timber. I supposed that

Jissock had eventually been intending to fire his test shots deeper still inside the network of caves and passages which seemed to radiate from this point. He was, I recalled, a geologist, but I still wondered what size of explosion he'd had in mind, or whether anybody cared if the front of the building fell off when they pressed the button.

There was a scraping sound as Amanda dragged one of the boxes of dynamite along the passage from the chamber behind me. I went over to a concrete table near the passage entrance and took the stoppers out of several carboys of fluid, all unlabelled. Two of them contained acetone and one had no smell at all; probably purified cooling water for the laser equipment. On the next table there was about a thousand pounds' worth of optical bench gear, an East German infinite-persistence oscilloscope, and a corroded EHT power-pack from which Jissock had hoped to get six kilovolts if the fuses didn't blow, or so the label said.

'Good grief,' said Amanda. She hauled the box of explosive into the centre of the working area and stared around. 'Is this all?'

'This is the lot. Except for whatever's down that side-tunnel,' I said, pointing.

'I was expecting it to look a bit different,' she said.

'You've been reading too much science-fiction,' I told her. 'This what you get when you spend thirty or forty thousand pounds instead of half a million.'

'It looks like my next-door neighbour's garden shed, only worse.'

'Yes,' I said. 'Somebody's pathetically under-financed dream of power. Maybe your next-door neighbour has one too.'

'You're sorry you came back.'

'You bet I am. But a little less sorry now I've satisfied my curiosity.'

She kicked the box of dynamite gently. 'Where ought we to put this?' she asked.

'I don't think it matters,' I said, 'so long as we do it quickly.'

I went back and dragged in another box while she set the air fuse. When I came into the cave again she was tying a bundle of three dynamite sticks around the little pencil with a length of wire. She pushed the wrapped sticks inside the first box and I dumped the second one on top of it, and then she released the spring plunger on the fuse and we walked quickly away from Jissock's untidy and ill-thought-out legacy to science, hoping that our luck and Yancy's capacity for attracting attention would hold out for a few more minutes.

TWENTY-SIX

As IT turned out everything stayed peaceful until I reached the outermost of the steel bulkhead doors, beyond the double right-angled kink in the passageway and about ten yards from the thin wooden door which marked where the underground system emerged into the corridors of the building itself.

Looking back on it later, it was some satisfaction to realize that if things had stayed peaceful for a mere five seconds longer we'd probably both have wound up dead. As it was I had almost stepped through the bulkhead when I saw the splintered outer door being wrenched open, and I had almost an entire second to step smartly back again and swing the steel door half-closed before Drakon sighted along the passage and loosed off a shot which sounded like the crack of doom in the narrow tube of masonry and bedrock. I tried to pretend I was a sheet of tissue paper flattened behind the lip of the bulkhead. I hadn't got the door shut all the way, and I didn't want to play High Noon out in the middle of the passage with a spare foot each side of me for the ricochets to squeeze by. The same throught evidently occurred to Drakon, because I heard the wooden door creak as he retreated.

I knew that he couldn't lock us in, which was something. Not much, but something. The fact still remained that getting out meant charging along ten yards of tunnel into the barrel of his gun, and time was running out. I pulled the door cautiously closed, leaving the latch cocked up, and went back to where Amanda was standing behind the right-and-left kink. I couldn't see what difference it would make if Drakon gained ten yards by advancing as far as the bulkhead door, and anyway he had no reason to try.

'Boxed in,' I said to Amanda. 'And it looks as though we have somewhere between ten and fifteen minutes to think of the way out.' I didn't need all that time. The way out was quite clear, and the longer I had to think about it, the less likely I was to try.

'That's too long,' said Amanda. 'It was Drakon, wasn't it?'

'Yes.'

'Then we don't want him to go and get any help,' she said, and started to walk back towards the rock chamber.

'What the hell are you playing at?' I shouted after her. I saw her cross the chamber and open the innermost door, the one which led back to all that dynamite, and I thought she'd gone bad. Twenty seconds later she reappeared, trotting unconcerned and catlike towards me and leaving all the intervening doors open.

'Three minutes now,' she said. 'Or perhaps a bit less. I pushed the plunger threequarters of the way down the tube.' She tapped the bulging outline of the gun in my pocket. 'Well, I'm not staying around here for a quarter of an hour waiting for something to happen. You'll have to go and open that door again' – she trod on my toes as she edged past me and pointed – 'or the compression from the blast might burst our eardrums.'

'I'm getting too old for this,' I said. 'You went back in there and shortened the fuse by rather more than ten minutes?'

'It's the sensible thing,' she said.

'Oh sure.'

'It's one of the advantages of air fuses. You can change your mind, longer or shorter, any time up to the actual detonation.'

'I see. After that it's a bit more difficult. And you've deliberately made sure that the blast will travel all the way out along this passage instead of being confined behind a couple of nice thick steel doors.'

'Oh come on,' she said. 'Forty-eight sticks? Nothing's going to happen this far out except a lot of smoke and a bit of a shock-wave. You'd better keep your mouth open, you've seen pictures of people firing big field-guns. It equalizes the pressure inside and outside your ears. Now go and open that door, if you feel like it.'

'I'll tell you what I feel like, and that's the wad in a shotgun cartridge,' I said. I walked along the fifty feet of passage again to the outer steel door, and pushed it open a couple of inches. Drakon fired again as I pushed. He wasn't going to the trouble of telling us to come out with our hands up or any such nonsense. It wasn't that sort of situation. He had us like rabbits in a burrow, and he knew it. He had no time for histrionics and he would have no rules about not shooting girls. We'd been unreasonable and irritating, but mostly we were a disposal problem.

I lay down on the floor and counted up to a hundred, slowly. Somewhere around eighty Drakon's gun went off again, but he had nothing to shoot at except a couple of inches of crack around the edge of the door. There was a monstrous, crackling thud behind me and I felt myself pressed in a fist of air. The steel door flew open and clanged against the wall, and after a bit smoke and dust started to billow around the angle in the passage behind me and I heard Amanda coughing delicately.

I rolled over and almost sat up, but I didn't because the next thing that happened was that Drakon stumbled down the passage towards me. I couldn't think what he was doing. Perhaps he thought we were dead.

Amanda shot him as he clambered through the open bulkhead door and he tripped over me and fell to his knees. He still had the gun in his hand, and I thrashed around to try to get mine out from under my chest. He got up and went on past me. There was a tiny spitting sound as Amanda fired again, and then Drakon was past her, too, and staggering down the smoke-filled passage and around the double angle, shouting unintelligible words and clutching at his arm. I got to my feet and stumbled to where Amanda was still lying on the passage floor, trying to extract the spent rounds from the Derringer. The lights had gone out, around the angle in the tunnel. I put my head around the corner, and I could make out Drakon's figure surrounded by smoke and silhouetted against a full orange glow of fire, and then the smoke closed in around him and he was gone. There shouldn't have been any fire; it must be the acetone in the carboys, or a circuit arcing.

I pulled Amanda to her feet and we headed, coughing, for the outer wooden door. Beyond it I could hear confused shouts and running footsteps. If there was a fire back there inside the mountain, we had no time to stand around and work out plans of campaign. I burst out into the corridor and there, five or six doors down, was Bratling.

If he'd borrowed one of the machine carbines it would have been just too bad, and I'd have ended up looking like something that had been through the meat grinder. But I suppose carbines were unofficerlike weapons, and he'd got a revolver instead.

'Jolly good show, squire,' he said pleasantly. He smiled to emphasize his approval, and pulled the trigger. About six square inches of the plywood door-edge ripped away just above my left hand, which I noticed in a detached sort of way was still holding the handle. I came clumsily towards him, knowing that he must hit me the second time however inaccurate the average revolver is, and the gun – his gun – in my hand exploded almost by reflex. Bratling swung around in a graceful backward arc, through the open doorway of the room from which he'd emerged. The ends of his fingers on the side of the doorframe stayed in sight after the rest of him had vanished, and then the fingers themselves loosened and vanished too. One of his feet, showing four inches of diamond-patterned sock above the suède boot, shot out along the ground and protruded into the corridor, turning over as though it were no longer connected to his now invisible body.

Amanda came up behind me and took the gun from my hand. As we passed the open doorway inside which Bratling lay face up and in almost the exact position of those cut-out figures they use on practice ranges, I saw Koniec beyond him leaning out of one of the front windows of the building. I wondered why he didn't turn round, until I saw that he was dead too, propped nearly upright by his carbine which had jammed across one of the glassless window-panes and the sill. Joseph and Mercedes were nowhere around.

We went down the last flight of the main stairway, and out

through the front door on to the narrow terrace at the head of the steps down to the landing platform. I hoped Yancy would recognize us from across the gorge, and that he could stop Mercedes or Joseph from firing at us if they were at an upstairs window, or on the roof. Then I looked across and saw his hand waving against the skyline opposite us. There was a stammer of fire from somewhere overhead and the hand-waving stopped abruptly, to be followed a few seconds later by the flat boom of the assault rifle. Smoke was beginning to drift from behind the far end of the building, and we still had a couple of hundred feet or more of stairway to descend before we reached the relative safety of the bottom of the gorge. Amanda stopped when we were at the level of the landing platform and surveyed the helicopter, but not for long. She pattered down the zigzag steps and overtook me, and a few minutes later we were out and running across the stream towards the cover of the far rocks.

As we reached them, the first of the two explosions, muffled and rumbling, shook the ground under us. I spun round in time to see glass leap out from the curved ranks of windows and fall in a crystal shower down the face of the cliff beneath. Then the second and larger blast came, and about a quarter of the building's frontage split away and dissolved from under the feet of the two small figures on the roof, carrying them down in a slow avalanche of rubble which poured earthwards behind the helicopter platform and out of sight.

The water of the stream was still running a muddy brown when Yancy came down into the gorge, carrying the assault rifle at the trail and with the binoculars slung around his neck. He wanted to know why I always overdid things, but he cheered up when we climbed back to the helicopter and found it almost as good as new. I kept thinking that the rest of the building might drop on us, and I wasn't nearly as confident in Yancy's ability to fly an unfamiliar Russian machine as he seemed to be, but most of the time I wished he'd stop chatting up Amanda and let me get some sleep.

TWENTY-SEVEN

SOME TIME after we crossed the border into Yugoslavia again, he diverted his attention to me.

'So tell me about Jissock.'

'What do you want to know about him?' I asked.

'Ah, come on,' said Yancy.

'It's simple,' I said. 'He just wanted somebody to talk to, and the only person he found after the end of World War Two was Drakon. Jissock was a scientist of sorts, probably an idealist and almost certainly a nut. We try to make our country fit for heroes and nuts to live in, but mostly we don't succeed. Drakon succeeded as far as Jissock was concerned. I dare say he told Jissock a whole sheaf of lies about the cause of international scientific cooperation, but that doesn't matter. They gave him a home, even if it was a hole in the rock, and they listened to what he had to say. They were wrong and everybody else was right, but that doesn't matter either.'

'So?'

'So one day they made the mistake of paying him seventeen thousand pounds. They probably thought he was a capitalist and it would make him very happy. Then he woke up one morning and found that he'd sold out for dirty old money, just like everybody else, and he couldn't take the idea. So he tried to get home again.'

Yancy corrected trim. We flew another mile, or five, or maybe ten.

Finally he said, 'You mean that's the whole scene?'

'Yes,' I said. 'That's the whole scene.'

'Well, okay,' he said. I could see that he was trying to work out how to explain it to US Intelligence, and that they wouldn't like it very much as an explanation for anything at all.

Nobody back in Bayswater liked it very much either, but then I didn't expect them to and I didn't care.

McKellar had been given a temporary office at Seeker, because Driver decided that Seeker personnel were getting their faces too well known in Whitehall, or that's the way I heard it from Higsbee. Higsbee also said they'd had three all-night sessions running when the tapes came through from four seismographs detailing an unexplained explosion in north-eastern Albania. I was glad to hear that other people had been losing sleep too.

McKellar and Driver took a whole morning off to explain the difficulties I'd caused them by arriving in Yugoslavia with neither permission nor passport, together with Amanda Grayle (also without passport) and in the company of a United States citizen flying a Russian-built helicopter across from Albania.

'It's a pity you couldn't have left us there and saved a whole lot of embarrassment,' I said. 'But of course you had to have some sort of report,' and then Driver went on to list all the other things he didn't care for, like our leaving pieces of Rock Baby about the place for Yugoslav Security to find and assemble. I told him not to worry; if they found the laser crystal as well they'd drive themselves crazy trying to fit it together with the other bits. But McKellar only started to complain about the crystal too.

'You have cost this department fifteen thousand US dollars,' McKellar said eventually. I supposed he meant they'd paid Tito fifteen thousand dollars to bail us out, but in any case Driver wanted to have things clear.

'He has cost DSS fifteen thousand dollars,' he said carefully. Nobody offered to get me back my job, not that I'd been expecting it, so I left. In Scotland, a week or so later, the business of the fifteen thousand dollars suddenly made me want to laugh. I shook Amanda gently until she woke up and told her about it, but she only said 'So what?' and went straight back to sleep again.

MARTIN WOODHOUSE

ROCK BABY (25p) 5/-

'Has the same combination of crisp Balchinesque buttonholing style, plus technological expertise, as his brilliant debut, TREE FROG'—*The Observer*

'Even better than TREE FROG ... a delightful amalgam of sardonic comment and fast-moving action'—*Books and Bookmen*

'Splendidly enjoyable'—*The Times Literary Supplement*

TREE FROG (17½p) 3/6

'An exciting story of top-secret intelligence stuff ...'—*The Guardian*

'A thriller based on up-to-the-minute affairs in the world of atomic science, computers, pilotless aircraft, and the use of these latest ingredients in the stirring up of cold war ... there must be a large readership for this clever piece of work'—*Country Life*

'Goes into top half of cold war fiction league'—*Evening Standard*

ALEXANDER CORDELL

The Bright Cantonese (25p) 5/-
Mei Kayling, a beautiful, fanatical Eurasian member of the Red Guard espionage service is used as bait to discover whether the atomic bomb dropped on China by America was intentional or accidental...

'A chilling novel which seems to penetrate to the heart of Chinese fanaticism'—*Daily Express*

The Sinews of Love (25p) 5/-
'The background of present-day Hong Kong, with its fascinating complex of ancient tradition and modern corruption, is brilliantly painted'—*Daily Telegraph*

The Rape of the Fair Country (30p) 6/-
'Will give pleasure to tens of thousands of people... will surely be the best-written best-seller of this year'—
Sunday Times

The Hosts of Rebecca (30p) 6/-
'Running over with lust and strength... sin and righteousness'—*The Times*